KENTUCKY WALTZ

To Kim
Best wishes

Kentucky Waltz

Collected Short Fiction

Garry Barker

WIND PUBLICATIONS

Kentucky Waltz. Copyright © 2007 by Garry Barker. All rights reserved. Printed in the United States of America. No part of this book may be reproduced in any manner except for brief quotations embodied in critical articles or reviews. For information address Wind Publications, 600 Overbrook Dr., Nicholasville, KY 40356.

First edition

International Standard Book Number   978-1-893239-67-8
Library of Congress Control Number   2007935005

Acknowledgments

"Thanksgiving Visitor" — First appeared in *M Magazine*, and won that publication's 2000 fiction competition.

"A Matter Of Vision" — First appeared in *The Mountain Spirit Magazine* and won the 1986 Catholic Press Association 3rd Place Award for Fiction. Also appeared in *Mountain Passage & Other Stories*.

"River City Run" — First appeared in *Appalachian Heritage* and then in *Mountain Passage & Other Stories*.

"White Sports Coat" — First appeared in *Potato Eyes* and was nominated for the O. Henry Award.

"Cassie Faye" — Appeared originally in *Appalachian Heritage*; winner of the Plattner Award for Excellence in Writing for 2000.

"Merry Christmas" — Appeared in *Mountain Passage & Other Stories*

"The Blue Goose" — First appeared in *Grab-a-Nickel* then in *All Night Dog*.

"Nine Holes" — Appeared originally in *Appalachian Heritage*.

"The Liberation of Elsie Watts" — Originally appeared in *Fire On The Mountain*, then in *The Mountain Spirit*, where it won the national 1985 Best Short Story award from the Catholic Press Association. The story was then selected *for The Uneven Ground: An Appalachian Anthology*, published in 1985 by Kentucke Imprints, and was then included *in Mountain Passage & Other Stories*.

"Kentucky Waltz" — When my father was in his deathbed, my youngest brother, Jon, flew a US Army Blackhawk helicopter to Flemingsburg and brought it down to window level to salute Daddy. Until Jon retired from active duty I could not write the story, and as written it is a highly fictionalized version. I only wish that I could have been there to see it in person. The poem included was written by my niece, Rebecca Atchison, then 18, and was published in *Appalachian Heritage* magazine, as was, years later, the entire story.

"Hellcat" — First appeared in *Appalachian Heritage*; chosen for *Groundwater: a Collection of Contemporary Kentucky Fiction*, published in 1992 by The Lexington Press, Inc.

"Fire On The Mountain" — The title story from *Fire On The Mountain*, published in 1983.

"Big Game" — First appeared in *Inscape,* the literary magazine of Morehead State University, where it was the 1985 fiction winner, then in *Mountain Passage & Other Stories.*

"The Bitter Creek Appalachian Symposium" — First appeared in the *Journal of the Appalachian Studies Association.* The poem "Bitter Creek Breakdown" appeared in *Appalachian Heritage* and later became the title poem in the chapbook.

Contents

Thanksgiving Visitor	1
A Matter of Vision	11
River City Run	22
White Sports Coat	32
Cassie Faye	40
Merry Christmas	50
A Higher Education	60
The Blue Goose	71
Nine Holes	81
The Liberation of Elsie Watts	94
Kentucky Waltz	104
Final Liberation	115
Hellcat	123
Hellcat II: The Burying	132
Fire On The Mountain	140
Big Game	156
New York, New York	163
The Bitter Creek Appalachian Symposium	173

For Danetta

Foreword

Maybe the very first popular song I ever heard, over my grandfather's big battery powered Philco radio in Gimlet, Kentucky, was Bill Monroe's 1946 classic "Kentucky Waltz."

I would have been almost three years old at the time, and I'd already had my first haircut, hard-soled shoes, and formal portrait, all part of a day which began well before daylight in Elliott County when Grandma hitched the mules to the Studebaker wagon and we set out for Olive Hill, over Mauk Ridge and down Sinking Creek, and we came back up the mountain late that night by starlight.

That tinted portrait sat on Grandma's mantle until her death, and now it hangs in my living room, just above the CD player that brings Bill Monroe and the Bluegrass Boys, Lester Flat and Earl Scruggs and the Foggy Mountain Boys, the Osborne Brothers, Ricky Skaggs, Keith Whitley, Ralph Stanley, and even, yes, the fictitious "Soggy Bottom Boys" to life in four-speaker stereo.

"Kentucky Waltz" is still one of my favorites, but on the same CD is Bill's haunting instrumental "End of My Days," a tune I value more and more as the end of my days comes closer and closer.

This is not, though, a book about Bluegrass music. The title story draws more on a son's final salute to his dying father than on the music, though Bluegrass is an integral part of the tale.

I have often been told that some of my short stories would make good country songs, because they are drawn from the exact same place and people, but my musical talents are limited to manipulating the remote control switch.

These stories are the ones that have won awards or have been selected for anthologies, or have not appeared in one of my previous books, with a few exceptions. "Fire On The Mountain," the title story of my first book in 1983, is simply a personal favorite, one I think deserves another reading.

"The Liberation of Elsie Watts" was also in that first book, and "Elsie," based on my mother, shows up in about thirty more stories including, in this book, "Thanksgiving Visitor," "River City Run," "White Sports Coat," "Cassie Faye," "A Matter of Vision," "Nine Holes," "A Higher Education," "Merry Christmas," "Kentucky Waltz," and "Final Liberation."

My mother was born in a log cabin on Mauk Ridge in Elliott County, over eight decades ago, on the farm that's still part of the family. She was the mother of nine children; I was the third, the "war baby" born just before our father left for the US Navy and active duty in the English Channel. Mom died on December 30, 2001.

My mother gave me strength, inspiration, consolation, and creativity every day of my life, and will do so until the end of my own days. This book is really about her, and about a way of life that's largely gone now. Both my mother and the simple, hard, and often funny way of living will last, though, at least as long as I do.

— Garry Barker

Thanksgiving Visitor

The late November rain poured down cold and relentless for the fourth straight day. The barnyard muck was ankle deep, sucking with every slow step, as Harper Watts trudged back toward the house with a bucket of fresh milk in one hand and a flickering kerosene lantern in the other.

Harper kicked open the gate with one muddy foot, then followed a path of flat rocks toward the shadow of the tiny farmhouse. On the back porch he sat down his bucket and lantern to shake off water and to unbuckle ragged overshoes. He pulled the boots off wearily, disgusted at the holes and rusted buckles, but new overshoes could not be found. Rubber was for the war effort, and except for those who could afford to buy on the black market there were no new boots or tires to be had.

Harper took off his cap and shook away rain, unbuttoned his waterlogged mackinaw coat, gathered up his lantern and milk bucket and went inside. There, huddled in a dark corner away from the dim yellow lamplight, Margie Ward sat trembling and sniffling. "What's the matter?" Harper asked his wife's fifteen-year-old sister. "What is it, girl?"

Margie looked up and whimpered. "The baby's coming."

"Is that all? Why are you bawling about that?" He hung his coat on a peg by the door. "Where is she?"

"In the bed," sniffled Margie.

"You make me some coffee," ordered Harper. "And build up the fires. This place is colder'n a coal mine. Get a move on, girl." He smiled. "Babies have been being born for a long time, Margie. This ain't the first one ever to come." Harper went straight to the musty bedroom, where Elsie lay rolled up in quilts. "Is it time?" he asked gently. "Or is Margie just being Margie?"

Elsie smiled weakly. "It's time." She held her abdomen and sat up. "Margie is scared to death, Harper. Would you go for Doc Winters?"

Harper shrugged. "If you say so." He sat down in a chair pulled up close to the bed. "But Margie ain't the only one scared, is she?"

"No," admitted Elsie. "With the other two, my mother was with me the whole time."

"Evie's a hundred mile from here," Harper said wearily. He groaned. "Babies pick the damnedest times to bring theirselves. The mud is axle deep out yonder, and it ain't stopped raining for a week." Harper smiled. "But I'll bring you a doctor if we have to swim back in here." He stood. "Which we might have to. Creek's up, and the tires on my car is as slick as Sam's bald head. Let me get me a dry shirt on and I'll head out."

As Harper buttoned his flannel shirt he checked on the two children, already asleep in the loft, and to see if Margie was stoking up the fires in the cookstove and heatstove. "I'm going in to Otway to get Doc Winters," he told Margie. "It might be a hour or two, the way it's raining. You stay close to Elsie. She's a mite anxious."

"She's not the only one," whimpered Margie.

Harper chuckled. "You'll be a fine midwife," he said. "Ain't nothing to it, bringing babies. I bet Evie has caught her a hundred of 'em."

"I ain't Momma," whimpered Margie.

"And she ain't here," Harper said firmly, "so it's up to you."

He poured steaming coffee into a cracked china cup, sloshed some out into the saucer to cool, sipped gingerly and made a wry face. "I hope you're better at birthing babies than you are at making coffee. This stuff'd walk if it was to ever get loose." Harper smiled gently. "It'll be okay, Margie. I promise."

"Just you hurry up and bring that baby doctor back here," the girl pleaded. "You can make your own durn coffee when you get back."

Harper laughed and reached for his waterlogged coat. "I'll do that." He shook water off his cap, and bent to peer out at the blackness. "I hope the car'll start."

"Just go on," said Margie, her voice rising.

"Easy, girl," chuckled Harper. "Light that lantern for me while I get on my overshoes." Bundled, lantern in hand, Harper paused at the door. "I'll be right back."

"Hurry up," pleaded Margie.

Harper's square old Chevrolet sat sunk in mud under the maple tree. He crawled in, fumbled with switches, set the throttle and choke, and toed the starter button. There was only a soft groan. "Damned old battery," sighed Harper. He made sure the gearshift was in neutral, reached down the in the floor for the crank handle, and slid back out into the rain. He slipped in the mud, cursed, then squatted to fit the crank into the slot. He perched the lantern on a fender, bent, and jerked at the crank. On the fifth try, the motor spat and gurgled. "Come on, damn you," wailed Harper. He threw his weight into twirling the slippery crank handle.

The old car suddenly sputtered to life, shuddering, and Harper ran to feather the choke. The lantern shook itself off the fender, and Harper swore again. He gunned the rattling old engine, made sure it was going to keep on running, started out again but decided the broken lantern could lie where it fell.

The single windshield wiper slapped erratically and smeared the rain. Harper switched on the pale headlights, shifted to low gear, and jerked the Chevy loose from its deep tracks. He skidded, revved the weary motor, and slithered down toward the creek crossing. He stopped twenty feet away to stare at the swirling muddy current. "I'll never make it," he said softly. With calloused fingers Harper rolled and lit a cigarette, studied the rushing water, and made his decision. He backed up fifty feet to get a running start, and roared toward the creek at full throttle, angled upstream to allow for the strong current.

The high-riding Chevrolet skidded, floated, and clawed its way across, caught a gravel sandbar and lurched toward the steep far bank. Harper hung on grimly, gunned the car up the bank, and stopped at the top to take a deep breath and laugh at his trembling hands. Then he drove on, headed downstream, hoping the creek wouldn't be up over the road yet.

From the window, Margie watched until Harper's yellow lights vanished in the darkness. Then she walked slowly to the little bedroom.

"He's gone for the doctor," Margie said glumly, "but I wouldn't bet no money that they'd ever git back here."

Elsie smiled weakly. "Harper will make it."

"Probably, he'll get to town and go to playing poker and drinking moonshine," snorted Margie. "We won't see him for a week."

Elsie laughed. "Why are you so mad at Harper?"

Margie stiffened. "First the man drug you and the youngens off to that old coal camp in West Virginia, then over to Gallipolis so's he could work all of one whole day in the factory, then here to this Ohio swamp farm where it ain't quit raining since we got here, and all the time you with the baby due any minute." Margie bit back angry tears. "Why couldn't Harper just have stayed at home 'til the baby come?"

"They wasn't no work back home," Elsie said softly.

"Leastways there you had a roof over your head and food to eat," sniffed Margie. "And they wasn't no durned creek trying its best to come right up in the house with you. How come Harper thinks he's too good to raise a crop like the rest of 'em?"

"Harper don't think he's too good," said Elsie. "You know that as well as I do. He's just trying to get ahead."

"He may be a trying," said Margie, "but it looks to me like he's going backwards most of the time."

"It's the war," Elsie said lamely.

"The war." Margie squared thin shoulders. "I'm sick to my death of the durn war. Everbody gone, no sugar, no shoes, no fun."

"People are getting killed," said Elsie. "Our brothers, and Harper's brothers, they're all over there fighting right now."

"And that's where Harper would druther be," blurted Margie. "That's how come he won't stay put nowheres, won't work in a factory, and won't stay at home where he belongs of a night. He wants to go, too, and probably get hisself killed or crippled."

Elsie stared grimly at the faded flowered wallpaper, avoiding Margie's indignant glare. Finally she turned. "Maybe you're right," she whispered. "And maybe Harper is right, for wanting to do his part. Maybe I ought to let him go."

"And then what'll you do?" demanded Margie. "Set and starve? You with two youngens already and another'n coming tonight?" She stamped her foot. "All men ever want to do is fight. Fight, drink whiskey, and make babies." Margie blushed.

Elsie giggled. "That last part, that's what you're a wanting to do."

"And wind up like you, laying there with your belly stuck up? A baby on the way, and the creek so high the doctor'd have to have wings to get over here? Nossir, not me. I ain't never having me no man nor no babies."

Elsie smiled, then winced.

"Oh, Lordy," moaned Margie. "Is it coming?"

"Soon," said Elsie, through gritted teeth.

Margie ran to the window to peer out hopefully. "Damn you to hell, Harper Watts!" she wailed. "Hurry up and get yourself back here!"

Fifteen miles east, Harper Watts pounded hard on the front door of the ramshackle Winters family farmhouse. After ten minutes, Harper saw lights come on and heard a chain rattle. "Hold your horses," complained the high-pitched voice from inside. "You've done woke up the dead, and ever damned watchdog from here to Ironton." The door cracked. "What's the matter?"

Dr. Reuben Winters, past seventy, wrapped in a ragged robe, rubbed his swollen eyes. "Harper Watts? That you?"

Harper stepped in out of the rain. "The baby's coming, Doc. Right now."

Winters chuckled. "And you expect me to leave my warm dry house and go across a flood to deliver it? I'm an old man, Harper. Go wake up that young doctor over at Portsmouth."

"Elsie, she wants you," insisted Harper.

"Elsie, hell," Winters grumbled good-naturedly. "It's you that figures I won't charge very much." He yawned and scratched. "Have you got a boat?"

"A what?" asked Harper.

"A boat, damnit," laughed Winters. "The Ohio River is already licking at my back door. Where you live, it'll be an island."

"We don't need no boat," Harper said impatiently. "Hurry up."

"I'm hurrying as fast as I can," grumbled Winters. He pointed. "Pour you a drink while I get me some clothes on."

Harper paced, gulped down two tumblers of expensive bourbon whiskey, and finally heard Winters come back down the steps. The old doctor poured himself a shot, downed it, smacked his lips and reached for a rain slicker. "Where's my bag?" He found the worn old black case, snapped it open, and added a full bottle of whiskey. "We'd better take my car," he said, "or, better still, the farm truck. Can you drive a Reo, Harper?"

"I can drive anything that's got wheels," said Harper. "Where's it at?"

The big red flatbed truck started easily. Harper pulled up from the stock barn to the house to pick up Winters, who climbed happily up into the cab. "If anything'll make it," he said, "it'll be this old truck."

Harper drove slowly, dim headlights peeking into the heavy rain, impatient with the slow progress.

"Settle down, son," Doc Winters said gently. "Elsie is as healthy as a horse, and she's done had two babies. They ain't one thing to worry about." He dug in his bag for the bottle, twisted off the top, and took a long pull.

"Take it easy on that stuff," warned Harper.

Winters grinned, capped the bottle, and tucked it gently back into his bag. "I'm a better doctor drunk," he said, "than most of 'em are stone sober."

Harper chuckled. "That's what you said about playing poker, too, that night you lost $200 over in Nelson Hunt's barn."

Elsie gasped at the pain and clenched Margie's hand. "It's time," she said.

Margie stared. "What do I do?"

"Catch the baby," said Elsie.

"What?" Margie's eyes widened.

"Just do it, Margie," moaned Elsie.

"Oh, Lord," whimpered Margie. "There's its head."

When the baby came, Margie stood helplessly, her hands full. "What do I do with it?" she asked frantically. Margie looked around, looked down at her handful, and plopped the newborn down on Elsie's belly.

Elsie stirred. "Is it okay?" she asked weakly.

"It's a him," Margie announced proudly. "And I reckon he's a doing just fine. Right now he's laying there looking up at the light bulb and scratching his belly." She giggled. "I swear he is, Elsie."

Elsie laughed. "Don't you think we better finish up?"

When the baby was clean, wrapped in a blanket and tucked in beside Elsie on fresh sheets, Margie beamed. "We done it, didn't we? We brung a baby."

"We sure did," smiled Elsie. "A big healthy boy baby."

"What's his name going to be?" asked Margie.

"You brought him," said Elsie. "You name him."

"Really?" Margie grinned. "Can I?"

Elsie nodded, and Margie pondered. "What about Vernon Mack?" she asked. "After the both of his grand-daddies?"

"I like that," Elsie said softly. She looked out the window at the gray drizzly dawn. "Margie, do you remember what day it is?"

"It's Vernon's birthday," said Margie.

"It's Thanksgiving Day," said Elsie.

Margie sighed. "I reckon that means I got to do the cooking?"

"Yes," laughed Elsie. "What little we have." She stared out at the soft rain. "I wonder where Harper is at?"

"Somewheres drunk, I'd bet," sniffed Margie, "while we stay here and do all the work."

Margie was half right. Harper and Reuben Winters, trapped in the truck in four feet of floodwater, had finished off Doc's fifth just before daylight, and now they were trying to figure out how to get to shore. Harper finally saw the low-hanging oak limb just overhead. "There's us a ladder," he grinned. He swung out the window, reached and grabbed, and pulled himself up onto the roof of the truck. "Come on out, Doc."

Winters peered out gloomily. "Take my bag," he finally said, "and I'll give it a try."

An hour later Harper and the weary old physician stood on the muddy hillside and looked back down at the truck. "It's getting deeper," said Harper. "It's up over the steering wheel."

"I reckon we ain't going to drown," Winters said sourly. "But we still can't get to your place, neither."

"Yes we can," grinned Harper. "Remember the old swinging bridge?"

It was a fierce, evenly matched battle, but Margie finally killed the muddy hen. She staggered to her feet, dragged the hen to the chopping block, and used Harper's big axe to chop off its head. "There, durn you," she said. "That'll teach you to flog me."

The muddy, bloody girl came dripping into the house, slung the hen into a washpan of scalding water and tried to dry herself. "Pick off all of them feathers," she told four-year-old Priscilla. "You can help, Roy." The big eyed two-year-old hid behind the cookstove.

"Chicken and dumplings," grumbled Margie. "A body'd think we had company coming." She poured rubbing alcohol into a plate, lit it, and singed the hairs off the old hen. Margie carried the carcass and a sharp knife to the bedroom. "How," she asked, "do you cut up one these things?"

Doc Winters was wheezing, staggering, by the time they reached the old bridge. He took one look at rotted floorboards, rusted cables, and muddy floodwater, and sat down on a jutting rock. "I ain't going," he said.

"The hell you ain't," replied Harper. "You got a baby to bring."

"Harper," the old doctor said wearily, "there are just two things in this old world that scare me. One's a setting hen, and the other'n is a swinging bridge."

"In that case, Doc," grinned Harper, "you're going first. I ain't taking no chances. You get yourself acrosst there, and I'll bring your doctor bag with me." He chuckled. "It's not but two more mile to the house. I got a gallon of Kentucky moonshine in the corncrib."

Winters stood. "If a body's got to die, I reckon now's as good a time as any." He took a tentative first step onto the creaky bridge, and stared down at the rushing water. "Is that good shine you've got?"

"The best," promised Harper.

"It had better be," muttered Winters. He took another step, and clung to the cables. "If this damned rotten thing breaks, they'll find me in New Orleans."

"Go on," ordered Harper, "before I have to pick you up and pack you across."

On the opposite bank, Winters wiped off rain and cold sweat. "Where's the whiskey?" he asked weakly.

"Follow me," grinned Harper.

Margie sniffed at the cooking pot, wrinkled her nose, and went to the bedroom where Elsie was nursing the baby under the watchful eyes of the two older children. "It's ready to eat," she announced.

"Let's wait," said Elsie. "Harper will be here soon."

"Not unless he's sprouted him wings," said Margie. But she agreed. "A little while longer."

Back in the kitchen she rolled out biscuit dough and cut circles with a tin can. Margie shook down in the ashes in the cookstove, added more lumps of coal, and happened to look out the window. Two men came at a half-run, slipping in the mud, staggering, coming closer. "It's Harper!" she yelled happily. "And Doc Winters too!"

The doctor went straight to the bedroom, and came out beaming twenty minutes later. "Both of 'em are fine. Great." He sat down heavily. "You done good, girl." Winters rocked back and sighed. "Now, Harper. Where's that corn whiskey of yourn?"

Reuben Winters belched, wiped his mouth, and grinned at Margie. "You've delivered a fine baby boy and cooked up a feast, all in one day," he said. "If I was fifty years younger, I'd marry you in a minute."

Margie blushed happily.

"But I'd bet cash money," continued Winters, "that you've done got you a feller, and that you'll be going back to Kentucky as soon as that baby can travel."

"I ain't got a feller yet," Margie said shyly, "but I'd give my eye teeth to get back home."

"We're going," blurted Harper. "Before Christmas, if I can get the money together."

"And if you can get across that creek," chuckled Winters. "We may all have to winter here."

"If we do," grinned Harper, "I got a flock of hens and two more gallons of whiskey. We'd make it, if we had to."

Winters rolled his glass in his hand, studied the clear liquid, then gulped it down. "Mighty fine," he said, shuddering. Winters smiled across the table at Margie. "Can you play five stud poker, girl?"

"Margie Ward," Harper said proudly, "can do anything she sets her mind to."

"Then clear off this table," grinned Winters, "and deal the cards."

Five miles away, the backwaters of the Ohio River crept up and over the red cab of the old Reo flatbed truck. There was a gurgle as it vanished in a muddy swirl. The moon was high, full, shining brightly down on remote southern Ohio farmlands. By midnight, the flood crested, and slowly the waters began to recede. There was, still, in one hilltop farmhouse, a yellow light flickering from the kitchen window. Inside, Dr. Reuben Winters bet into Margie's full house and finally managed to finish losing the hundred dollars he'd set out to lose.

About enough, figured Winters, to get this Kentucky family moved back across the river to its rightful ridgetop home

A Matter Of Vision

When his mother wouldn't let him quit school halfway through the second grade, Vernon Watts settled things the only way he could figure out.

He went blind.

Not all the way blind, just enough to where it wasn't safe for a six year old to be wondering around the schoolyard or climbing up and down the school bus steps. Vernon could still see, up close, but couldn't read what Miss Hall wrote on the blackboard and couldn't see across the circle when the whole school played "Farmer in the Dell" on the muddy ball field.

Martha Hall, for almost thirty years the first and second grade teacher at the Goddard School, nervously edged her new 1949 Ford up the creek bed roadway toward the Watts family farmhouse, then had to brake hard to stop just short of the scowling boy and his bristled little brown and white dog.

Vernon hefted a smooth, heavy creek rock. "Go back," he ordered. Rex, the dog, added a growl, but his crooked tail was wagging. "Go away!" yelled Vernon. The white scar on his lower lip was clearly visible now.

Martha shut off the engine and shoved open the door.

"You better not get out," warned Vernon. "Rex, he's liable to eat you alive." He waved the little dog forward. "Sic her, Rex."

Rex advanced stiff-leggedly, tail still wagging, and offered a tentative growl. He stopped, and looked plaintively back to his young master. "Go on," ordered Vernon. Rex advanced apologetically.

Martha smiled. "Is this your dog, Vernon? He's much prettier than you told me he was. And I bet he's really good at treeing squirrels."

"Best in Kentucky," Vernon said proudly. "Manual Cox said he'd give me fifty dollars for Rex, but he ain't for sale. Not even for a million dollars."

Now totally confused, Rex sat down and cocked an ear to listen. Harper Watts broke the stalemate. "Git, you little varmint!" he swore. Rex scrambled, tucked his tail, vanished in thick scrub brush. "What are you doing?" Harper asked Vernon. "Lay down that rock and open the gate so's Miss Hall can drive on up to the house."

Harper sighed as Vernon ran to unhook the barbed wire gate. "Don't know what's got into that one," he grumbled. "Him and that durn dog has gone wild."

"Have you noticed that Vernon is having trouble seeing?" asked Martha. Harper shrugged. "Ain't paid much attention. Is he giving you trouble at school?"

"There's a little problem," admitted Martha. "That's why I drove out here to talk to you and Elsie."

"Come on up to the house," said Harper. "I'll hitch the gate and go catch Vernon."

"First I want to talk with just you and Elsie," said Martha. She drove slowly up to the weather-beaten farmhouse, eased through a cluster of cackling white hens, and parked close to Harper's muddy Dodge. Elsie was waiting, wringing her hands in a damp calico apron. "What is it now?" Elsie asked anxiously. "I'll thrash Roy to a inch of his life if he's been fighting at school again." She frowned. "Except, I can't say as I blame him for whipping Ezra Jackson for throwing them new overshoes down the toilet-hole."

Martha Hall laughed. "It's not Roy this time. I want to talk to you and Harper about Vernon."

"Vernon?" Elsie stared. "But he does the best of them all in school." She paused. "He did come home the other day, though, and ask me if he could quit school. And he says he can't see very good, but I never thought nothing of it. Is something really wrong?"

"I don't know," said Martha. "Have you ever had Vernon's eyes checked by a doctor?"

"No," Elsie said softly. She blushed. "I figured it was just Vernon making up another one of his stories."

"And that's probably what he's doing," admitted Miss Hall. "Sometimes Vernon's imagination does get a little out of control. But he won't talk in class any more, and says he can't see the blackboard." She sighed. "I can't help but wonder if it's all because he thought he'd go to the next room this year." Martha smiled. "When school started this year, Vernon was furious that he had to stay in my room another year."

"But why?" asked Elsie. "He always has liked you a lot."

"Vernon insisted he'd already finished with my room," laughed Martha. "He couldn't understand why he to stay there and do the second grade. The truth is, Mrs. Watts, that Vernon did do the first and second grades at the same time last year. His test scores put him at about a fourth grade level. So now he's bored, and a little bit of a problem."

"He don't behave?" Harper stiffened. "I'll tan his hide."

"Oh, no," Martha said quickly. "That wouldn't help."

"What can we do?" asked Elsie.

"First, I'd suggest you have him examined by a doctor," suggested Martha. "Just to make sure there's really nothing wrong."

"You mean he might need eyeglasses?" asked Elsie.

"Maybe," Martha said carefully. "Or maybe the problem is emotional."

"Emotional?" Harper pondered. "You mean Vernon is sick in the head?"

"That's not what I said," protested Martha. "It's just that, well, maybe Vernon's loss of vision is caused by something emotional."

"Nerves," blurted Elsie.

"Maybe," agreed Martha.

"Harper's brother Kenneth," said Elsie, "come home from the war with nerves. He couldn't hardly sleep or eat, hid under the bed half the time, and stayed drunk for most of two years."

"Kenneth, he was half shell-shocked," grunted Harper. "Vernon ain't been in no war. He just needs his bottom burnt good."

"That wouldn't do," Martha said firmly. "Vernon is brilliant, and very sensitive. Punishment now would just make it worse."

"Spends too much time with that damn dog," grumbled Harper. "Why, the boy near lives with Rex. Don't have a thing to do with people. Get rid of the dog, and Vernon'll be okay."

"Don't you dare touch that dog," warned Elsie. "Vernon has had Rex ever since the time he got his tongue cut off. Margie brung him the pup when she left to get married."

"Elsie is right," added Martha. "Right now, Vernon probably needs his dog more than ever."

"Is Vernon doing anything else at school?" asked Elsie.

"That he ain't supposed to do?"

Martha blushed lightly. "I can't get Vernon to do anything. Once I twisted his ear, sort of playing, mostly, and he hasn't opened his mouth since."

"Boy just don't want to go to school," insisted Harper. "Nothing that a hickory switch won't fix."

"That's really not a problem," said Martha. "If Vernon wasn't already younger than his classmates, we'd just skip him ahead a grade, but he truth is he wouldn't miss a thing if he didn't come to school for a while. I'd recommend that you take him to a doctor, first, then wait to see what happens."

"Is he really part blind?" asked Harper.

Martha shrugged. "Maybe. There may not be anything wrong with his eyes, but the partial blindness still could be very real."

"Don't make no sense to me," said Harper.

"I don't understand it either," said Martha. "But I do know Vernon is a very special child. Someday he could go to college, and become a doctor or an engineer."

Elsie walked to the car with Martha, gently shooed aside the kittens and chickens, smiled when she found Vernon and Rex standing guard over the new Ford. "We kept the cats off," announced Vernon. "So they wouldn't be muddy tracks all over."

"Thank you both very much," smiled Martha. She reached into her purse. "Here's a reward for you."

"It's a French harp!" said Vernon.

"A harmonica," corrected Martha. "I want you to play me a tune the next time I see you."

Saturday morning Elsie and Vernon waited two hours in the crowded office to see the doctor. After a series of examinations and charts, Dr. Sellers scratched his head. "Vernon says he can't see very good. All I can do is send him somewhere for better testing or to Maysville to get glasses fitted."

"You go wait outside, Vernon," ordered Elsie. "I got to talk to the doctor."

She came out twenty minutes later, and took Vernon with her to the drug store. The tiny green pills came in a yellow bottle. Harper and the rest of the children were waiting in the Dodge. "What'd he say?" asked Harper.

"I got medicine," Elsie said grimly.

"And I got two red suckers," announced Vernon. "One for me, and one for Rex."

At home Elsie shook out two pills. Vernon gagged and the pills came back up. Elsie spooned apple butter and tried again. After a ten minute struggle Vernon swallowed the melting medicine and bolted for the door. "You wait," said Elsie. She caught Vernon by his overalls straps. "From now on, you can't go outside of the yard. It ain't safe for you to go running all over."

"In the yard?" wailed Vernon.

"You can't see good enough to go out in the woods," said Elsie. "When your eyes gets better, then you can go up on the mountain again."

Elsie smiled, watched Vernon feed half his candy to Rex, and grinned at Harper. "What's them pills for?" he asked.

"Nerves," said Elsie.

"Well," demanded Harper. "Is he blind or ain't he?"

"He thinks he is," said Elsie. She smiled softly. "When it's handy to be."

"You mean he's just pretending to be?" asked Harper.

"Probably," said Elsie. "But it's real to him."

Harper stared, perplexed, then shrugged. "He's your youngen."

"He's our youngen," countered Elsie.

"I never meant nothing by that," protested Harper. "I mean, you and Vernon, you all get along better, since I was gone the whole time he was a baby." Harper searched for words. "All I'm a trying to say, Elsie, is for you to do whatever you think is best."

Elsie smiled.

Harper flinched. "What's that screeching noise?" he asked.

Elsie grinned. "That's Vernon, playing the harmonica Miss Hall give him."

"Well," grunted Harper, "he better get his eyesight back. He dang sure ain't going to make a living playing music."

A pained howl from Rex punctuated their laughter, and from the barn the bull bellowed plaintively.

Monday morning Elsie sent Priscilla off to school with orders to bring home Vernon's lessons, then kept a sharp eye out that the boy and dog didn't slip out of the yard. Vernon now pretended to swallow the pills, fed four of them to Rex, then worried all afternoon that his groggy dog might be dying. Rex recovered enough to go squirrel hunting, after supper, with Harper and Manual Cox. Manual, a trucker who hauled coal or watermelons depending on the season, again tried to buy Rex.

"Sixty dollars," grinned Manual. He rolled three crumpled twenties in his fingers. "That's a lot of cash for a little cur dog."

"Rex ain't a cur dog," protested Vernon. "He's a Shepard."

"He can damn sure tree a squirrel," said Manual. He pondered, and added another twenty. Then another. "A hundred bucks," he chuckled. "I'm a even bigger fool than I knowed."

"Rex ain't for sale," whispered Vernon.

"Everthing's for sale, boy," chuckled Manual. "Ain't that so, Harper?"

"It's Vernon's dog," Harper said quietly. "It's up to him."

"You mean you'd let that boy turn down a hundred dollars? As hard up as you all are?" Manual grinned slyly. "You better think it over, Harp."

"Ain't no thinking to be done," snapped Harper. "Vernon has done told you no."

"Then I reckon that's that," grinned Manual. He winked. "Let's you and me go out and take a look at my truck, Harper."

The two old friends left chuckling.

"Is Daddy going to sell Rex?" whispered Vernon.

"No," Elsie said wearily. "He's going out to get a drink of Manual Cox's moonshine."

"I don't like Manual," Vernon said softly.

"That's one thing," Elsie said tiredly, "that I'm starting to agree with you about. Come on. It's time for your medicine." Vernon gagged down the pills, practiced his harmonica playing for a while, then slept heavily. The roar of the big truck leaving, before daylight, woke him, but Vernon slipped quickly back into drugged sleep.

When Vernon did get up, Rex wouldn't come when called.

"He's probably gone to visit some pretty little girl dog," grinned Harper. "He'll be back."

"Manual took him," sniffled Vernon. "He stole Rex."

"I bet he's right," snapped Elsie.

"Just a dadgummed minute now," protested Harper. "You all are saying Manual took the dog and you don't know nothing for sure. Why, Rex is gone lots of mornings."

"No he ain't," Vernon insisted stubbornly.

"No he ain't," echoed Elsie. "I'm the one that feeds him ever morning, so I ought to know."

Harper thoughtfully gnawed a biscuit, then shrugged. "Tell you what," he finally said. "If the dog ain't home by Saturday, I'll drive over to Grayson and see if Manual has got him." Harper slurped coffee from a chipped saucer. "If he has got Rex, you don't have to worry none. A man is going to take real good care of a hundred dollar hound dog."

"Rex ain't a hound," sniffed Vernon.

"All the same," said Harper, "your dog will get fed and watered and took care of. Now, I don't want to here no more about it. I got corn to cut."

"And you," Elsie told Vernon, "can get your mind off it by doing your school lessons."

"Would it be all right to pray, Momma?" asked Vernon. "To get Rex back home?"

"Sure it would," Elsie said gently. "I reckon that God, he's got all kinds of animals, and He'd know what it's like to have your dog missing."

When Elsie carried cold water to the cornfield at mid-morning, she waited until Harper quenched his thirst before she spoke. "One thing I got to know," she said, "is did you sell Rex to Manual Cox? Last night, while the two of you was drinking?"

"No, I never," sputtered Harper. "Much as we need the money right now, I told Manual to keep his hands off of that dog." He rolled a cigarette with clumsy fingers and struck a match. "Do you really think I'd sell the boy's pup?"

"I didn't think so," said Elsie, "but I had to know for sure." She smiled. "Besides that, if Rex is okay this could all help Vernon."

"How's that?" asked Harper.

"Vernon is doing his lessons, playing that French harp, and doing everything I say to do." She giggled. "And do you know what else? I do believe Vernon's eyesight is better."

Harper sucked the last drag from his cigarette and grinned. "So you reckon Vernon will be able to see when we go to get the dog Sunday?"

Elsie nodded. "But," she added, "I thought you were the one who swore Manual didn't take the dog."

"Shucks, Elsie," grinned Harper, "Manual couldn't no more keep from taking that dog than you could keep the sun from coming up of the morning. He's got Rex, and when we show up Sunday morning he'll swear he found him asleep in the back of the truck and was just getting ready to bring the boy's pup home."

Elsie stared. "Why do you put up with him, Harper?"

"Because," Harper said softly, "it was Manual Cox that crawled out under machine gun fire to drag me back to the foxhole when I was hit in '44. The man saved my life, Elsie." He grinned. "And, besides that, he's always got a gallon of the best moonshine in ten counties."

"Then how come all you ever take is a sip or two?" asked Elsie with a smile.

"Because you told me you'd send me packing if I ever come in drunk again," chuckled Harper. "And I know you're a woman of your word, Elsie Watts."

Vernon grieved, prayed, and carefully behaved. He did not argue with Priscilla and Roy, helped take care of the babies, did his arithmetic and spelling, and practiced his harmonica playing. By Friday afternoon he could produce sounds vaguely resembling music. "Why don't you let him out of the yard?" suggested Harper. "To my way of thinking, that

French harp playing would sound mighty good if it was being done somewheres on the other side of the mountain."

"Not until I know he can see," smiled Elsie.

Sunday morning Vernon was up early. He took his harmonica and went outside to sit in the porch swing and practice a dreary version of a familiar hymn. As the thick fog lifted up off the narrow valley, Vernon stared intently down the creek bed roadway. There was something moving, something small, something brown and white. "That's Rex!" yelled Vernon. He flew off the high porch, running hard, scattered sleepy chickens and sluggish kittens.

Harper came out and stood with his hands cupped over his eyes. "I don't see a thing," he finally announced. "Just Vernon, running down through there like a plumb fool."

"Maybe your eyes ain't as good as Vernon's," laughed Elsie. She took Harper's arm. "Does that look like a blind boy to you?" Vernon scooted under the barbed wire gate and skimmed over the rocks, fairly flying, and the tired little dog limped faster as the boy got closer. Vernon swept Rex up in his arms, whimpering with joy, and the dog feebly licked the tears from the boy's face. Rex was black with coal soot, and a frayed rope dangled from his neck. His feet were raw and bleeding, and his crooked tail wagged tiredly. Vernon gently carried him back to the house.

Elsie wiped away her tears, and Harper turned gruffly away to roll a cigarette.

Martha Hall was shaking down the grate to get a fire going in the iron potbellied stove, to ward off the early autumn chill in her classroom, when she heard a car outside. She checked her watch. The buses weren't due for another twenty minutes. Martha stood up just as the door flew open and a brown and white dog bounced into the room. "Rex?" asked Martha. "Are you Rex?"

The dog wagged happily. Then, from outside in the morning haze, came the shrill, halting notes of a harmonica, "Amazing Grace" in bagpipe cadence.

Around the corner, marching proudly, cheeks puffed and harmonica wailing, came Vernon Watts.

"Oh, my," whispered Martha.

Harper Watts, grinning ear to ear, carried Vernon's lunch pail and notebooks. Vernon stopped, blew the final ragged notes, and waited expectantly.

"Why, Vernon, I just don't know what to say." Martha stooped and wrapped the boy in a hug, then laughed as Rex danced up to lick her face. "I'm so proud of you," said Martha.

"My cows was mighty proud to send that French harp off to school, too," chuckled Harper. "Vernon couldn't wait for the bus. I brung him on early so he could play for you."

Vernon hung his head. "I can see now, too, " he said shyly.

Martha glanced at Harper. He nodded, and shrugged. "Beats me," he offered lamely. "Boy's got eyes like a chicken hawk."

"Priscilla told me last week that Rex was missing," said Martha. "How did you find him?"

"He come home all by hisself," Vernon said proudly. "Rex walked a hundred miles."

"More like forty," Harper corrected softly. He grinned. "You never in your life seen two happier little fellers than them two yesterday morning."

"I know that's true," Martha said softly. She met Harper's stare. "I don't guess we'll ever know, will we, just what has happened?"

Harper grinned. "You might ask Elsie one of these days." He handed Vernon the dinner pail. "You behave," he ordered, "and put Rex in the car. He can help me farm today whilst you're here learning to be a doctor."

Martha watched as Vernon lifted Rex into the old Dodge and bent to hug the dejected dog.

"He will, you know," Martha suddenly said to Harper. "Vernon will be a doctor, or lawyer, or writer, or whatever he decides he wants to be. He'll go to college, and maybe even medical school. He can do it!" Martha stopped and blushed. "I guess I get as carried away as Vernon sometimes. I'm sorry."

"Ain't no call to be sorry," Harper said wearily. "The reason we moved here, down off of Caney Creek, was to get where they was decent schools for the youngens." He sighed. "Times are changing. Youngens has got to learn new ways. Now, me, I don't know nothing but a team of mules and a double-shovel plow, but Vernon, he's gonna have to learn about jet airplanes and telephones and television and such as that. I seen it all coming, during the war, and I aim for mine to be ready for it."

"They will be," said Martha.

"I know," grinned Harper. He twisted calloused hands. "Twixt you and Elsie, they ain't got no choice."

Vernon came running with his harmonica ready. "Want to hear me play some more?" he asked.

"I got to go," Harper said quickly, already walking toward the car. "Nice talking to you, Miss Hall." He escaped in a rattle of pistons and bearings.

Martha sighed. "Okay, Vernon. Play."

They marched side by side toward the schoolhouse, Martha's arm draped over Vernon's thin shoulders, to the jerky tempo of "Turkey in the Straw."

Halfway there, Martha Hall lifted her skirts and danced the buck and wing and hoped nobody was watching.

River City Run

Vernon stood up too fast and smacked headfirst into the cobwebbed barn beam. He sat down openmouthed, stunned, knees suddenly weak and watery.

"You all right, boy?" asked Harper. "Let me take a look at the top of your head."

"No." Vernon pulled his Cincinnati Reds baseball cap down tighter and tried to stop the spinning and flashing. He felt warmth seeping from the cut under the cap, gritted his teeth and reached for another stick of tobacco. "It ain't nothing," mumbled Vernon. "I ain't hurt." He shoved the tobacco to Harper.

"He hit hisself on the head, Harper," chuckled Manual Cox. "Can't hurt a Watts, hitting him on the head. Let's get this stuff loaded on up and hit the road."

Working in the dim yellow light of a kerosene lantern, Vernon and Harper loaded the sticks of stripped burley tobacco onto Manual's old truck and covered the load with a stiff, dirty tarpaulin. Vernon ducked under the truck to snug the ropes and had to grab onto the wheels when the dizziness struck.

"You sure you're okay?" asked Harper.

Vernon nodded. "Some dizzy, is all." He crawled out, stood, and rubbed his swollen eyes. "It's just from getting up so early."

"The boy's got growing pains," laughed Manual. "He growed a foot since last year. Bumps into lights, trips over the doorsteps, can't even hold onto a glass of milk without spilling it. This one's going to be a big man, Harper, but just yet he ain't got used to being near six feet tall."

Harper smiled tiredly. "I guess you're right," he finally said. Vernon tugged his cap down tighter. "Go set in the truck," ordered Harper.

Dawn was breaking when the truckload of tobacco finally rattled down Mudsock Road. Manual fumbled with the heater controls and light switches, flipped on the radio, geared down for the steep descent and stopped for the intersection at Mt. Hope. The old Chevrolet roared, backfired as Manual double-clutched and shifted, and slowly picked up speed. After he had worked up to high gear Manual rolled down the window to spit, lowered the volume on the radio, and grinned at Vernon. "First time to the tobaccer market?" he asked.

Vernon nodded. "I never been to Maysville before." The throb in his head was easing off some now. "Momma let me miss school to come."

"Elsie ain't no fool," chuckled Manual. "She knows a pimple-faced boy has got to get him a look at the big city."

"Some big city," grunted Harper. "Maysville ain't nothing but beer joints and tobacco warehouses."

"It ain't Paris, France," agreed Manual. "But it sure beats hell out of Mauk Ridge." He guided the truck with the gaudy plastic spinner clamped to the wheel. Manual glanced across at his old friend, sighed, slowed the truck and listened to the popping exhaust as they rolled downhill into the county seat of Finch County. "Finchburg, Kentucky," intoned Manual. "The friendly town that hospitality built." He chuckled. "They do got a right friendly jailer, at that. Last time they locked me up, old Willard went and got my jug out of the truck and me and him set in the cell and drunk it ever bit. When he let me go I had to sleep it off in the truck before I could drive home." He braked the truck to a stop at the traffic light, and pointed. "Jail's up yonder by the courthouse."

"You don't stop roaring that muffler," warned Harper, "that's where we'll all be."

Manual eased the truck away from the light and upshifted gently. "Your pappy tries to act like he ain't never raised no hell, Vernon, but don't you believe one word of it. Old Harper used to be the drinkingest, fightingest little feller on the ridge afore Elsie got aholt of him and settled him down."

"Shut up, Manual," Harper said with a sleepy grin. "The boy don't need no encouragement."

They crossed the Mason County line and threaded through a row of dismal roadhouses, bleak in the foggy morning. "Now, a man can get hisself killed in this burg," said Manual. He down-shifted for the hill. "They's a fight ever night in Spencer's and most of them old boys packs knives and pistols."

Vernon dozed for half an hour and woke as the truck's protesting engine and creaky brakes held them back going down the Maysville hill. "Are we there yet?" asked Vernon.

"Coming right up on Bob's Bar," announced Manual. "Best looking waitresses in fifteen counties."

"And that's Maysville down yonder," said Harper.

Vernon stared down at church spires, smokestacks, acres of flat tobacco warehouse roofs, the elegant old bridge, and in the background the muddy waters of the Ohio River. "Better close that mouth, boy," chuckled Manual. "You'll catch you a bushel of bugs."

"It's big," whispered Vernon.

"Right smart of a town," agreed Harper. "Maybe after we unload we can drive downtown. Maybe even go across the bridge to Ohio and back."

"Could we?" Vernon leaned forward, eager to not miss a sight. "I never seen so many houses and stores and stuff."

"You've kept this youngen up on the ridge too long, Harper," complained Manual. "What would Vernon do if he ever seen Cincinnati?"

"He'll see Cincinnati, all in good time," said Harper. "Vernon's one youngen that ain't going to spend all his life stuck on Mauk Ridge. He's a scholar, Vernon is. Might make a doctor someday."

"Not if he don't set back so I can see to drive," said Manual. He swung the truck down a narrow street lined with beer joints and used car lots, sidewalks already busy with roughly dressed farmers, and stopped at the Kentucky King tobacco warehouse. "This the one, Harper?"

"Just follow the other trucks," said Harper.

Manual drove through huge double doors and Vernon gasped. "Big, ain't it?" chuckled Manual. "A body could put all of Finch County in here and have room left over for Soldier." He parked and swung out to meet the warehouse crew.

"Climb up there and hand it down, Vernon," directed Harper. "These boys'll do the rest."

Warehouse workers slid the hands of tobacco off the split hickory sticks, neatly stacked the leaves on round flat baskets, and sorted the crop into four grades. When the crop was tagged and weighed, Harper swore softly. "Not but 1500 pound to the acre. I was hoping for a whole lot more this time."

"You're going to have to stop raising this pretty stuff," said Manual, "and grow you some real tobaccer. Now they got that new kind, Kentucky 21, why last year Earl Allen growed it and got 2500 pounds a acre."

"That damned old black tobacco?" Harper snorted. "My burley, it'll bring a nickel a pound more than any of that stuff'll get."

"Yeah," agreed Manual, "but people like Earl Allen will go home with about $500 more a acre than you'll get. If you're going to grow a crop you're going to have to use the new seed and sock the fertilize to it. Hell, Harper, pretty tobacco don't pay no more."

"I reckon not," sighed Harper. "But a body ought to be able to make a living growing it right."

"That's how come I'm a trucker and not a farmer," said Manual. "If you and Buck had of stuck with it when you was running that truck, you'd be rolling in the cash right now instead of grubbing out a living."

"Reckon I'd be as rich as you?" grinned Harper. "I like to go home at night, Manual. We do all right, Elsie and me, farming."

Manual snorted. "If you could raise up crops the way you make youngens, you might get rich."

"I'm rich enough," growled Harper. His face tightened. "But if the damn prices don't go up, a body ain't going to be able to make it another year."

Vernon was busy inspecting the long rows of tobacco baskets, each tagged and weighed, waiting for the auctioneer. He shivered and wished he'd worn long underwear.

"You cold, boy?" asked Harper. "They's a stove over there in that little room."

"Let's go warm ourselves up in The Black Cat," said Manual. "And get us some dinner."

"What's The Black Cat?" asked Vernon.

"Best eating and drinking place in all of Maysville," announced Manual. "Harper, it's high time we showed this boy the good life. I'll buy."

Harper hesitated. "That's a rough joint."

"Not in the broad daylight," groaned Manual. "Let's go." He wheeled the empty truck down an alley, swung left, and roared toward the flood wall. He parked in front of a drab building with a broken neon sign. "You ever been to a restaurant?" he asked Vernon.

"Nope." Vernon stared at the flickering sign and the dim interior of The Black Cat. "Is that a beer joint?"

"Hell, you could call it that," laughed Manual, "but they got good looking waitresses and the best hamburgers you ever et."

"What's a hamburger?" asked Vernon.

"Harper," groaned Manual, "you've got to start letting these youngens come down off of the mountain ever now and then."

Harper held the door open for Vernon and Manual. Vernon stopped, just inside, awed by the tinny jukebox and the powerful stench of beer and stale cooking grease, by the assortment of derelicts and farmers who crowded the booths and tables.

"Quit gawking," Harper said quietly. "Let's set over yonder."

Vernon slid into a ragged corner booth. "Take off your cap, boy," chuckled Manual. "Was you raised in a barn?"

Vernon reached for his cap. It wouldn't come off.

Harper scowled. "Take that damn cap off, Vernon."

"I can't," whispered Vernon. "It's stuck."

"Stuck?" Harper leaned closer. "Why's it stuck?"

Vernon squirmed. "It's blood," he blurted. "From where I hit my head this morning. My cap is stuck to my hair."

"The hell you say," grunted Manual. He yanked at the cap and Vernon yelped. Manual ripped the cap loose. "Lord have mercy, Harper," he groaned. "Elsie will kill the both of us when she sees that."

Harper stared at the dried, matted blood on Vernon's head. "Boy," he said finally, "would you mind putting that cap back on?"

They sat in uneasy silence until the waitress arrived with plastic menus and a throaty welcome. "What'll it be, fellers?"

Manual brightened. "One hot waitress with nothing on, to go. Howdy, Mabel." His grin showed dirty teeth. "Been a while, ain't it?"

"Be a longer while afore you get more out of me than beer and burgers," snapped Mabel. She chewed busily on her gum and rested her stocky frame against the booth. "Want a beer, hon?" she asked Vernon.

"No," he stammered, staring at the oilcloth. "I ain't old enough."

"I never would have guessed that," Mabel laughed, "if you hadn't of told me."

"Get me a cold Falls City," said Manual, "and the same for my buddy Harper."

"Two Cities coming up," said Mabel. "What for the red-faced young one here?"

"Pepsi," said Harper.

"Cat got your tongue, sonny?" Mabel leaned over to tease Vernon and the buttons of her short white uniform strained. Vernon turned bright red. "Look at them big brown eyes, would you," sighed Mabel. "In a year or two he'll have to whup off the girls with a stick." Laughing, she swished off to get the drinks.

"Look at that behind," Manual said admiringly. "Wouldn't that keep a feller warm on a winter night?"

Mabel returned to plop sweaty tall-necked bottles on the table. "Ready to eat?" she asked. "What'll it be?"

"Hamburgers all around," said Manual, "with fries. On me today."

"I'll put yours on you and theirs on plates," said Mabel.

Vernon giggled.

Harper salted his beer and drank greedily. "Two more, Mabel," yelled Manual.

"I'd better not," Harper protested weakly.

"What the hell, Harper?" chuckled Manual. "A man don't sell his crop but onct a year."

When Mabel brought the platters Vernon stared suspiciously at the greasy potatoes and dripping hamburger. "Douse it all with ketchup," advised Manual. "Then you won't notice how bad it tastes."

"Try the stuff without ketchup first," suggested Harper.

Vernon picked up the limp hamburger and shook off grease. "What's this made out of?" he asked. "Ham?"

"Beef," snorted Manual. "Damned ground up beef."

"But why — "

Manual shut the boy off. "I don't know why they call 'em hamburgers," he snapped. "Just shut up and eat it."

Vernon bit into the hamburger and chewed thoughtfully. "Good," he announced.

"Try them French fries," advised Harper.

Vernon bent over and busily cleaned his plate. Then he licked his fingers. "Eats like a young heathern," observed Manual. "Want another one, Vernon?"

Mabel brought another hamburger platter and two more beers. "Growing boys," grinned Manual. After his third beer Harper was grinning for different reasons. Vernon paused halfway through a mouthful. "Are you drunk, Daddy?" he asked.

"Hell no he ain't drunk," spat Manual. "Two more Cities, Mabel."

Vernon's eyes widened as Harper drained another tall bottle. "Momma said if you all got drunk I was to hide the truck keys."

"Ain't nobody drunk, damnit," Harper said thickly. He pulled out his railroad watch. "But the crop sells in a half a hour, so we'd best git."

Manual dug in his pocket for two quarters and slapped them down on the wet table. "Is that all that this costs?" asked Vernon.

"Hell, boy, that there is just the tip," snorted Manual. "It's for Mabel."

"Why?" asked Vernon. "Don't Mabel get paid for working?"

"Not enough to live on, hon," laughed Mabel. She scooped up the quarters and handed Manual the ticket. "Ya'll come back now. You hear? Especially the youngen, soon as he grows up a little." She winked and Vernon blushed fiercely.

Manual patted Mabel's corseted fanny and ducked her fist. "Pleasure doing business with you, Mabel," he said. "Some night when I can stay longer I'll be back."

"That's what they all tell me," laughed Mabel.

Harper stumbled going out the door. "Out of practice, old son?" laughed Manual. "They was a time, Vernon, when your old daddy'd have him six beers before breakfast and then set into some serious drinking."

In the cold warehouse the auctioneer's singsong chant totally confused Vernon. The selling happened too fast, and only his father's glum face gave Vernon a clue as to what their tobacco had brought. "Was it real bad?" he asked.

Harper smiled weakly. "Not so good. Down some from last year." He inspected the tags and sighed. "About $750 a acre, and half of that goes to Lawson, so we'll get about $1600, all told."

"That's a lot," said Vernon.

Harper chuckled, his eyes dim and weary. "Aw, hell," he finally said. "It'll pay off the bank and most of the grocery bill." He sighed and rolled and lit a cigarette with trembling gnarled fingers. "We'll get by, Vernon. We always do, somehow."

"Where's Manual?" asked Vernon.

"Probably gone to get him a bottle," said Harper. "He'll be back by the time we get our check."

They waited in the crowded little room, filled with odors of sweat, whiskey, kerosene, and tobacco, until the man behind the cage called for Harper Watts and Lem Lawson. Lawson, the Morehead merchant who owned the farm which Harper cropped, was visibly angry. "Can't you do no better, Watts?" he growled. "Next year I might have to find me somebody that knows how to grow burley."

"I do the best I know how," Harper said quietly. "If that ain't good enough, go find you another man."

Lawson backed away, frightened by the soft cold voice and steady brown eyes. "I never meant nothing, Harper," he apologized. "You know how I go on."

Harper glared, big fists clenched, then slumped. "Yeah," he said. "I know how you go on." He turned to Vernon. "Let's find Manual and go home, son."

"Was Mr. Lawson mad?" Vernon asked as they walked outside. "Is he going to make us move?"

"He was just running at the mouth," said Harper. "And, no, he ain't gonna make us move. Lem knows they ain't anybody else that'd work as hard as we do for next to nothing." Harper sighed. "I'll do a little trucking, come spring, to get us by."

They walked slowly down the narrow sidewalk until Harper suddenly stopped. "Now do you see why I want you to stay in school?" he asked abruptly. "You see why I don't want you and the rest of 'em to farm all your lives?"

They found the truck, with a door hanging open, but no Manual. "Where is he this time?" Harper asked angrily. He slammed the door and kicked savagely at a tire.

Vernon edged back, wide-eyed. Harper took a deep breath, fumbled for the makings and rolled a cigarette. "Get in, Vernon," he said. "We'll go to The Black Cat and get Manual."

Mabel met them at the front door. "Am I ever glad to see you," she said. "I thought I was stuck with him."

"Get me a fifth of Old Crow," said Harper. "I'll get Manual and take him home."

Vernon followed as Harper threaded his way through the noisy bar. Manual was perched on a high stool, grinning. "Pull up a chair, old son," he said happily. "You too, young Vern. Let's drink to burley tobaccer, and to how it makes a rich man for a day out of a poor old hillside farmer."

"Let's go, Manual," Harper said softly.

"Go?" Manual swayed. "Hell, we just got here." He drained his glass. "Hit me again, Mabel, and bring the boy here a short beer."

Mabel handed Harper a bottle and change. "Take out what he owes you," said Harper. "We'll be going now."

Manual shook his head sadly. "You've gone and got old, Harper. They was a time . . . " Manual slid down off the stool and draped a limp arm around Vernon's shoulders. "Next year, son, you and me will come by ourselves and leave your old wore out pappy at home where he belongs."

Harper slid under the wheel and handed the bottle across to Manual, who uncapped it and drank the top two inches. "Good," he grunted. "You okay to drive, Harper?"

It was much colder now, and the truck's noisy heater did little to warm the cab. Vernon shivered, and Harper wiped the fogged windshield with his forearm. Manual passed the bottle back and Harper drank grimly, guiding the truck with one hand on the spinner. He double-clutched and downshifted for climbing the Maysville hill, and Manual winced as gears crunched loudly.

They stopped at the county line for another bottle. Vernon huddled, sick from the exhaust fumes and the stench of raw bourbon, and watched the jerky wipers fight the cold drizzle. Harper reached for the bottle.

"Don't drink no more," pleaded Vernon.

Harper hesitated, then tipped the fifth. "Grow up, boy," he growled. "Just grow up, would you?"

Vernon sank back against the ragged cold seat and tried to not touch either man.

The drizzle turned into a heavy, spattering snow which quickly blanketed muddy hillsides, and the gray gloom of twilight darkened the hollows.

Vernon fought back the tears, watched his father's grim face, and hoped they'd drop him off at home before they went to the bootlegger's for another bottle.

White Sports Coat

The year Harper Watts made a deal with Otto Wilson to live rent-free in return for fixing up the abandoned old farmhouse was the year Vernon Watts was an eighth grader, six gangly feet of awkward knees and elbows and a blushing awareness that girls were somehow different. It was the year of Elvis rocking on the radio, of Marty Robbins crooning about "A White Sports Coat," of Ted Kluzewski hammering the baseball for the Cincinnati Reds.

Ducktailed, sideburned, third baseman for the Hilltop School Wildcats, Vernon Watts was learning to shave cautiously with Harper's heavy brass razor, to shift gears in the blue cigar shaped Buick Roadmaster, to smoke stolen Lucky Strike cigarettes, and to nervously take part in the kissing games which were part of every community gathering.

Vernon had grown a foot taller in less than a year, sprouted chin-whiskers and chest hair, and suffered through a change of voice and outlook. He was on the verge of something. Vernon didn't know exactly what it was, but whatever was coming had something to do with leaving part of life as he knew it behind. Most of the rapid changes, Vernon decided, were good. For one thing, he could hit a baseball and now was chosen first instead of last. He was on the school team, playing third base with an old first baseman's mitt, batting cleanup. Against the Plummers Mills school he'd hit line drives off the schoolhouse roof but been more concerned with the three girls who sat close to third base and giggled as they sprawled to flash skinny legs and white cotton underwear. Watching, blushing, Vernon had made a reflex catch of a hard-hit ball down the line but then self consciously spun and slung the ball twenty feet over the first baseman's head.

Late in the game Vernon came on to pitch and struck out the first two batters before nerves and the watching girls got to him. Two walks and a hit batter loaded the bases, and the next hitter waited for a waist-high fastball. The home run cost Hilltop School the game and ended Vernon's pitching career, but Beulah Watson consoled him down the ravine in right field. Beulah stuck her tongue in Vernon's mouth and bit his ear before he retreated to catch the bus home and lie awake all night twisting restlessly.

By Monday morning Beulah was mysteriously aloof, the other girls giggled whenever they saw Vernon, and he was simply confused. Vernon's confusion multiplied when Miss Cook, the teacher, unveiled a graduation program she'd ordered and informed Vernon that, as class valedictorian, he would memorize and deliver the prewritten speech.

"Why me?" he asked weakly.

"The valedictorian is the person in the class with the best grades," said Miss Cook. "That's you. You'll make the speech right after the principal finishes his talk."

Vernon numbly told his mother what was happening. Elsie was delighted. "You'll do good," she told Vernon. "But we've got to get you some decent clothes."

"Clothes?" Vernon stared. "Do I have to dress up?"

"Of course you do," said Elsie.

"How?" asked Vernon. "I ain't got a suit."

"We'll take care of that right now," said Elsie. She reached for the Montgomery Ward catalog. "It's high time we got you one. Next year you'll be in high school. Which one of these do you like?"

Vernon selected a white sports coat and gray trousers, twenty dollars worth. Elsie, who'd never heard of Marty Robbins or Patsy Cline and their song, scowled. "Are you sure? A nice blue suit would be lots better for more stuff."

"Does the white one cost too much?" asked Vernon.

"I can pay on time," said Elsie, "if it's what you want."

Elsie sent in the order with a five dollar down payment, and Vernon started memorizing his speech. At the Hilltop School in 1956, eighth grade graduation was a major community event. Fewer than a fourth of the new graduates would go on to high school. Most would accept their places on the farms, as field workers and housewives, young adults in a society which saw little need for schooling past eight years.

Vernon Watts was part of an exception to the rule. Already his older sister and brother were high school students, and Vernon, winner of a statewide essay competition and acknowledged as the best speller in the county, was expected to bring some overdue glory to remote Hilltop School. There was even talk of college someday for the shy youngster, talk which Elsie Watts discouraged.

"College is for rich people," she told Vernon gently. "We'll do good just to get you through high school. Don't get your hopes up for something that can't be." She sighed and recited the familiar refrain. "God must love poor people, He made so many of us. We'll do our best, Vernon, but don't get your heart set on college."

Vernon didn't really question Elsie's advice. The needs of rural Finch County were served well enough, most thought, by basic reading and arithmetic and enough writing to get by. After graduation there would be, for the few years before the draft or the lure of Ohio factories took the young men away, welcome fulltime help with tobacco and corn crops. The girls were destined to loose their youthful bloom far too soon to the rigors of childbirth and hard farm living, to become old women at thirty and worn-out shells at forty.

Of Vernon's class of war babies, largest in the school's history, most of those who would go to high school were the fortunate sons and daughters of the few well-to-do landowners and storekeepers in the rugged eastern end of Finch County.

"You mark my words," neighbor Jess Jackson firmly told Harper Watts. "That boy of yours, Vernon, he won't set foot back in Creech County after he's growed. He'll be too good for the likes of us."

"I hope that's not the case," said Harper. "But, if it was to come to that, I'd just set back and be proud of him, and know that I helped him get there. If Vernon has to leave to find what he's looking for, then that's what he has to do. If he didn't have a mind of his own, I don't reckon he'd be mine and Elsie's anyhow."

Vernon, happily ignorant of the discussions of his future, had already committed his speech to memory. He didn't know what some of the words meant, or just how to say them, but he did have them all in the right order and could say them loud.

The package came from Montgomery Ward, and Elsie made Vernon wash before he tried on the pants and jacket. The coat hung baggy over Vernon's thin shoulders, and the gray pants were four inches too big around at the waist. Elsie measured, pinned up the waistband, and barely tacked the cloth together. "Is that all?" protested Vernon. "They'll bust loose. My britches will fall off while I'm up in front of all them people."

"No they won't," said Elsie, her voice muffled by a mouth full of pins. "Hold still. And don't get these things dirty."

Monday before graduation was Eighth Grade Day at the Finch County High School, a day when every potential freshman was bussed to the big WPA schoolhouse in Finchburg. Vernon saw Roy at the school but Roy wouldn't even speak. Prissy introduced Vernon to her friends, seniors at the school, who giggled as his ears burned bright red. Vernon strutted back to the bus and was still feeling cocky as they unloaded back at Hilltop School.

Chester Conners, a hulking sixteen-year-old classmate held back three times, took exception to Vernon's arrogant excitement about high school and told him so. Vernon bristled, his good sense dimmed by the presence of Beulah Watson and her friends, and he counterattacked. "We're not all too dumb to go to high school," Vernon told Chester. "Some of us can read and write."

"Did you say I was dumb?" growled Chester. He shoved Vernon against the wall. "Well? Did you?"

Vernon gulped and started sweating. Beulah Watson came up close. "Don't let dumb old Chester push you around, Vernon," Beulah snapped. With her hands on her hips, Beulah waited. Vernon closed his eyes and swung. Chester, happily surprised to get hit first, punched Vernon in the belly. The next thing Vernon saw, and the last thing, was Chester's right fist slashing toward his face.

Vernon woke up on the oiled oak floor, surrounded by anxious teachers and classmates. Vernon felt for his nose, found it, and stared at the fresh blood on his hand. Miss Cook and two boys helped Vernon up, and he saw for the first time the blood spattered down the front of his best shirt and jeans. Vernon staggered back into a chair.

Beulah Watson proceeded to give Chester Conners an angry tongue-lashing. Chester, confused and frightened, was led away to the principal's office. Vernon, for being foolish enough to attack a classmate three years older and sixty pounds heavier, got the hero's treatment. The girls and smaller children ogled the dried blood and Vernon's swollen face, and the boys offered to gang up and whip Chester. Beulah stood proudly close and basked in Vernon's newfound glory. She sat beside him on the bus home and nobody teased Vernon about it. Elsie's reception was less admiring. "You've ruined your best school clothes," she muttered as she put the bloodstained shirt and pants into cold water to soak. "Fighting at school." Elsie shook her head in disgust. "I thought you was different, Vernon."

Harper, with a puzzled grin, inspected Vernon's nose. "What I want to know," asked Harper, "is what does the other feller look like?"

"Chester has got a sore hand," laughed Roy, "where Vernon hit him with that big old nose." But outside, after supper, Roy asked about the necessary vengeance. "Me and Joe will stomp Chester," growled Roy. "We'll hold him while you hit him."

"But I started the fight," protested Vernon. "I hit Chester first."

Roy stared. "You? Hit Chester Conners? He's bigger than I am."

"I hit him, " Vernon said dully.

Roy grinned. "You ain't got much sense, Vernon, but you sure ain't a sissy. Me and Joe will help you next time."

"Ain't going to be no next time," said Vernon.

Roy shrugged. "Don't ever say I didn't offer."

The next morning Vernon held his breath as he climbed onto the bus, but Chester Conners wasn't in his usual back seat. Vernon relaxed and spent the day enjoying the respect his swollen face brought. At recess Beulah ran her hands gently over the bruises, and planted a firm kiss on Vernon's cheek. He blushed and retreated. "Don't you like getting kissed?" asked Beulah.

"Yeah." Vernon grinned foolishly.

"I'll do better than that little old peck," said Beulah, "at my party Friday night."

"Party?"

"At our house, Friday night after graduation," Beulah said smugly. "You'll come, won't you?"

"How am I supposed to get there?" asked Vernon.

"They can drop you off on the way home," said Beulah. "Don't you want to come, Vernon?"

"I want to." Vernon fidgeted. "What do you do at a party?"

"Play games," teased Beulah. "I'll teach you."

Elsie Watts did not like the idea of a party for eighth graders at the Watson home. "Let the boy go," chuckled Harper. "He's big enough."

"It ain't Vernon that worries me," sniffed Elsie. "It's that sassy little Beulah Watson."

Harper grinned. "I recollect a sassy girl I knowed once."

Elsie blushed. "That was different."

On graduation night Vernon dressed carefully, in Roy's new white shirt which was only a little bit too big and his new clothes. "You still didn't fix these," said Vernon as he pulled on the gray pants. "They're still not sewed good."

"They'll do," said Elsie. She stood back to admire him. "My, but don't you look all grown up."

Vernon tugged at Harper's tie and shuffled. "Feels awful."

"Better get yourself used to it," beamed Harper. "One of these days that's what you'll wear all of the time."

"Not me," grunted Vernon.

The school lunchroom was jammed with sweaty parents and relatives as the graduating class marched proudly into place. Chester Conners was missing, but thirty-five blushing eighth graders were present for the honors. When the time came Vernon recited his speech. There was much applause. Few, including Vernon, had any idea what he had just said, but everyone agreed he said it well despite a slight lisp attributed to the swelling in his face.

The diplomas were handed out to much yelling and clapping. Then it was over. For most of the class, school was over. Forever. Harper dropped Vernon off at the Watson farm. "Don't mess up the clothes," warned Elsie. "Walk home on the road instead of coming through the woods."

Inside Vernon took a glass of Kool-Aid and sat stiffly, watching. Some were dancing. One group of boys went outside to smoke. Girls clumped together, boys huddled in a group. Beulah broke the stalemate. "Let's play post office," she suggested.

The kissing game rotated until Vernon was in the dark pantry with Beulah. She attacked more with enthusiasm than skill, and her sharp teeth cut Vernon's bruised lip. He pulled away and Beulah pursued. Somebody banged on the door. "Let's go out the window," whispered Beulah. She was already climbing, strong legs bared as she straddled the windowjamb. "Come on, Vernon."

In the corncrib Beulah came swarming to Vernon. He froze when she guided his hand to her small breast. "What's wrong?" she asked.

"I better go," Vernon said.

"Why?" pouted Beulah. "I thought you liked me."

"I do," stammered Vernon.

"I don't bite," said Beulah. She grinned. "Not much."

Two hours later, dazed, Vernon walked the three miles home. On the road, as Elsie had ordered. Elsie was awake, waiting. "Give me the pants," she said. Vernon emptied his pockets and stepped out. Elsie inspected the trousers and laughed at Vernon, standing cross-legged in his underwear. "Go to bed," Elsie said gently. She smiled. "But first go wipe that lipstick off of your face."

Saturday morning Vernon slept late, wondered when he saw sunshine why Harper hadn't got him up to work, and went down-stairs. Elsie was busy with needle and thread, working on the gray pants. "How does it feel?" she asked Vernon.

"How does what feel?"

"Why, being an eighth grade graduate," beamed Elsie. "That's what." "Why are you sewing on my britches now?" asked Vernon. "It's all over."

"I know what I'm doing," said Elsie. She had removed the darts she'd used to make the pants smaller at the waist, and had reattached every tag and label. "I'm sending these back. For the same money we can get you school clothes for a whole year."

"Can you do that?" asked Vernon. "I wore them."

"That's why I said to be careful," beamed Elsie. She still had the original wrappings, and was carefully folding the jacket. "When would you ever wear this again?"

"I don't know," blurted Vernon, "but it ain't right to send them back after I wore them."

Elsie stiffened. "Being a eighth grade graduate don't make you big enough to tell me what's right and what ain't."

"I don't reckon," Vernon said softly, "that being a eighth grade graduate makes me big enough to do anything." He went outside and found his old dog Rex and sat humped up with him in the sunshine. Somehow this special day, this day when he was supposed to feel so proud, was turning out wrong. Vernon's face was sore, and his lips were chapped from Beulah's enthusiasm.

Maybe, figured Vernon, he'd be better off to be like Chester Conners and just farm all the time. Vernon hugged Rex closer, and the dog growled a good-natured warning. "Not you too," wailed Vernon. Rex solemnly licked Vernon's face.

"Don't let that dog lick on you," scolded Elsie. "No telling what he's been eating." She handed Vernon a package and a limp dollar bill. "Take this to the mailbox."

As he walked, scuffing dust with his heavy workshoes, Vernon laughed at the gloomy dog who tracked at his heels. "Get up from there." Vernon made a quick move and Rex skipped sideways, barked happily, circled and attacked from the rear. Vernon and Rex played in dusty confusion, mixing laughter and frantic yelping.

Harper Watts, watching from the hillside, leaned on his plow to rest and smile. "Play ever chance you get, son," Harper said softly. "You got precious little playtime left now."

In time Vernon retrieved the brown package and slapped off the dust. He trudged on toward the mailbox, stooped and slow, on his way now to mail the packet to Chicago and get back, in a week or so, the dreary work clothes of reality.

Cassie Faye

The summer of Vernon Watts' fifteenth year, he met Cassie Faye McCormick.

Cassie was a very grown-up fourteen, the only daughter of Mudsock bootlegger Minnie McCormick, a high-spirited country girl impatient to get on with life and living.

High schooler Vernon Watts caught Cassie's eye. Vernon's slim body, long sideburns, slicked-back ducktail hairdo, shiny black eyes, and scholar's reputation intrigued Cassie Faye, whose exposure to men was more to Minnie's unwashed, beer-breathed and beer-bellied regular customers.

Cassie Faye had been an elementary school classmate of Reba, Vernon's sister, before quitting after six grades. Cassie quit with her mother's full approval; Minnie saw no need for a girl to graduate even eighth grade, and Cassie Faye had grown weary of the persistent snide comments about her mother's profession. But the Watts children, including Vernon, treated Cassie with friendly open respect, and Vernon always offered a shy smile whenever he passed by Minnie's old mobile home.

Dark, budding Cassie Faye, who now methodically tracked Vernon's movements, found out that he and Buford Farley swam often in the big mossy pond in the apple orchard. She finally found the two boys splashing naked there after a day in the hayfields.

Vernon who saw Cassie Faye coming, thin cotton dress short over slender brown legs, blushed and backed out into deeper waters. Buford grinned, puffed out his stocky chest, stood as tall as he could on short bowed legs. "Come on in, Cassie Faye," he yelled.

Vernon sank lower into the murky water. "Shut up, Buford," he whispered urgently. "She's a girl."

"I know that much, you fool," grinned Buford. "Why do you think I want to get her all wet?"

Cassie Faye walked slowly to the pond's edge.

"Did you bring us some beer?" asked Buford.

Cassie scowled, toed Buford's dusty shirt and pants where they lay in the clay, then smiled. "How would you like some wet pants?" she asked. "And socks and underwear?"

"How do you know them are mine and not Vernon's?" asked Buford.

Cassie sniffed. "They stink," she drawled, "and the legs of these britches are little bitty."

Vernon giggled. Feisty Buford, a full foot shorter than Vernon's six-feet-one, glared. Cassie stood with a hand on one hip, an imitation of Minnie's business stance, and stared boldly at Vernon, who sank lower and lower. "You'll drown yourself," Cassie finally said, smiling.

"You coming in?" Buford asked eagerly.

Cassie stared, shrugged, dipped a bare toe in muddy water.

"Come on," urged Buford. "It's warm."

Cassie waded in, up to her knees. Vernon's eyes widened. Cassie laughed, came further, dress swirling up in the water, floating. Buford suddenly hit the surface with both palms, and sent a spray of tepid water toward Cassie. She shrieked, caught the water in her face and down her chest, then stood with her arms wrapped around her breasts, brown hard nipples thrust against wet cotton.

Vernon lost his footing and went under. He came up gagging, shook the water out of his eyes, tried not to stare.

"God-a-mighty," gasped Buford.

"Dumb boys," Cassie said scornfully. She turned, waded to the shore, and climbed out. The thin wet dress clung to every curve, and water streamed down both brown legs. Cassie shook herself, and swung her hips as she walked away.

Vernon and Buford watched, frozen, until Cassie Faye was gone. Then there was a sudden frenzy of splashing, yelling, punching, and rowdy sheer exuberance, a celebration of Cassie's sexual presence.

After they dressed, Buford punched Vernon's shoulder. "Cassie Faye's got the hots for you, Highpockets," he said. "She wants your body."

"Naw," blushed Vernon. "Maybe she thought I was Roy." He grinned. "Only Roy, he would have drug her right off to the bushes."

"I sure would like to," Buford said wistfully. "Did you ever see the like, Vernon?"

"Nope," Vernon admitted. "I never did."

"Not even from Beulah Watson?" grinned Buford.

"*I* got more curves than Beulah's got," Vernon said absently. His mind still saw clinging wet cotton, water sliding smoothly down slim brown legs. "But," he added, "until today I sure didn't know Cassie Faye looked that good."

"Me neither," said Buford. "Heck, Vernon, she's as pretty as Sarah Collier."

"Prettier, almost," Vernon said softly. He walked home in a daze, preoccupied and stumbling, totally unaware that he was being watched. Cassie Faye McCormick followed from a safe distance, watched Vernon stoop in the front yard to pet a little beagle pup, smiled as he tripped up the front porch steps.

Two days later a drizzling rain washed out work in the hayfields and tobacco patches, and Vernon Watts walked restlessly through the woods alone in early afternoon. He wound up on the hill overlooking Minnie's dreary mobile home business site, stood for ten minutes staring down at the clutter and faded shell.

Cassie looked out the window and saw him, pulled on a scarf and threadbare short jacket, and ducked out the door. She intercepted Vernon near Alton Razor's barn. "Want to come in out of the rain?" she asked. Cassie led the way to an open door. Vernon followed, stepped into musty animal and tobacco smells and gloomy darkness, took off his water-soaked cap and wrung it out.

"Up in the hayloft," suggested Cassie, "you can see out for two miles." She scrambled up the crude ladder, legs flashing. "Come on," she called back. "It's warmer up here too."

Vernon scraped mud off his feet and climbed, hesitated at the top then followed Cassie across to a shuttered window. She shoved the hinged shutters open. "See?"

From the top of the ridge they looked down at foggy hillsides, winding fence rows, rows of corn and tobacco hugged to winding contours, houses and barns shrouded in filmy mist. "Ain't it pretty?" Cassie asked softly.

Vernon, not trusting his voice, just nodded.

"Can't you talk?" grinned Cassie.

"Yeah." Vernon cleared his throat. "Some."

"Some must be about all," said Cassie. "I was starting to wonder if you was tongue-tied."

Vernon shrugged. "You make me nervous."

"I make you nervous?" Cassie laughed, sat down on a bale of hay with her skirt tucked between her legs. "You're the one that's the big deal in high school and stuff, that wins all the prizes and gets your name in the paper about ever week."

Vernon blushed proudly. "That ain't nothing. Just schoolwork." He shoved his hands deep in his pockets and squirmed.

"Do you still go with Beulah Watson?" blurted Cassie.

"I don't go with nobody," protested Vernon. He felt the blush creep hotly up the back of his neck. "Do you?"

"On dates?" Cassie sighed and shook her head. "Momma says two more years first. She said she got married when she wasn't but thirteen and she ain't about to have me turn out the same way."

Vernon stared. In the shaft of pale light from the window, Cassie was half in shadows, darkly mysterious and sculptural. Then she laughed, reached up and took off the scarf, shook loose her curls, shrugged off the jacket. Cassie smiled. "You could sit here by me," she suggested.

Vernon grinned foolishly, took an awkward seat at the other end of the hay bale, blushed some more and twisted his hands anxiously.

"I don't bite," grinned Cassie Faye. She scooted across. "Do you think I'm pretty, Vernon?"

"Real pretty," whispered Vernon.

"Well?" Cassie leaned closer. "Don't you want to kiss me?"

Cassie's face was an inch from Vernon's. Her eyes were closed, her lips puckered. He edged closer, and their lips touched. Vernon jerked away. Cassie opened her eyes. "A real kiss," she protested. "Not that old peck."

This time Cassie did the kissing, with hard and aggressive lips, and she slipped both her arms around Vernon's neck. He stiffened, finally relaxed, and reached for her. Vernon lost his balance and fell, dragged Cassie off with him, and they landed in a laughing tangle, Cassie clinging, Vernon on the bottom. She was warm, all hard and soft at once, sprawled languidly across Vernon's chest. She wiggled over, dress up to her hips, to lie full on top of him. Vernon looked up with a puzzled smile.

"How did we wind up like this?" asked Cassie, smiling. She made no move to get away.

"I don't know," mumbled Vernon. "But I kind of like it."

"Me too," said Cassie. The next kiss was long and lingering, exploring, and finally Vernon's hands slid instinctively down to Cassie Faye's waist. They were both breathing heavily, and Cassie's firm little breasts were pressed to Vernon's heaving chest.

Then Cassie lifted herself up on both arms, smiled down at Vernon, rolled over and reached for the hem of her flimsy dress. She pulled it up and off, quickly, sat naked except for white panties. Vernon gasped, and stared. "Now take your shirt off," whispered Cassie.

He did, fumbling with every button. Cassie smiled and snuggled close, and arched up her body to help Vernon slide the white panties down over her scuffed knees.

Vernon walked toward home in a happy daze, a crooked grin maybe permanently affixed, his gait a cross between an arrogant swagger and a hesitating stumble. He wanted to yell, wanted to cry, wanted to tell the world what he'd just done, wanted to keep it all a deep dark secret.

Elsie watched from the clothesline, clothespins in her mouth, wondering what great thing her eccentric second son had now discovered about the world, smiled as he tripped up the front steps.

"Are you okay, Vernon?" she asked.

His foolish grin and sudden red face triggered Elsie's suspicions. "Where have you been?" she demanded.

"Out walking around," mumbled Vernon. "Nowheres."

Elsie walked closer. "Your shirt is buttoned up crooked," she said. "And how'd you skin your neck?"

Vernon blushed brighter. "I fell."

Elsie, hands on her hips, stared at Vernon, who wilted. "After supper," she said firmly, "you and me had better talk."

Supper lay heavy in Vernon's stomach, fresh beans and cornbread turned suddenly hard and tasteless, but Elsie pretended to not notice. Then, while the girls washed dishes, she followed Vernon out to the old metal lawn chairs in the back yard. "Who is she?" Elsie asked. "Buleah Watson?"

"No," blurted Vernon, red again already. He eyed the grass. "Cassie Faye McCormick," he whispered.

Elsie scowled. "Minnie's girl?"

Vernon nodded.

"What'd you do?"

Vernon's bright face was answer enough for Elsie. "Oh, My God, Vernon," she said disgustedly. "Go wash yourself off."

Vernon stiffened. "What's so bad about Cassie Faye?"

Elsie groaned. "She growed up in a bootleg joint. She quit school after sixth grade. She ain't but thirteen years old."

"Fourteen," corrected Vernon.

"My Lord," whispered Elsie. She wrung her hands and blushed. "Did you use anything?"

Vernon stared blankly.

Elsie blew out her breath and slumped. "What if Cassie has a baby now?" she asked.

"A baby?" Vernon blinked. "Why, we ain't old enough for that." He waited. "We ain't, are we?"

Elsie sighed, nodded, sank lower in her chair. "I got to explain some stuff to you," she finally said, "that I was hoping you didn't need to know just yet." Elsie's explanation was short, terse, and blunt. Vernon tried to sink under the chair, wished now he'd never gone walking in the rain.

"So you stay away from Cassie Faye McCormick," concluded Elsie. "And hope you ain't caught nothing and ain't already about to be a daddy."

Vernon laid awake all night, stumbled off to work for Jake Howard at daybreak, labored glumly all day and finally wore down Jake's good humor. "What's wrong, boy?" Jake finally asked. "I not see you act so funny since your little dog get killed on highway."

Vernon shrugged, offered a weak grin, gave no explanation and started walking across the ridge toward home. Halfway there, Cassie Faye was waiting for him, perched on a fallen log, thin dress high over her thighs. She smiled. "Ain't you glad to see me, Vernon?"

"No," said Vernon. He looked away. "And I can't see you no more, ever," he mumbled.

"Why?" demanded Cassie. She grinned. "Are you afraid of me?"

"Nope," said Vernon. He dared now to turn and look at her, smiling and cross-legged, eager and impish, and his fierce resolve melted instantly away.

Vernon missed supper, avoided Elsie, left for work at daylight the next morning.

For a month, Vernon and Cassie Faye spent every free minute together. They swam naked in the pond, romped in thick wet grass, spent Sunday afternoons deep in the woods with a picnic basket and an old quilt, mated frequently and frantically.

Buford Farley complained. "You don't ever come to the store no more, Vernon. You stopped playing baseball, and you act all goofy now. What's the matter with you, anyhow?"

"Nothing," Vernon replied happily. "Not a thing."

Elsie finally could stand idly by no longer. She walked over to see Minnie McCormick, came home grim and distracted, said nothing but watched sadly as Vernon wolfed down his supper and left happily.

Elsie sat in the back yard far into the night, waiting, was still there when Vernon finally came home well after midnight. He saw her, started to leave, but came over and sat down heavily.

"Where have you been?" Elsie asked gently.

"Walking," said Vernon. "Nowhere. Everywhere." His voice shook. "Cassie Faye is gone. Over to Dayton, to live with her aunt Jennie."

"I know," said Elsie.

"You already know?" Vernon stiffened. "How come?"

Elsie sighed. "I talked to Minnie, this morning. For a long time. About you and Cassie." She groped for words. "Vernon, Cassie is just fourteen. You're just fifteen. What the two of you have been doing, it ain't right, and you know it. It had to stop, before . . . " Elsie's voice trailed away. "You know why."

"You run Cassie off?" Vernon asked stiffly.

"Nobody run her off," said Elsie. "We didn't have to. Cassie wanted to go. The minute Minnie mentioned it, Cassie Fay was ready to pack up and leave."

"I don't believe that," Vernon said dully.

"It's the truth," insisted Elsie. "Cassie couldn't wait to get gone."

Vernon sagged, stared glumly at his mother, then rested his head down in his hands.

"Vernon," Elsie said softly, "Cassie Faye is just a wild little girl. What you and her done, it don't mean a thing to her except fun. The way she was raised, she didn't know any different, and it didn't matter who would have come along. It would have been just the same, for you or anybody else she seen."

"No," whispered Vernon. "That's not so."

"She's gone," snapped Elsie. "So it don't really matter no more, does it?"

"Matters to me," mumbled Vernon.

"What matters," Elsie said wearily, "is that you learn the difference between what you and Cassie Faye was doing and the way it is between growed-up men and women."

"What's the difference?" asked Vernon. "I don't see none."

"There's more to it than acting like two old hounds in heat," Elsie said tightly. "You got to care about each other, and want to spend the rest of your lives with each other. To think about the future, not just about what feels good." She sighed. "You got a chance, Vernon. You might even go to college, in two years, and Lord knows what, after that. But not if you have to quit school and get married, and especially not if you marry somebody like Cassie Faye."

"I like Cassie Faye," Vernon said stubbornly.

"I know what it is that you like," snapped Elsie, "and for that part, it don't matter one bit what her name is."

Vernon blushed in the darkness.

"Let this all be a lesson to you," said Elsie. "You were lucky this time. But, if you ever get a nice girl pregnant, Vernon, you'll have to marry her."

Vernon grinned weakly. "Does that mean it's okay to get girls that are not nice pregnant?"

"What that means," snapped Elsie, "is to keep your britches zipped until you know what you're doing." She stood. "Go to bed. You have to help Jake cut tobacco in the morning."

Vernon went slowly on into the house, and Harper slipped out of the darkness to join Elsie. "A big help you are," she said. "Hiding in the dark to listen, and not helping me one bit."

Harper chuckled. "You done fine, all by yourself."

"You think it's funny, don't you?" Elsie asked sharply. "Vernon and that fourteen year old wildcat running naked all over the ridge?"

"Boy's got to sow his oats," grinned Harper. "Vernon will be okay."

"*He* will," Elsie agreed coldly. "But what about the girl? She left here crying her eyes out, kicking and squalling, yelling for Vernon, trying to get Minnie to let her see him just one more time. What about Cassie Faye, Harper? What's to come of her?"

He lit a limp cigarette. "She'll get over it. Up in Dayton, she'll find plenty of stuff to keep her busy."

"That's what I'm afraid of," Elsie said softly.

Harper stubbed out the cigarette. "We got nine of our own to worry about. We can't take care of the bootlegger's girl too."

"I won't sleep tonight," said Elsie, "wondering about that poor little girl."

Harper scowled. "She ain't in a family way, is she?"

"No," said Elsie. She shrugged. "At least, not that we know about."

"But she could have been," grunted Harper, "and that's why you're so wound up."

"I guess," said Elsie. She blushed. "Vernon, it just don't seem like he's old enough to be out . . ."

"Tomcatting?" Harper grinned. "Hell, Elsie, just because the boy reads books and draws pictures don't mean he ain't human like the rest of us."

"I know," sighed Elsie. "I just hope he don't let all that keep him from his school."

"I'd reckon," smiled Harper, "that a feller could do both. Don't you think?"

He chuckled, shook his head, and followed Elsie on into the house.

Merry Christmas

Vernon Watts' first real girlfriend was the daughter of a Finchburg building contractor.

Vernon, almost seventeen and a senior at the Finch County High School, didn't arrange his first date with Sarah Collier. One of her friends, Patsy Kilgore, grinned and told Vernon how Sarah said he was cute and she'd go out with him if he wanted to. The negotiations took three days, through Patsy, before Sarah stopped Vernon in the hallway to say yes, Saturday night would be great.

On the school bus home, Buford Farley rubbed it in. "Old skinny Vernon Watts has got a date with the richest girl in Finch County." Buford grinned happily. "Hey, Highpockets, where are you going to get a suit and necktie and a fancy enough car to go driving up to old Buck Collier's big house?" He punched Vernon's shoulder. "Dang it all, Vernon. How'd you do it?"

Vernon shrugged. "Just comes natural. Don't you ever watch how the women just fall around my feet?"

"Yeah. Little bitty girls and white haired old women do," snorted Buford. "Heck, Vernon, Sarah Collier is about the prettiest girl in the whole school, and a cheerleader, and her daddy's rich." He sighed. "Do you need to borrow some clothes? Or some money?"

"Nope," said Vernon. "I'll get by." But as he swung down off the bus, surrounded by the smaller Watts children, Vernon wasn't so sure. He walked slowly up the rutted roadway, pondering.

From a distance, it was easy to see why Vernon's nickname was "Highpockets." Over six feet tall, barely 125 pounds, all wiry muscle from hard farm work, Vernon seemed to be mostly legs. Just today the drama teacher, after choosing Vernon for a role in the senior play, had wondered aloud when he'd ever grow a chest and shoulders, and this morning Elsie had complained gently that it was hard to find britches to fit a six footer with a twenty-four-inch waistline.

Vernon's mother was waiting on the porch, a puzzled smile on her face. "Is something the matter?" asked Elsie. "I can tell, from your face. What is it, Vernon?"

He grinned sheepishly. "I got me a date with Sarah Collier. Saturday."

Elsie stared. "You are the beatingest youngen," she finally said. "Last year you come home and tell me you aim to be president of the whole school, and now you say you're going out with Buck Collier's girl." She sighed. "Vernon, don't go and get yourself into something that'll get you hurt."

"Ain't I good enough for Sarah Collier?" smiled Vernon.

"It ain't that. You're as good as anybody." Elsie twisted her apron. "It's just that I worry about you sometimes."

"That I might go and get above my raising?" Vernon laughed. "Momma, don't start on that stuff about how God must love poor people because he made so many of us."

"That's the truth," insisted Elsie. "I don't want them people in town to laugh at you."

"They don't," Vernon said quietly. "I am the president of the student council now, Momma. I've won almost every award they give at school. Just because we live way out here and aren't rich doesn't mean I have to be ashamed."

"I still worry," fretted Elsie. "Now, Prissy and Roy, when they was in high school, they never got into all that stuff."

Vernon's dark eyes sparkled, and in them Elsie saw Harper Watts' young fire and devilment, the youthful eagerness which had dimmed now after many years of hard work and frustration. "I don't want you getting hurt," she repeated lamely.

Vernon laughed. "Don't you worry about me. I don't reckon God will mind if one or two of us tries to quit being poor."

"You do so good in school," said Elsie. "And I know you want to go to college. And I know we ain't got money for that."

"I'll get a scholarship," Vernon said confidently, "and I'll work." He grinned. "But Saturday, if Daddy will let me use the car, I got me a date with the prettiest girl I ever saw."

At the supper table, Harper grinned and told Vernon to take the Dodge Saturday night. "It ain't a Buick, like that girl is used to, but I reckon it'll get you there and back." He shook his head admiringly. "Going out with my boss's girl. See if you can get me a raise, Vernon. Buck Collier has durn near worked me to death for a dollar a hour."

"You'll do no such thing," snapped Elsie. "And when you go in that house, don't you drag in no mud on your feet."

Saturday morning Vernon was in Jake Howard's barn at dawn with a pitchfork in his hands. He cleaned stalls all day, collected four dollars and hurried home to clean up for his date. Vernon scrubbed himself with hot water from the wash pan, shaved carefully with Harper's big brass razor, and slicked down his ducktail with Wild Root Cream Oil. He pulled on khaki pants with tightly pegged legs and a buckle at the back, turned up the back of his shirt collar, and slipped on scuffed old saddle oxfords.

"Ain't you going to polish them nasty shoes?" asked Elsie.

"You don't polish this kind," Vernon said absently. "How do I look?"

"Just like your daddy used to," Elsie said wistfully. "Except half a foot taller and your hair ain't as black." She sighed. "I'm grateful you ain't as bad to fight as Harper used to be."

"I never was nearly as bad as you let on," chuckled Harper. "You need a couple of dollars, boy?"

"I got money," said Vernon.

"Car's got gas," said Harper. "Now, you remember to pump up the brakes, and don't forget she won't go into second gear unless you double clutch."

"I been driving for five years," said Vernon. "Don't you worry about me."

The old green Dodge coughed and started. Vernon's dogs yapped excitedly and followed him to the end of the lane. On the outskirts of Finchburg, Vernon started sweating.

"Lord," he groaned softly. "What have I gone and got myself into?"

Vernon parked in the Collier's long paved driveway and nervously patted down his hair before he knocked on the door. Buck Collier shoved it open. "I'm Vernon Watts," stammered Vernon. "Is Sarah home?"

"Come on in," Collier said gruffly. "Are you Harper's boy?"

"Yessir," said Vernon.

"Good man, Harper Watts," growled Collier. "Good worker." He studied Vernon. "You're the one that's so good in school?"

"I guess so," said Vernon, squirming.

"Your daddy talks about you a lot."

"Really?" Vernon blushed. "I mean, he don't ever say anything to me one way or the other."

"Well, he's mighty proud of you," said Collier.

Sarah came into the room smiling. "Hi, Vernon. I see you've met Daddy."

"Hello," mumbled Vernon. He stared. Sarah was simply beautiful in soft wool, and Vernon wondered if the snag in the car seat would tear her sweater. "Where are we going?" asked Sarah.

"I don't know," gulped Vernon. "The movie?"

"Sounds great," said Sarah. "Daddy, would you tell Mother I've gone?" She handed her jacket to Vernon, who grimly held it at arm's length.

Buck Collier chuckled. "She means for you to help her put it on, son. Trying to act all grown up tonight." He took Sarah's coat and slipped it over her arms, then turned to Vernon. "I hear good things about you. When you graduate, come and see me about a job."

"I'll be going to college," Vernon said softly.

Collier shrugged. "You'll need summer work. Going to the University?"

Vernon shook his head. "I don't know where yet, but Kentucky is too expensive."

"Don't matter where you go, as long as you go," said Collier. "I got one boy's an engineer, one that's a CPA, and what I really wanted was somebody to take over the business." He grinned and winked. "Maybe Sarah can learn to run a crew."

"Let's go," said Sarah, "before Daddy has me wearing a nail apron and driving a pickup truck."

That night Vernon fell hopelessly in love. Sarah was funny, bright, warm, and she kissed Vernon ardently when he took her home. "Tomorrow night?" she asked.

Vernon calculated his cash reserves. "Maybe," he hedged, "but we've already seen the movie."

"You could come here and watch television," said Sarah.

"Yeah," Vernon said quickly. "That'd be fun."

Elsie was still up when he got home. Vernon tossed her his jacket. "You got to help me figure out how to put one of these on a girl," he laughed. "Rich people don't put on their own coats."

Sunday night Vernon left his class ring with Sarah, and Monday morning she moved her books into his locker at the school. They went to basketball games, where Vernon proudly watched Sarah lead cheers, to the movie on Saturday, to Sarah's to watch TV on Sunday, and were inseparable at school. Sarah quietly warned her friends to not smoke or talk dirty around Vernon, who was shocked by girls who did such things, and she fiercely put a stop to all comments about Vernon's lack of a car, clothes, and cash.

Sarah's mother took to the shy, softspoken boy, and praised his school achievements. After a month, Vernon was almost at ease in the Collier's modern home with its lush carpets, three bathrooms, color television, and central heat. "It really is something," he told Elsie, who struggled to maintain her large household with an outdoor toilet, water from a cistern by the barn, coalfired stoves, and seven children crammed into two bedrooms. "Someday," swore Vernon, "we'll get you a house like that."

"I won't hold my breath," Elsie said dryly.

Buck Collier surprised Vernon the most. On a rainy Saturday night he tossed Vernon the keys to the new white Buick. "Go on, drive it," insisted Collier. Vernon, faced with power steering, power brakes, and an automatic transmission for the first time, poked along so carefully that Sarah laughed.

"Sometimes you're so much like a little old man," she teased. "Are you always so scared?"

To prove her wrong, Vernon floorboarded the Buick and couldn't handle the skid, and narrowly missed a cattle truck. "Let me drive," squealed Sarah. "Your daddy would kill me," Vernon protested weakly.

Sarah insisted, Vernon surrendered, and Sarah promptly drove the Buick off the highway into a weed-choked ditch. Vernon pushed, Sarah spun the tires, and they finally worked the car free. At a friend's house they hosed off the mud and looked for damage. Vernon finally breathed again when there were no dents or scratches. He used his last dollar for gas to get the Buick home, and was relieved to get back behind the wheel of Harper's old Dodge.

The next night Vernon and Sarah had their first fight. She wanted to go see a new movie, and Vernon was too stubborn to admit he didn't have any money. "Momma's right," he whispered as he drove home. "I got no business hanging around with rich people." But Monday morning Sarah was bright and affectionate, and Vernon's fears were soothed.

Vernon's sister Reba, a freshman at the high school, scoffed at Sarah Collier's reasons for dating Vernon. "She just thinks it's a big deal to go out with the student council president," said Reba. "If you wasn't such a big shot at school she'd be ashamed to be seem with you."

Vernon's schoolwork suffered, and his teachers were blunt. "I'm very disappointed in you," said Miss Willard, the English teacher. "Vernon, you and I both know that to go to college you have to win a scholarship. You've been mooning around, staring off into space, for a month. I know Sarah Collier is pretty, but your future is a little more important than a cute girlfriend."

Vernon was subdued that night, quieter than usual when Buck Collier met him at the door. "Come in here," said Collier. He led Vernon into the den with its crackling fireplace. "I need to talk to you." Vernon squirmed as Collier finished off a drink and lit an expensive cigar. "I've been thinking," began Collier. "You need money for college, and I need help in my business." He leaned forward. "I'm going to offer you a business proposition. Don't say yes or no tonight. Think on it first. I'll help pay your way through the university, and give you work summers and vacations, if you'll agree to come back and work with me after you graduate." Collier shrugged. "Maybe in time you could be a partner. I've got fifty acres at the edge of town, and pretty soon I'm going to build a hundred new houses out there. Collier Estates, I call it. Your daddy will be hanging windows and doors out there for ten years. But, I can't do all that by myself."

Collier chuckled as he watched Vernon's face. "What I'm offering you," he said softly, "has absolutely nothing to do with Sarah. I'm talking business. I need a good hard working young man to help me out."

"I don't know," Vernon said hesitantly. "Do you really mean it?"

"Every word," said Collier.

Sarah pushed the door open. "Is Daddy trying to scare you off? What are you two doing in here with the door shut?"

"Talking business," grinned Collier. "Ours, not yours. Think it over, Vernon. I'm dead serious."

In the car Vernon told Sarah what her father had just proposed. "That's great," she said. "We could go to the university together."

"I couldn't just take his money like that," whispered Vernon.

"Don't be silly," laughed Sarah. "You'd earn every cent. Daddy would work you to death."

Elsie shared Vernon's uneasiness about Buck Collier's offer. "Why's he being so good to you?" she asked.

"Neither one of his sons is interested in the business," explained Vernon.

"Do you have to marry the girl?" asked Elsie.

"No." Vernon grinned. "But that wouldn't be so bad, would it? And I wouldn't have to worry about college."

"They's more to this world than college," snapped Elsie, "and more to marrying than pretty."

For his 17th birthday at Thanksgiving, Sarah gave Vernon expensive leather gloves from a Lexington men's store. "These won't last long in the tobacco patch," joked Vernon.

"I wanted you to have something nice," said Sarah. Vernon felt that her emphasis was on "something" and bristled. "I didn't mean that the way it sounded," protested Sarah. "Please don't get all mad and stubborn just because I gave you a gift."

"You don't have to feel sorry for me," said Vernon. "I'll get by."

"I don't feel sorry for you," protested Sarah. "I gave you a birthday present. Because I wanted to. Can't you just accept that? Sometimes, Vernon, you make me so mad when you act so stubborn. You're not the only person in the world whose family doesn't have a lot of money, you know."

"I'm the only one in this room," growled Vernon. But he smiled. "I'm sorry. I guess I got too big a chip on my shoulder, don't I?"

"Yes," Sarah agreed emphatically. "And if I didn't like you so much I'd take those gloves back and throw them in the fireplace."

Elsie examined Vernon's new gloves admiringly. "You take care of these," she admonished. "You've never had nothing this nice before." Elsie smiled. "I'll help you pick out something really nice to give Sarah for Christmas."

Elsie was as good as her word. Two weeks later she led Vernon into the drug store. "See?" she said proudly.

It was an oriental jewelry box, black with red decoration, the prettiest thing Vernon had ever seen.

"How much?" he asked.

"Just five dollars," said Elsie. "And I'm paying for it out of my egg money."

Vernon smiled. "Have you finally decided to like Sarah?"

"I figured I might as well," grinned Elsie. "Seeing as how you're as good as married to her."

Vernon waited smugly for Christmas.

"What if she don't like it?" pestered Reba. "What if Sarah thinks that old box is ugly?"

"She won't," said Vernon. He proudly inspected the wrappings and ribbons. "This is just right for Sarah."

"She's stuck up," said Reba. "Sarah Collier is just plain old stuck up, is all."

"You're just jealous," grinned Vernon. "Jealous of her and me both."

"Jealous of a cheerleader and a idiot?" Reba smiled evilly. "I hope she pinches her finger in that ugly old jewelry box. And I bet she gets you some sissy necktie."

"You'll see," Vernon said smugly.

On Christmas Eve Vernon splashed on some extra Old Spice, and even polished his old saddle oxfords. He drove into town with Sarah's bright package safely beside him in the front seat. Buck Collier insisted that Vernon taste eggnog laced with bourbon, and Sarah's mother had a basket of fruitcake and candies for Elsie. Finally, Sarah and Vernon were alone.

"Open it," said Vernon.

"You first," said Sarah.

Vernon tugged at the ribbons, stopped to admire the elegant box, uncovered a soft blue cashmere sweater. "Try it on," Sarah said happily. "Mother and I went all over Lexington trying to find just the right one."

Vernon pulled the incredibly soft sweater over his head. "Look okay?" he asked.

"Perfect," smiled Sarah.

"Now open yours," said Vernon. He waited anxiously as she struggled with ribbon and tape. Sarah gently lifted out the jewelry box and opened a drawer. "A music box!" she squealed.

Vernon's heart stopped.

Sarah opened another drawer and waited. "How do you make it play?"

"You don't," Vernon said dully.

"Don't tease me," protested Sarah. "How do you make the music play?"

"It ain't a music box," whispered Vernon. "It's just a box." He stared at what until now had been so beautiful. "Momma found it for you," he finally said. "But it don't make music."

"That doesn't matter," said Sarah. "It's beautiful, Vernon."

"No it ain't," he said. "It's just a cheap, ugly little box that don't even make music." He blinked. "I got to go."

"Vernon, I love my jewelry box," pleaded Sarah. "Please, don't get mad at me."

"I ain't mad," Vernon said gruffly. "I just got to go. To help fix up Christmas stuff for the little ones."

"I'm sorry I acted like such a baby," said Sarah. "Won't you believe me?"

"Sure." Vernon shrugged. "No big deal."

"Don't be mad," said Sarah. "Please."

Vernon stood, stiff and uncertain.

"Are you just going to walk off?" asked Sarah. "Just leave?"

"No," whispered Vernon. "But I got to go."

"Don't forget your sweater," snapped Sarah. She spun and stared at the wall. Vernon hesitated, then grabbed the package and fled. Sarah walked to the door to watch him go.

"Goodbye, Vernon," she whispered into the swirling snowflakes. "Merry Christmas."

A Higher Education

The end of his senior year romance with Sarah Collier didn't stop Vernon from applying for a job with the Collier Lumber Company after his high school graduation in June.

"For the summer?" asked Buck.

Vernon shrugged. "Maybe fulltime."

"What about college?" Buck asked gruffly. "If I spend all summer getting you trained, and then you up and leave, I've wasted a bunch of time and money."

"I don't know yet," said Vernon.

"Well." Buck sat back. "What can you do?"

Vernon bristled. "Anything," he snapped. "I can drive a truck, stack lumber, paint, drive nails, and anything else that comes along in the way of work."

Collier grinned. "Can you run a cash register? What I need, just for the summer, is a sales clerk."

"I'd rather do outside work," said Vernon.

"I've got a job for you, if you want it," said Buck. "Sales, some delivery, inventory, a little bookkeeping. Take it or leave it."

Vernon took it, at seventy five cents an hour, and soon discovered that an office job had its problems. The yard and construction crews sneered openly at Vernon. "The way to get a easy job," they laughed, "is to make up to Buck's girl." There was envy, that Harper Watts' boy could move in the Colliers' social circle, and the jealousy took the form of cruel jabs. "You don't sweat a whole lot, do you?" grinned a crew foreman. "Does little Miss Sarah come by ever day and fan you?"

After two miserable weeks Vernon went to Buck Collier. "I don't know what I'm doing in here," pleaded Vernon. "Let me do some real work. Put me on a crew."

Buck grinned. "Getting to you, aren't they?"

"Yes," Vernon admitted glumly.

"I've been watching," said Buck. He thought it over. "Tell you what, Vernon. Billy Jessup broke his foot and will be out most of a month. I want you to take Billy's place."

"On the barn crew?" Vernon wilted.

Buck chuckled. "You want to show this bunch you're a man, don't you?"

Barn foreman Henry Wells took one look at the skinny replacement and groaned. "You're the one they call 'Highpockets,' ain't you?" Henry asked wearily. Vernon hung his head and nodded. Henry grinned. "Come on, son. Let's go stack some lumber."

Vernon spent his first day on the barn crew stacking rough oak timbers, twenty-foot beams for rafters. Muscular Frank McNeill broke Vernon in, worked him to the verge of collapse, then grinned and shared the water jug. "You work good," said Frank.

"Thanks," gasped Vernon. "You've about killed me."

"Gets worser tomorrow," grinned Frank.

"How could it?" groaned Vernon.

"You'll see," said Frank.

Vernon saw. At daybreak a flatbed truck was waiting with a load of freshly creosoted poles. "Ever see a pole barn, Highpockets?" asked Henry Wells. "We're about to put one up."

Under a blistering sun Vernon, Frank, and the two other barn builders, Johnny Bryan and Eck Rose, wrestled the tall, sticky poles into place. Vernon, as was his habit when working outside, peeled off his shirt. In mid-afternoon, dizzy and stinging, Vernon splashed out into a muddy farm pond to scrub off the smeared creosote. The others howled. "Why don't you just lick yourself, Highpockets?" yelled Eck Rose. "Like an old tomcat?"

"Laugh all you want to," Vernon yelled back, "but this stuff is killing me."

"You better toughen up, boy," grinned Eck. "A real man, he can drink creosote for breakfast."

That night Vernon, weak and burning, went to bed early. He woke up still sick to his stomach, peeling, red and raw across his chest and upper arms. "You better not go to work," cautioned Elsie.

"Got to," grunted Vernon. "I'm not about to be the only one that doesn't show up."

Vernon was the only one who did show. Worried Henry Wells relaxed. "Eck and Johnny are both in the hospital," said Henry, "and Frankie ought to be. I tried to find you last night, but you don't have a phone and nobody was sure where you live." Henry inspected Vernon. "Are you okay?"

"Except for my hide peeling off," grinned Vernon. "What are we going to do today?"

"Go out to the barn job," chuckled Henry, "and make like we're working."

Buck Collier stopped Vernon. "Are you all right?" asked Buck.

Vernon nodded. "I'm okay. But even if I wasn't, I'd still be here."

"Want your office job back?" asked Buck.

"Nope." Vernon straightened his shoulders. "We got a barn to build." Two days later the rest of the crew was back on the job, and it was time to hang rafters. "This was Billy's job before he got hurt," said Henry. "Highpockets, do you think you can nail 'em?"

"Tell me how," Vernon said grimly. Balanced thirty feet in the air on a four inch beam, Vernon caught the long rafters which were lowered from each side. "What now?" he gasped.

"Just nail them together," said Henry.

"How?" protested Vernon. "I ain't got but two hands."

Henry chuckled. "You want Frank to come and help?"

"No," snarled Vernon. He grimly balanced the rafters in one hand, dug in his apron for a handful of twenty-penny nails, and stuck them in his mouth. Vernon clawed his new hammer free and tried to drive a nail. He dropped it, swore, and tried again. The second nail bent.

"Let me do it," offered Frank.

Vernon shook his head. He finally got a nail started, pounded it home, did another, then grinned down at the crew. "Is this all they is to it?"

"You scrawny little rooster," chuckled Henry. He turned to Frank, who was watching anxiously. "That schoolboy might just do, Frankie. He ain't got any sense, but he's a tough little son-of-a-gun."

"He's gonna get hurt," mumbled Frank.

"Naw." Henry watched as Vernon finished nailing the rafters and swung easily back to safer beams. "Vernon climbs like a monkey. He's been up in a tobacco barn since he was a baby, so working thirty feet up in the air ain't nothing new to him." Henry raised his voice. "High-pockets, you're getting yourself what I'd call a higher education. You come down from there and get some ice water."

As Vernon gulped and splashed water down his chest, peeled and cracked from creosote burns, Henry again suggested that the job of tying the rafters was a little much. "No," insisted Vernon. He grinned. "But, it's enough. It don't get any harder, does it?"

"Yes," said Henry. "Along about three o'clock, when that sun hits just right, when you're already wore plumb out, you'll get to wondering if quitting time will ever get here."

"And it won't," grinned Eck. "Henry'll work us till dark if we don't tell him when it's four-thirty."

"Henry, he's a slave driver," added Johnny Bryan. "Someday we're gonna drop a rafter on him. Wouldn't hurt Henry, though, if we hit him on the head."

"Eck and Johnny is joking," Frank told Vernon solemnly. "They like Henry."

Vernon smiled at Frank, so simple and serious. "I kind of figured that much," Vernon said softly.

"You're okay, too," added Frank. "You work."

"We all work, on this crew," interrupted Henry. "Let's get back to it."

When Vernon crawled down to the ground at quitting time his arms were trembling from exhaustion. They gathered up the scattered tools and the water jug, and loaded them into the back of Henry's old blue '53 Ford. "You okay?" Henry quietly asked Vernon. "Buck said for me to keep a eye on you. And to tell you the office job is still yours whenever you want it."

"We've got a barn to build," grinned Vernon.

"So I'll see you bright and early," chuckled Henry. "Go get some rest."

For the rest of the month Vernon worked on Henry Wells' barn crew. They framed out the barn, nailed on tin roofing and hemlock siding, mounted sliding doors and laid in tier rails for hanging tobacco. Buck Collier came out to inspect the job.

"Looks good to me," Buck finally said. "Clean up the place and come back to town." Buck took Vernon aside. "Billy Jessup will be back at work Monday. I want you to come back to the office." Buck scowled. "If it'll make you feel any better, you can work in the yard part of the time."

"Whatever," shrugged Vernon. "I think it'll go lots better now."

Henry laughed. "That office doesn't sound so bad after building a barn, does it? But I'll tell you what, Buck. This boy is a worker. He can come on my crew anytime he wants to." Henry punched Vernon's shoulder playfully, then turned back to Buck. "Got us another barn to build?"

"You've got about a week of roofing first," said Collier. "The widow Carmicheal is driving me crazy, wanting her roof patched, and all the other crews are tied up. Fix Sadie's roof, then we've got a big barn over in Lewis County."

At home Vernon told his mother about finishing the barn. "And," he added, "Monday I go back to selling nails and paint. Working in the office."

"Ain't you glad?" asked Elsie.

"I'm not sure," said Vernon. "I like working on the barn crew. I know how to do everything. In the office, I always have to ask."

"I'd think you'd be tickled to death to get inside work," admonished Elsie. "That's part of why you been going to school." She pulled a letter from her apron pocket. "This come today. From Berea College."

Vernon tore open the envelope and read quickly. "They've accepted me, even though I applied late. And it says to not worry about money, to come on anyway and they'll find a way to get me through."

Elsie beamed. "A college student. The first one ever, from either side of the family."

Vernon slumped against a porchpost. "Not just yet," he said softly. "College would mean four more years. Doing without, working like a mule, not having a penny to spend. I might would rather work regular at the lumber yard."

"You do that," snapped Elsie, "and I swear I'll go see if Jake Howard still wants to buy you."

On Monday morning Vernon reported for work in the office. The crews, friendly now, chided Vernon as he weighed out nails, charged out lumber and hardware to jobs, and rushed to collect the supplies each foreman ordered. "Don't get all sweaty, Highpockets," warned Eck Rose. "Some good looking woman might come in here and buy a nail, and we don't want you to scare her away because you stink like a hog."

The work crews cleared out, and for the next two hours Vernon was busy with walk-in customers. There was a lull before lunch and another flurry of business in the early afternoon. Buck Collier's phone jangled just before three o'clock, and the big man stumbled out from behind his desk. "It's Henry," Buck said hoarsely.

"What about Henry?" demanded Vernon.

"He fell off of the roof," mumbled Buck.

"What is it?" snapped the bookkeeper. "Is Henry hurt?"

"He's dead," whispered Buck. "Henry is dead." Buck leaned against a counter, trembling. "Henry tripped, up on the roof, slid off and landed headfirst on some rocks. He was dead before they got him to the doctor."

Buck, Vernon, and the bookkeeper sat, stunned, until the front door swung open. Eck, Johnny, Frank, and Billy Jessup filed in. "We quit," Eck said wearily. "Ever man of us."

"Go on home," whispered Buck. "Take tomorrow off with pay. Come back Wednesday and we'll talk about it."

"Ain't nothing to talk about," said Johnny. "Unless you got work where I don't even have to climb a stepladder."

"We'll see," said Buck. "Go on home now."

Vernon lamely followed the men out the door. "I'm glad you wasn't there, Highpockets," said Eck. "Poor old Henry, he was gone before I got down off of the ladder."

Frank was crying softly. "Henry was good to me," he sobbed. "Nobody else ever was."

Buck Collier interrupted. "Come with me, Vernon," Buck said gruffly. In Buck's new pickup Vernon squirmed. "Where are we going?" he asked.

"To gather up Henry's tools and stuff," said Buck, staring straight ahead, "and to bring his car back to the yard." Buck drove angrily. "Henry Wells," he finally said, "worked for me for over thirty years. Started with me. Like family. Sarah loved Henry. Everybody did." Buck twisted for a quick look at Vernon. "You go to college," blurted Buck. "Get yourself out of this."

Vernon didn't respond. At Sadie Carmichael's place Buck pulled off onto a winding gravel drive, slowly approached the big house, and parked up close to Henry's old Ford. "Do we have to do this right now?" pleaded Vernon.

"Yes," snapped Buck. "The thieves and vultures will carry off anything we leave loose. Soon as word gets around, half the county will drive out here to gawk and look for blood. Go see if the keys are in Henry's car."

They were. Buck pointed out the tools that needed to be loaded. "Bring it all back to the yard," he told Vernon. "Don't worry about the heavy stuff. The next crew will need it all. I've got to go. To the funeral home."

Vernon, alone, gathered up Henry's saws, hammers, wrecking bars, and other small tools, and locked them into the trunk of the old Ford. Then he slid into the driver's seat. Henry's water cooler, lunch pail, a worn denim jacket, and the day's charge slips cluttered the passenger's side. Vernon started the engine, backed out carefully, and eased around the graveled circle.

A battered Plymouth sedan rattled up from the highway and stopped. The driver leaned out the window. "This where the man got killed?" he asked.

Vernon nodded.

"Where'd he land?" the man asked eagerly. "Did he fall from all the way up on top?"

"I don't know," Vernon said hoarsely.

"Landed headfirst on a rock, they said," grinned the beefy farmer. "Split open his skull like a ripe pumpkin."

Vernon gagged, stomped the gas pedal, and slung gravel as he cut over into the grass to go around the Plymouth. Back on the steep driveway he was going too fast; Vernon had to lock up the brakes and slide to a stop at the edge of the highway. The motor died. Vernon slumped over the steering wheel and gasped for breath. He lifted his head as another car pulled in beside him. "Is this where the man got killed?" asked a blonde woman.

Vernon swore, and gunned Henry's car out onto the pavement. At seventy the front wheels bobbled violently, and Vernon let off the gas. He was crying, cursing softly, as he drove into Finchburg. At the stoplight somebody recognized the car. "Is Henry Wells really dead?" asked an overalled farmer.

"Yes!" wailed Vernon. He lurched away, and whipped the old Ford angrily into the lumber yard. Bookkeeper Phil Kitchens walked quickly to meet him. "Take it easy, Vernon," Phil said gently. "Take a deep breath. Put the car under the shed, lock it, and bring me the keys."

Vernon nosed the car into a lumber shed, locked both doors, and avoided the stares as he walked grimly to the office. Phil Kitchens stared at Vernon. "Sit down," he said quietly. Phil fumbled in a drawer of Buck Collier's desk and came up with a fifth of bourbon, half full, and filled a tumbler. "Drink this," he ordered.

Vernon gulped down half the contents, gagged and kept it down, closed his eyes and grimaced as the whiskey burned its way to his stomach. Then he blew out his breath and drank the rest. Phil poured again, inspected the bottle, turned it up and gulped down the remaining two inches of bourbon. Vernon slumped, cradled the glass in his trembling hands, and finally looked up at Phil Kitchens. "Everybody wants to see the blood," Vernon whispered. "It's like a big circus."

"People are people," Phil said softly. "Don't let 'em get to you." He sighed. "Here I sit, telling you how to act, and me, I'm shaking life a leaf." Buck Collier arrived twenty minutes later, shook the empty whiskey bottle and went to the storage bins for a new fifth. He poured himself a stiff drink. "The funeral is Wednesday at two," Buck growled. "Tell everybody to be there. A day off with pay." Buck finished off his drink and noticed Vernon, wide-eyed and watching. "I'm sorry," said Buck. "Thanks. Why don't you go on home now."

"I'd better drive Vernon home," said Phil, "and explain to his mother why he smells like sour mash."

"Good," grunted Buck. "Thanks again, Vernon."

The trip home, the next day, and the day of the funeral blurred. Vernon stumbled out of the church and was suddenly aware of the rawboned, heavily tanned work crews, uncomfortable in dress clothes, even Frank McNeill sweating in an undersized wool suit. Before Vernon could get to Frankie, Sarah Collier intercepted him. "How have you been, Vernon?" she asked quietly.

Vernon felt every eye on him, and he blushed furiously. "Okay, I guess," he mumbled. "What about you? How have you spent the summer?"

"Swimming, mostly," said Sarah. She inspected Vernon. "But you have a better tan than me. And you've gained weight." She blushed. "Muscles."

"From building barns," mumbled Vernon.

"Are you going to college in September?" asked Sarah.

"Probably," said Vernon. He shrugged. "Mostly I just work, like some old man." Vernon met Sarah's bold stare. "Would you want to go out sometime?"

"Sure. When?"

"Tonight?"

Sarah smiled. "Seven o'clock." She started away then turned back. "You look nice, Vernon, all dressed up." Sarah joined her parents in the big Buick. There was a soft chuckle, and Vernon turned.

Eck and Johnny, grinning, stood two yards away. Eck shrugged. "Me, I don't see nothing wrong with making a date at a funeral. Do you, Johnny?"

"Nope," grinned Johnny, "especially with something that looks as good as that."

Vernon smiled. "Are you coming back to work?"

"In the morning," sighed Eck. "Man's got to eat, no matter what. Buck wants me to run the barn crew now, at a dime a hour more, so tomorrow I reckon Johnny and me will go back to that roof job."

"What about Frankie?" asked Vernon.

"Him and Billy, they'll be there," said Eck, "but that leaves us a man short. Want your old job back?"

Vernon shook his head. "Mr. Collier wants me to stay in the office."

"You mean Miss Collier," grinned Eck. "Highpockets, ten years from now we'll be working for you. When that comes about I want a big raise."

"If that ever happens," smiled Vernon, "I'll give you both double your pay. But don't go spend the money just yet."

Vernon drove slowly along the ridge in Harper's old Dodge, and slowed as he topped the hill above Jacob Howard's sprawling jumble of barns, cribs, silos, loading chutes, and machinery. Jake was bent over a hay baler. Vernon smiled and pulled into the barnyard.

"Hey, Vernon," Jake yelled happily. "Come here and fix this mess I make."

Vernon inspected the tangle of string and gears and shook his head. "Get me a knife and a screwdriver." In five minutes the gears were clear. "Good as new," announced Vernon.

Jake beamed proudly. "Still the good worker. Big man now. Go to college soon, I hear."

"I guess so," shrugged Vernon, "if I can scrape up enough money for clothes and stuff."

"I help?" offered Jake.

"I appreciate the offer," said Vernon, "but I couldn't let you do that."

"Stubborn," grinned Jake. "Like your poppa."

Vernon smiled. "Did you really try to buy me once?"

"Not buy, like cow or mule," said Jacob.

"Wanted you to live here."

"Thanks," grinned Vernon. "Thanks a lot, Mr. Howard."

"Why you thank me?" Jake, puzzled, grinned.

"For being you, I reckon," laughed Vernon. He walked back to the car, waved to Jake, and drove on.

Elsie watched her tall son, who whistled as he cleaned up for his date with Sarah Collier. "What's got into you?" Elsie asked. "You come home from a funeral happy as a lark, and now you've put on so much Old Spice my eyes is watering."

"I don't know," grinned Vernon. "Maybe I grew up."

"Lord," snorted Elsie. She sighed, wiped her hands on her apron, and worked around Vernon as she prepared supper. "You won't be eighteen until Thanksgiving," said Elsie. "What makes you think you've growed up? Working around that bunch at the lumber yard?"

"They all like me," said Vernon. "That means a lot to me. I showed 'em all I can work. They treat me like a man."

"That bunch treating you like a man," Elsie said flatly, "don't make you one."

"I know that," grinned Vernon. "I know a lot I didn't know a month ago. Henry Wells, one day, said I was getting a higher education working on the barn crew. Henry didn't know how right he was."

Elsie pondered. "I think," she finally said, "that they's going to be a lot of stuff about you that I won't understand."

"Maybe so," smiled Vernon. "But, if it's any comfort, I probably won't understand either. I just want to see what happens."

Elsie smiled, then laughed. "Ain't you something?"

"Ain't you glad you didn't sell me to Jake Howard?" teased Vernon.

"I'm not sure," smiled Elsie. "You ask me again in about twenty years."

The Blue Goose

One tire was flat and the other three were bald. Drooped, faded, spattered with bird droppings, the old Plymouth rested in a row of equally drab vehicles parked in a row between the sales lot and the junkyard. These cars could go either way, depending on whether the buyer first needed used parts or a whole car.

Vernon Watts needed a whole car. Ossie Doyle offered him the pick of the lineup for fifty dollars. "Do any of them run?" Vernon asked with a tired smile.

"They did when we parked 'em," shrugged Ossie. "Fifty bucks, cash money, and you can try all of them and see if they's one you want."

"What about the blue Plymouth?" asked Vernon.

Ossie beamed. "Be like new with a tuneup and some tires. Solid as a rock. Just 95,000 miles and not a speck of rust."

Vernon tugged open the door and sniffed at the musty odor. "What year is it?"

"A 1948 four door Voyager," said Ossie.

"Will parts off of a '50 Dodge fit it?" asked Vernon.

"Same car," shrugged Ossie. "Has Harper still got that old green Dodge?"

Vernon blushed. "I blew the engine last summer. But we've still got it, down by the barn."

"Then this here little Plymouth is exactly what you want," promised Ossie. "You got plenty of parts, and I guarantee you this old motor don't burn a drop of oil."

"Will you get it started and tune it up?" asked Vernon.

"For fifty dollars?" Ossie laughed. "Son, I'm trying to do you a favor. If I start fixing it, the price goes up. To $200."

"I'll take it," said Vernon, "if I can get it to run."

"Costs you fifty bucks to find out," said Ossie. "Take it or leave it, as she sets."

Vernon slowly counted out five tens. "We'll come and get it in the morning." He watched Ossie pocket a week's wages. "Will all the papers be ready?"

"Tell you what," beamed Ossie. "I'll throw in the transfer and license." He hesitated. "How old are you?"

"Eighteen," said Vernon. "Why?"

"Harper will have to sign for you," said Ossie. "In Kentucky, you're not old enough."

"He'll sign," sighed Vernon. "Tomorrow."

Vernon walked from the car lot to the poolroom uptown and found his older brother Roy. "I bought it," he announced.

"It'll never hit a lick," grinned Roy.

Harper Watts was even less pleased with Vernon's deal. "I ain't signing anything," he said. "Why do you want an old junker of a car anyhow?"

"I need to get to work, and get home at night," said Vernon. "It's fifteen miles each way. I'm tired of hitching and walking. You don't want me driving your car. How am I supposed to get anywhere?"

"You blowed up one car last summer," complained Harper, "and now you've about ruint my Ford."

"So sign the papers," shrugged Vernon, "and you won't ever have to worry about that anymore."

"You get a car," grumbled Harper, "you'll get to running around, get yourself in debt, and you won't go back to school. You got two more years of college to go."

Vernon groaned. "Getting a car," he said, "will mean I have a way to get to work and earn the money I need to go back to school."

"I don't want to," said Harper, "but I'll sign for you. Will the thing even run?"

"I don't know," smiled Vernon.

"You don't know?" Harper shook his head. "You bought a car and don't even know if it'll run?"

"Yep." Vernon blushed.

"Lord," snorted Harper. "What is it they teach you in college?"

Saturday morning Vernon and Roy gathered up tools, a bag of used sparkplugs, a tire pump, and jumper cables. As they drove toward Finchburg Vernon sorted out six plugs that matched. Roy cleaned and installed the plugs while Vernon pumped up tires, then they hooked up the jumper cables to the old battery. Roy shrugged. "Give it a try."

Vernon tapped the throttle, pulled out the choke knob, and anxiously twisted the ignition key. The old motor turned reluctantly. "Keep trying," yelled Roy as he worked at the carburetor. "It's about to start."

The engine finally caught, coughed, backfired, and blew out a huge cloud of black smoke. Roy jumped back, unhooked the cables, and bent over to inspect the clattering motor. "Shove in the choke," he called.

Vernon did, and the engine quieted. "Sounds pretty good," Roy said wonderingly. "I'll follow you home. Got any gas?"

Vernon checked. "Not a drop." He shifted gears and slipped the clutch to break the car away from where it had sunk down in thick gravel, then launched it across the street to a gas station. "Yours?" asked the attendant. Vernon nodded. "Better get you some tires," the boy grinned, pointing to the right front.

"The tube is sticking out of that one."

Vernon drove home slowly, wobbling, testing the steering and brakes, and parked in the front yard. "Runs good," he announced bravely.

"Four different sizes of tires," said Roy, hunkering close to inspect the old Plymouth, "and no muffler. Floorboards is rusted out, and the seats are rotted."

"The radio plays," grinned Vernon. "The overdrive works."

"Don't do you no good without tires," said Roy. He pondered. "You got twenty dollars?"

"Yeah," Vernon said cautiously.

"Joe Carpenter blew the motor in his old Ford last week. He's got four recapped tires, wheels and all, for twenty bucks." Roy stood up. "They'll bolt on. Want me to go get them?"

Vernon took out a twenty, and ruefully counted what little he had left. While Roy was gone for the wheels Vernon found an old tractor muffler and clamped it on. The engine ran quiet and smooth. Some sheet metal covered the holes in the floor. When Roy returned they jacked up the car and mounted the wheels.

"At least you can drive it now," said Roy, wiping sweat. He backed away and grinned. "The Blue Goose."

"What?" asked Vernon.

"Your car," smiled Roy. "It's The Blue Goose."

"Why?"

"Hell. Why not?"

Vernon shrugged and smiled. "Okay by me." Vernon drove down by the pond and scrubbed for two hours, then rubbed on cleaner and polish. To his great surprise the faded surface gave way to brilliant two-tone paint, light blue with a darker roof. "Doggone," said Harper. "Looks like a new car now."

Vernon stood back to admire the gloss. "Who'd have thought that was under all that bird manure?"

"Not me," said Harper. "Looked to me like you'd wasted ever penny, but now I ain't so sure. How does it run?"

"Like a sewing machine," grinned Vernon. At dusk he drove proudly into Finchburg, cruised the street twice then parked behind the Dairy Bar. High school classmate Roy Tackett pulled his sparkling red 1959 Impala up close and joined Vernon on the bench. "Where'd you ever find that?" asked Roy. "Did some old maid have it parked in a barn?"

"Got it at the junkyard," said Vernon.

"No kidding?" Roy looked closer. "Looks brand new on the outside."

"So will the inside," said Vernon, "by the time I get through."

With next Saturday's paycheck Vernon bought rubber floor mats and plastic seat covers at the Western Auto store and spent all afternoon installing them. Then, proudly, he hung a miniature pair of foam white dice cubes from the rear view mirror.

"How much has it cost you so far?" asked Harper.

"Not much," Vernon said quickly. "About a hundred."

"That hundred, and ever penny you make the rest of the summer," said Harper. "How do you figure to pay for school come September?"

"I'll manage," said Vernon.

"How?" Harper demanded glumly.

"I've got one job," said Vernon, "and Edd Miller said I can work nights and weekends at the Ashland station."

"We got a crop to raise," reminded Harper.

"I'll get the tobacco in the barn before I leave for school," Vernon said stubbornly. "Somehow."

That night Vernon joined his friends in Finchburg and was pleasantly surprised when they chose to cruise the town in the immaculate old Plymouth instead of one of the newer Chevrolets. The Blue Goose was reverse status in the car-conscious little town, a slow-moving and old-maidish contradiction to the powerful new vehicles. Sprawling with legs out the open windows, yelling at the girls, horn honking and foam dice swaying, Vernon and his high school buddies cruised happily. Later, Vernon hauled five giggling girls whose enjoyment of The Blue Goose was marred only by one girl's assumption that Vernon's choice of the ungainly old Plymouth was a deliberate act to get attention.

"Nope," said Vernon. "That's not the case. This is all I can afford. I'd whole lots rather have Kenny's new Chevy."

"What kind of place is it that you go to school?" Becky Todd suddenly asked. "Do they have a football team? Is everybody as smart as they say?"

"Smarter," grinned Vernon. "We don't have a football team, though, and nobody has any money."

"Why did you go there?" persisted Becky. "Kentucky offered you a scholarship, and Morehead, and probably ten more colleges. Why'd you pick that goofy place? They won't even let you keep a car there, and you have to work."

"And they lock up the girls every night at six," laughed Vernon. "You wouldn't like it, Becky."

"I sure wouldn't," she agreed. After a minute she asked "Are the girls there pretty?"

"A few," shrugged Vernon.

They met a white Buick and Vernon twisted to stare.

"That's her," snapped Becky.

Vernon grinned. "Who?"

"Your precious Sarah Collier." Becky sniffed. "Stuck up as ever, her and her big car and her fancy clothes from Lexington." She studied Vernon. "Why'd you and her break up, anyhow?"

Vernon smiled. "Her mother decided we were spending too much time parked."

"You did spend a lot of time out on Smith Road," said Becky. "You and miss stuck up."

"Jealous?" asked Vernon. "I'll take you out there. Unless you're ashamed to be seen in my old car."

Becky stared boldly. "Let's go."

Ten minutes later Vernon shut off the engine and pulled Becky across the seat. "Wait a minute," she protested. For hour they necked and wrestled in the front seat, sweating, before Becky pulled away and straightened her clothes.

"Take 'em off," suggested Vernon.

"Don't you wish," snapped Becky. She tugged at her twisted skirt. "Is this what they learn you in college?"

"No," laughed Vernon. "At school we've got big old lights everywhere, and a dean of women who watches every move I make."

"Why do you go to college anyway?" asked Becky. "They offered you a good job at the new factory, like Kenny. He makes over a hundred a week, already. That's more than teachers get."

"I'm not going to be a teacher," said Vernon.

"What, then?" demanded Becky.

Vernon shrugged. "Who knows? I just always wanted to go to college, and my teachers always said I should go. And I like it, too, except for not ever having any money."

"When you finish," Becky said seriously, "you'll never come back here. Will you?"

"I don't know." Vernon laughed nervously. "I might join the Navy and see the world."

"But you won't ever come back," Becky said emphatically.

He shrugged. "Maybe not. At least not at first."

"Never," insisted Becky. "You're different."

"You mean weird, don't you?"

"Not exactly," squirmed Becky. "It's just that you always knew stuff, in school, that nobody else did, and you won everything, and now you go to that funny college. It's like you've always known you were going to do something different from the rest of us." Becky struggled for words. "Just different," she said lamely.

"Poor is what you mean," Vernon said stiffly. "I go to that funny college because I don't have enough money to go anywhere else. I work hard because I want out. Not just out of here, but out of having to work in construction or farm all my life."

"Are you going to be a doctor?" asked Becky.

"No," said Vernon. "Not a doctor or a teacher."

"Then what?" asked Becky.

"I don't know. First a college degree, then I'll figure out the rest. Two more years of working, doing without, and going to chapel twice a week." Vernon groaned. "And, all the time, Kenny and the rest of my high school buddies are driving new cars and rolling in cash. By the time I graduate they'll be making more money than I will in my first job."

"So why bother?" asked Becky.

"Like you said, I'm different." Vernon twisted. "My uncle was a Navy pilot. You didn't know that, did you? Paul was killed in World War II, in the South Pacific. He was just 29, and I wasn't but about four when it happened." He started the engine and backed slowly down the logging trail and back out onto the road. "Maybe I want to match what Paul did." Vernon laughed suddenly. "That's why we're in this old Plymouth instead of a new convertible."

"I like your car," said Becky. "It's . . . "

"Different?" asked Vernon, smiling.

Over the next few weeks Vernon found out just how correct Harper had been about the expense of owning a car. Gas and minor repairs—a brake line, a radiator hose, a rebuilt generator—took big chunks of Vernon's dollar-an-hour paycheck, and his new mobility meant more money spent on fun. Dates, weekend trips, and constant cruising ate Vernon's wages. He was not able to save for fall term expenses, and in early August started looking for a fulltime job. "I'll drop out for a year and make some money," he told Elsie, "then go back and finish."

"You could sell that car," his mother suggested. "It's worth a lot more now than what you paid."

"Then I'd just have to start all over again next summer," said Vernon. Vernon did get an offer of fulltime employment from his boss at the construction company. "As an apprentice carpenter for a few years," said Buck Collier, "to learn the trade so you could run a crew. Then you'd be a foreman, then I'll give you all the crews." Buck sat back. "Sort of like what I offered you a few years ago."

"I really just need to work for one year," explained Vernon. "The job I'm doing now would be okay with me."

Collier sighed. "We don't need an extra clerk in the winter when things are slow. Sorry, Vernon."

Other potential jobs offered the same story. The bottled gas plant needed an assistant manager, and there was an opening on a survey crew, but both places insisted on long term commitments. But for just a year, not even a reliable minimum wage job was available.

"You're crazy," said Roy. "That gas place offered you $125 a week to start. Surveyors make really big money. What do you need with college anyhow?"

"I don't know," Vernon said wearily. "Maybe I'll sell my car."

A service station owner quickly offered $500, and others wanted The Blue Goose. The venerable Plymouth was a rare find. Vernon fretted, wrestled with the decision, and finally—the week before he was to leave for school—reached a painful conclusion. "I'm going to sell it," he told Elsie. Vernon smiled wistfully. "I guess I'm not ready to give up on college just yet."

"I know how much you love that old car," said Elsie, "and I wish they was a way I could help you keep it. But school is more important."

"I know," groaned Vernon. Then he scowled. "But next summer I'll work two or three jobs and let Daddy raise his own tobacco. That way I can earn enough to get me another car and go back to school."

On Sunday Vernon lovingly washed and waxed the old Plymouth, scrubbed the interior, and was rubbing the long hood with a soft cloth when Harper joined him under the big oak tree.

"Looks sharp," offered Harper.

Vernon didn't respond.

"Have you really sold it?" asked Harper.

"I guess," mumbled Vernon. "Tomorrow I have to let Edd Miller know for sure."

"You turned down them jobs they offered you?" asked Harper.

Vernon nodded.

Harper stuffed something into Vernon's shirt pocket. "Keep your car," he said gruffly, then spun and stalked away toward the barn.

Harper was gone before Vernon unfolded the check for $500. It was stubbed "for labor." Vernon smiled, and followed his father to the shed. Harper was busy sharpening the tobacco knives and spears. "I can't take this," said Vernon.

"You earned it," grunted Harper. He grinned. "Or, you will earn it, by the time the crop's in the barn." He tossed Vernon his worn old tobacco knife. "Can you still cut a thousand sticks a day? Or does book-learning slow a man down?" Harper reached into the old Army backpack for another knife. "I got the $500 from the bank," he said. "It's your share of this year's crop. I'll do it ever year you're in college. You get the fields plowed, the beds burnt and seeded, set the crop and plow it and hoe it, top and sucker it and get it in the barn. I'll get it stripped and sold."

"Why?" asked Vernon. "You can't afford to pay me."

"Can't afford not to," said Harper. He squatted to light a cigarette. "I can't hire that much work done for $500. You need the money, I need the help."

"I'll help anyway," Vernon said quietly. "I always have."

"I know that," said Harper. "If it wasn't so, I wouldn't be trying to help you out." he stubbed the cigarette and bent back to his work. "They's lots of folks watching you, Vernon. Them that thinks you can't make it. That it's foolish for people like us to even try to send a boy to college." Harper looked up and grinned. "By damn, one way or the other, I aim to get you through. If keeping that old car will help, keep it. Park her in the barn, and she'll be here weekends and Christmas for you."

That night Vernon took Becky to the drive-in movie. "Why are you so smug?" she asked. "Are you that happy about leaving me?"

"I'm just happy that I'm getting to go back to school," said Vernon.

"There'll be weekends and vacations," offered Becky. "We can still go out."

"I don't get back much," Vernon said softly.

"I get the idea," snapped Becky.

"No, it's not that," laughed Vernon. "It's just that with classes and work, even on Saturdays, I can't get away very often. Really."

Becky glared, then softened and relaxed. "You really are strange," she finally said. "What is it you want, anyway? Why is college so important? Are you too good for the rest of us?"

"College is my way out of being poor," Vernon said firmly. "And, I really do like learning new things and seeing new places. I'm not ready to give it up."

"Do you think the rest of us are giving up?" asked Becky.

"No," Vernon said quickly. "That's not what I meant. But, for me, it has to be this way. I don't want to wind up wondering, for the rest of my life, what would've happened if I'd finished college."

"You've got a lot more here than you know," said Becky. "Your mother and father, and lots of other people who want to help you."

"I know all that," said Vernon. "And I can't let all of those people down, can I? I'm sort of a test, I think sometimes, to see if it can be done. To see if a Mauk Ridge kid can make it through college." Vernon laughed. "And this old car has caused so much trouble. Everybody thought it'd cause me to drop out of school."

"You like this old car more than you like me," Becky grumbled good-naturedly. "You spend a lot more time with it."

"The Blue Goose is special," said Vernon. "It's my first car."

"And I'm sure not your first girl," sniffed Becky. "Or your last." She smiled. "I guess I'll do like the rest of them. I'll watch and see how you do out there in the world that you want to see so bad." She bent closer in mock fierceness. "Just don't you ever forget me and the old Blue Goose."

"I won't," Vernon promised.

And he didn't. Vernon's first new car was a bright yellow '64 Ford Mustang, and he nicknamed it "Becky." Vernon doubted that Becky would appreciate that fact, and never let her know, but he always smiled whenever he drove the nimble little car and he would never explain the name to his wife.

Nine Holes

When Vernon Watts read that a new golf course had been opened in Finch County, he brought along his clubs on the next visit to Kentucky. Vernon's golfing gear was a mixed lot: woods from K-Mart, rusted irons from a yard sale, a gooseneck putter won in a poker game, and yellow spiked shoes picked up in the Salvation Army Store in Asheville. Vernon's golf glove and orange XXXed balls came from the discount store on the bypass.

Vernon's game was equally inconsistent and colorful. Flailing, chopping, swinging from the heels, Vernon played at a sweaty half-trot. "If you'd slow down," grumbled Vernon's usual playing partner Russ Williams, "you might be good."

"Wouldn't be fun that way," grinned Vernon. "I like to play, not loaf around. It's the game, Russ. Not wearing a shirt that cost more than my car and sipping drinks at the clubhouse."

Vernon rolled into Finch County a week after his younger brother Lee got home from the Army and a Vietnam tour. Lee shared his beer with Vernon, and allowed as how he'd like to shoot a few golfs too. "I watched 'em play at the officer's club," said Lee. "Anything an officer can do has to be easy. Where can I get me a sack of bats?"

A phone call verified that clubs could be rented at the new Horse Mountain Country Club. "Country Club?" chuckled Vernon. "Since when is that copperhead den a country club?"

"Opened up a year ago," Harper Watts told his sons. "Senator Baker and some his buddies started it. Costs a hundred dollars a year to join up, and they won't let you play if you ain't a member."

"That's just if you live here," said Vernon. "Out-of-town players can pay a greens fee. I'm from North Carolina and Lee, he's from Saigon."

Just after noon the next day Lee drove up to Vernon's mother-in-law's house in a black '55 Chevy with fat tires, noisy dual exhausts, a tiny steering wheel, and a stuttering engine. Vernon tossed his clubs into the back seat. "This thing runs a little rough," yelled Vernon.

Lee grinned and handed across a beer. "Cam," he said.

"What?" asked Vernon.

Lee punched the throttle and snapped Vernon hard back against the seat. Beer splattered. Lee jerked the stubby gearshift, straightened up the spinning rear end, and leaned over. "I said," he yelled, "that it idles a little rough because of the racing cam." At ninety Lee shifted into high gear.

"Runs good," wailed Vernon, "but you better drop the parachute if you're going to get around this curve."

At the foot of Horse Mountain the narrow road veered sharply right and started climbing. Lee geared down, wrestled the car through the turns, and almost missed the cutoff. A homemade sign marked the entrance to the new country club. Lee threw gravel as he worked the car up a steep bulldozer cut. In the gap there was a small parking lot and a weathered, sagging barn. Lee stopped. "Is this it?"

"Must be," said Vernon. "Over there's a golf cart."

Lee drove up to the barn. Vernon unloaded his clubs and sat down to lace up his shoes. An overalled, tobacco chewing little man came grinning out from the barn. "I swear," chuckled Toad Walters, "Vernon and Lee Watts. I thought you two boys had left the country."

"Toad? What are you doing here?" Vernon shook the little man's hand. "I thought you lived in your poolroom. When did you take up golf?"

"I'm the manager," grinned Toad. "I reckon they figured I could make change and break up fights and keep my mouth shut, so they give me the job. Come on in, boys. I got a pool table in the barn."

"We come to shoot golfs, not eight-balls," said Lee. "Can you rent me some clubs?"

"Seeing as how it's you, Leroy," said Toad, "I'll dig out Senator Baker's rig. He don't ever use it anyhow." The inside of the old tobacco barn had been cleaned out and graveled. "Take the cart too," said Toad.

Lee drove the spanking new Harley Davidson cart out into the sunlight. State Senator Elmo Baker had spared no expense in outfitting himself. "All this thing needs," Lee said admiringly, "is a television set and some girls." Vernon loaded Lee's cooler onto the cart. "You boys drinking?" Toad asked warily.

"Just Pepsi," grinned Vernon. He looked around. "Just where is this golf course, Toad?"

Toad pointed. "Starts up yonder. Winds around the mountain and back to the other end of the barn."

Lee grunted. "Has this cart got four wheel drive?"

"Watch out for the copperheads!" Toad yelled after them.

At the first tee Vernon took out his driver and limbered up. "See a green anywhere?" he asked.

Lee peered out from under the brim of his cap. "Nope." he finally said. "But it looks like you'd go that way."

Vernon shrugged, teed up, tagged the ball long and low, and groaned as it hooked into the mountainside, caught a boulder, and kicked high in the air.

"That ought to scare off the snakes," observed Lee. "Now. Which one of these sticks do you use first?"

Vernon pointed to Elmo Baker's spotless persimmon three-wood. "Try that one. Keep your head down and your left arm straight." Lee chunked up dry grass. His second try sent the ball dribbling down the fairway. "Nothing to it," he grinned. "I'm driving the cart. You open the beer."

Ten tries later Lee was within nine iron range of the withered green. Vernon's ball had bounced into the clear where he now had a straight shot. "Watch the cowpiles," advised Lee as Vernon bent over his wedge. "You might mess up them yellow shoes." Vernon smiled, swung, and punched his shot twenty yards to the right of the green. "You're not exactly Jack Nicklaus," Lee said dryly. "Where did you learn how to play?"

"I didn't," replied Vernon. "I just like to walk around in the fields and drink beer."

The second hole was a par three with the tee high above a tiny green. "Heck," grunted Lee. "I'll just kick it off and let it roll down."

Vernon's iron shot flew 90 yards out, 150 yards straight down, and hit the center of the green. "Yeah," he grinned. But the ball bounced and flew off into a brush pile. "Hard as a rock," growled Vernon. Lee's shot dribbled slowly down the hill to the fringe of the putting surface. "See?" grinned Lee. "Told you. Now how do you reckon we get down there?"

They found a cart path, circled slowly and came out of the dense thicket just below the green. Vernon approached the brush pile warily. "Should of brung old Thunder," he said, "to go in there and run off the snakes. Only course I've ever played where you need to carry a shotgun and an axe."

"A lot like Nam," muttered Lee as he probed with his putter. "Except I don't reckon Toad has got these brush piles booby-trapped. Yonder's your ball."

Vernon studied, then stepped cautiously into the mess. "Stand back," he warned. "No telling where this thing will go." Vernon chopped down. Weeds, twigs, and dry mud exploded. The ball popped up, spun, and dribbled close to the flag. "Son-of-a-gun," grinned Vernon. "I didn't know I was that good." He went to the cart for his putter and a cold beer, then knelt close to Lee to study the green. "Pretty rough over there?" he asked softly.

"Rough enough," said Lee. He watched Vernon tap in his putt. "How was it you didn't have to go, Vernon?"

Vernon retrieved his ball and squatted beside Lee. "By the time the draft board got around to me," he said wearily, "I was out of college with a year old kid and an ulcer. They pestered me for a year then gave up and classified me 3A."

In the cart Vernon opened a beer for Lee. "Why did you volunteer?" asked Vernon.

Lee shrugged. "They were going to draft me. The draft board likes to get rid of hell-raisers, and that meant anybody named Watts was about to become a private."

"You could have gone Air Force or Navy," said Vernon.

"Yeah." Lee crumpled his can. "I could have." He shook his head. "But, you know me. I got about half lit one Saturday and went in to tell 'em I was ready to kick some tail in Vietnam. They signed me up in about two seconds."

The tee for number three was at the foot of a steep hill. "Some golf course," snorted Vernon. "How do you hit a golf ball straight up?"

"Have another cold beer," said Lee, "and hope that the Senator's cart here can climb that cliff."

Vernon's tee shot came rolling back down. His second try cleared the crest. "Wonder what's up there?" he mumbled.

Lee topped the hill and braked hard to keep the cart out of the muddy pond. Ripples tugged at the cattails, and a fresh boil of muddy water marked where Vernon's ball had landed. "Let's see you hit that one out," grinned Lee. "I believe I see an alligator over yonder."

"Just a water moccasin," growled Vernon. "Where'd your ball go?"

Lee pointed. "About a foot from that flag."

"How'd you do that?" asked Vernon.

"Kissed it off the ten ball with some reverse English," grinned Lee. He shrugged. "How the hell should I know? I smacked it, and there it is."

Vernon dropped a new ball, shanked it into tall grass, swore and slung his wedge into the pond. "One word," he growled at Lee, "and you go in next."

They found Vernon's ball nestled in thick dry grass. "You have to really blast this shot out," Vernon explained to Lee as he wiggled his hips to settle in. "Hit down on it." Vernon took a mighty swing. An inch under the grass was a huge limestone rock. Sparks flew. The crystal of Vernon's watch spun away crazily. Vernon staggered backwards and stared at his nine iron. The head was bent straight back. Both Vernon's forearms were numb. He sat down heavily. "I quit," Vernon said softly. "I frigging quit."

Lee leaned on his putter and smiled. "If I was you, I wouldn't set right there." Lee pointed. Vernon saw the snake and came up flailing, dropped his own club and grabbed Lee's putter to attack. He finished and tossed the bloody club back to Lee. "Your shot. You got a birdie and I got a copperhead."

"Cow-snake," grinned Lee.

"Shut up and play," snapped Vernon.

Number four was a par five, a dogleg left along an old logging trail. "Last time I was up here," remembered Lee, "was with Patsy Collins in her daddy's pickup truck. I sure got a hole-in-one that night. You remember Patsy?"

"Everbody remembers Patsy," said Vernon. "She gave half of Finch County the clap."

"You too?" asked Lee.

"Nope." Vernon grinned. "By Patsy's time I was pretty well gone from here, just back for summers and Christmas. Ever time I saw Patsy she was with you."

"That's when you were chasing Wendy," said Lee. "You didn't have a lick of sense."

"That's the honest to God truth," grunted Vernon. "Worse thing is I caught her. Or somebody got caught."

"Hell of a way to talk about your wife," said Lee.

"Hell of a wife," said Vernon. "Play."

Lee's drive hit the old trail and bounced off into thick brush. "Better take some lunch if you're going to go look for that one," said Vernon. His own shot was down the middle. Lee parked the cart, opened a beer, took a seven iron and went off whistling. He came back with his golf ball and a pair of tattered black bikini panties.

"Somebody still uses the old road," Lee grinned. He stuffed the frilly underwear down into Senator Baker's golf bag. "I'd like to hear Elmo explain them, the next time him and his wife is out here playing golf."

They played out the hole and parked in the shade to drink. "Well, Lee," Vernon said lazily, "what're you going to do, now that you're finished with the Army?"

"For a while," Lee said seriously, "I'm going to drink, chase women, and sleep. Take three or four showers a day, and sleep in a real bed. Try to heal up my rotted toes. Tell everbody I know that's draft age to move to Canada."

"I guess it was pretty bad," Vernon said quietly.

"Bad ain't the word for it," snorted Lee. "More like a damned nightmare. Little kids and women trying to kill you, a bunch of idiot college boy officers, and half of us so stoned most of the time we'd be giggling and shooting and not giving one damn about what we hit. You spend a year living in mud, bullets, and body bags, then they stick you on a jet and you're back in New Jersey trying to act civilized again. They hand you your Purple Heart and some discharge papers and send you on back to wherever you come from."

"I didn't know until last night that you got hit," said Vernon.

"Mom still doesn't know," Lee said softly. "I got it twice. Once through the butt and once in the leg, neither time bad enough to get sent home." Lee sighed and popped another beer. "This one ain't like Daddy's war, Vernon. We didn't even know who we were fighting, and we weren't allowed to win. Just count bodies and keep score, like a football game. If they'd have let us, we'd have started at the south end of that miserable country and wiped it clean all the way to the top."

"Sometimes I wish I'd gone," said Vernon. "I feel like I should have been over there with you guys."

"The hell you say," growled Lee. He smiled. "You'd have been an officer, and one of us might have had to slip a grenade under your bunk." Lee crumpled the aluminum can. "Where do we go next?" He eased the cart to the next tee, got out and groaned. Number six started out with a narrow chute between rows of tall oak trees. "I couldn't hit one through there in a year," groaned Lee.

Five lost balls later they saw the green. Four cows grazed around the flag. Vernon's iron shot thudded into a fat Guernsey, who twitched her tail and stolidly held her ground. Lee's shot screamed in low, hit a cow in the leg, and sent her bucking off into the thickets. The others followed. "Reminds me of that old Andy Griffith record," laughed Vernon. "What it was, was football."

"Putt around the cow-piles," grinned Lee. "I bet Arnold Palmer never had to play through a herd of milk cows."

On number seven Vernon hit a long drive to the edge of the woods, planted his feet firmly and wiggled his rear to settle in for the chip shot. Suddenly he screamed, danced sideways, threw his club and ripped off his shirt. The angry cloud of yellowjackets followed Vernon, swarming and stinging.

Lee howled. Vernon's left eye was swollen shut as they approached the eighth tee. "Want to call it a day?" asked Lee.

"I came to play nine holes," snarled Vernon, "and I'll play nine holes if it kills me." His second shot flew over the green, twenty yards up a steep grassy slope. "Park here and I'll go mountain climbing," Vernon said wearily.

"Walk? Not while I'm the driver." Lee laughed and hit the throttle. "Hang on, Vernon."

Halfway up the bank Lee lost power and turned left. The right side of the cart lifted slowly up off the ground. "Oh, hell," groaned Lee. "Jump, Vernon!"

Vernon went off the high side as the cart toppled left, scattering clubs. Lee dived to safety. The elegant new cart tumbled, rolled over twice, and slid to a stop. The fiberglass body lay on the green, six feet away from the frame and engine. Lee sat up and stared. Vernon crawled out from the weeds. "Well, hell," Vernon said softly. "Now you've done it, Lee. All the beer will be fizzy." He stood up grinning, and surveyed the wreckage. "I wonder," Vernon said thickly, "how much this mess is gonna cost us?"

"Not a cent," growled Lee. "We'll fix it. Help me gather up the parts." They gently lifted the fiberglass body back onto the frame. "See any baling wire anywhere?" asked Lee. An old fence yielded rusted strands. Lee crawled under the cart, fashioned crude body mounts, and backed out giggling.

"What's so funny?" asked Vernon.

"I was remembering," laughed Lee, "the time me and Rocky took Daddy's old pickup truck over to the river and wrecked it. We didn't know wet brakes wouldn't work. I crossed the river, it up on the doors, then must have been doing seventy when I come to the intersection. We had to build Rat Abrams a new fence, pay him for two rows of tobacco, and buy that cow." Lee sat back and laughed until tears streamed. "That old cow, she must have been fifty years old. Rat swore it was a two year old registered Holstein. Cost us $400."

"That wasn't so funny," said Vernon. "You tried to patch Daddy's truck and get him to believe a tree limb fell on it. That didn't work, and neither is this rusty old wire on a five-thousand-dollar golf cart."

Lee opened a fizzing beer, shook away the foam, and studied it over. "We'll threaten to sue Elmo Baker," he announced. "Damn anybody that'd rent out a booby-trapped golf cart to a veteran just back from the war. Danged if my leg ain't hurting. This piece of junk of Elmo's has damaged me."

Vernon shook his head wearily. "Let's go on home."

"Nope," Lee said solemnly. "We came to play nine holes."

Number nine was a par three, with an elevated tee looking down at the barn. "Five dollars says you can't hit that tin roof," Lee said suddenly.

Vernon grinned and switched clubs. "You're on."

Vernon's shot dropped onto the roof. He dug for more balls.

Twenty minutes later Lee carefully guided the cart up to the barn. Toad Walters came out fuming. "You crazy sonsabitches," sputtered Toad. "I been hid under a wagon for half a hour. It sounded like a war. You Wattses is all crazy."

"Where do you want me to put this thing?" asked Lee.

"I'll park it," said Toad.

"Nope," insisted Lee. "You work hard enough already. I'll help you." Toad pointed, and Lee eased the cart into its slot. He steadied the cart as he dismounted, but Toad wasn't watching anyway. Toad was staring at Vernon's swollen face.

"Yellowjackets," Vernon said grimly. "Toad, in nine holes of golf I've had to kill a snake, fight off a swarm of bees, milk a herd of cows, and clear off an acre of new ground. I lost one club, broke one, and used up two dozen balls. This ain't a golf course, Toad. It's an obstacle course."

They loaded clubs and Lee's cooler back into the black Chevy. "You drive," said Lee. "I've had enough wrecks for one day."

"You fellers come back," yelled Toad.

"We will," promised Lee. "The next time I get homesick for Vietnam I'll be right here."

Vernon started the car and nudged the gearshift. "Where to?"

"Minnie McCormick's house of bootleg beer," ordered Lee. "You're too drunk to drive any farther than that and I need Minnie's services."

Vernon hurried down the drive, missed a shift, and finally jerked the car out onto the pavement. "How do you drive this thing?" he asked. "I can't guide it, and it keeps trying to rear up."

"Pretend it's a golf cart," grinned Lee.

Vernon stood on the brakes and wrestled the Chevy through a curve. "Drives like a tank," he grumbled.

"How would you know?" asked Lee.

Vernon grinned, shook his head, and caught the muddy shortcut to Minnie's. "I see you still know how to get there," smiled Lee. "Finch County ain't plumb wore off of you yet."

The car was muddy to the windows when Vernon gunned across the creek and up to Minnie's barn. He shut off the clattering engine. "This," he explained to Lee, "is how the ones of us with good sense do business with Minnie and the girls. You crazy people park right out front where everybody can see you."

"Who cares?" asked Lee. "Your wife is going to kill you anyway when you go in drunk." Lee climbed out, stumbled, and clung to the door. "Hey, Minnie!" he bawled. "Get some cold beer out here for Jack Nicklaus and Arnie Palmer."

Minnie, all 200 pounds of her, was waiting on the back porch. "Law, Leroy Watts, you're a sight for sore eyes. And Vernon too. Where have you boys been?" Minnie looked around. "Where's them other two fellers? That Jack and Arnie?"

"That's us," beamed Lee. "Me and Vernon, we've been over at the country club shooting golfs."

"Did you get many?" the fat woman asked.

"We got the limit," grinned Lee. "We was afraid the game warden would come around so we quit. Minnie, honey, you got any cold Blue Ribbon?"

"I think maybe you've had enough, Lee," said Minnie.

"He's okay," said Vernon. "I'm driving."

Minnie sat down in a big hickory rocker and yelled for Cassie. A bony, tousled brunette came smiling to the back door, blushed happily when she saw Lee then froze when she noticed Vernon. "Go get Lee a sixpack," ordered Minnie.

"Make that a case," said Lee.

"A sixpack," said Minnie.

Cassie stared at Vernon. "Ain't you going to vote?" she asked. "Or did you get too good for beer when you went off to college and moved to North Carolina?"

"Hi, Cassie," Vernon said gently. "How you been?"

"Okay. Considering." Cassie studied Vernon carefully, coolly, then turned back to Minnie.

"Half a case," compromised Minnie. "Go get it, girl. Don't stand there with your teeth hanging out." Minnie rocked back and stared at Vernon. "I don't reckon Cassie has got over you yet."

"Fifteen years is a long time to carry a grudge," Vernon said quietly.

"Grudge, hell," snorted Minnie. "You don't know a thing about women, Vernon Watts, and you never did. Not when you was fifteen, running through the woods with Cassie, and not now."

"Oh, hell," sputtered Lee. "I forgot, Vernon. About you and Cassie."

"Never mind," Vernon said stiffly. "It's okay."

Cassie brought the beer in a brown grocery bag. "On the house, boys," Minnie said grandly. "For old times sake." Minnie sat back heavily. "You home for good now, Leroy?"

"Discharged, paid off, and home for good," grinned Lee.

"But Vernon, he's just passing through," said Cassie. "I'm surprised he still knowed how to get out here."

"I'm here for two weeks," said Vernon. "Maybe I'll come back out. We could talk."

Cassie sniffed. "I've had enough of your talk, Vernon Watts, to last me three or four lifetimes. You just stay up at that country club with your own kind."

Back in the car Lee chuckled evilly. "You could come back, Vernon. See if Cassie's still as willing as she always was."

Vernon shoved in the clutch. "You want to walk home, Lee?"

"Touchy, ain't you?" grinned Lee. He rode in silence, finished his beer and slung the can at a road sign, then opened another. Vernon declined. "You always stop just a little short, Vernon," Lee said seriously. "That's the difference in us. I get drunk and just keep on getting drunker until I wind up in jail. You get about half wild then back off."

"I've got a wife, kids, and a job," snapped Vernon. "My boss wouldn't be very happy to find out I spent my vacation in the Finch County jail."

"Lighten up, Vernon," grinned Lee. "You worry too much, and always have. There for a while, up on the golf course, I thought you'd learned how to have fun. Then Cassie jumps your case and you get all gloomy again. Hell, Vernon, what you and Cassie done when you was kids don't matter at all any more."

Vernon grinned tiredly. "Cassie was my first girl. I was fifteen, she was fourteen. She was pretty, too, back then. And wild as a mink. We about killed ourselves out in the brush piles."

"Since you took off," Lee said dryly, "they's been many a feller into Cassie's brushpile. You were just the first one, Vernon. If you hadn't come along, somebody else would have. You never made old Cass what she is. She was born that way."

Vernon circled Horse Mountain, peered back up at the golf course, and grinned. "I wonder if Toad has noticed yet that we tore up the Senator's golf cart?"

"Naw." Lee shrugged. "If he ever does notice, Toad will lie. If it had of been just me that rented it, I'd get my butt kicked, but since you was along it won't matter."

"What difference does it make that I was along?" asked Vernon.

"Hellfire," snorted Lee. "You're almost a movie star in these parts. You went to college, you got that big job, your name is in the papers all the time, you drive a Oldsmobile. You could get away with murder." Lee grinned. "Me, I'm just crazy old Leroy Watts. If I fart in public I get arrested."

"But you're a war hero now," said Vernon.

"Don't mean nothing," growled Lee, "except out at the VFW. Vietnam don't make no heroes, Vernon. Just screwed-up veterans or dead people, and I ain't real sure yet which one is worse. I haven't slept a whole night in over a year now."

Just outside town Lee pointed out a cement block building with an American flag flying. "Let me out there," he said. "My home away from home. The VFW Club." Vernon slowed and eased into the parking lot. "Tell Mom I'll be home when I get there," Lee said tiredly. "If I ever get there."

Vernon shut off the ignition. "Tell her yourself," he grinned. "If we ever get there."

A slow smile crossed Lee's thin face. "You coming in with me?" he asked.

"Can I?" asked Vernon.

"Hell yes," grinned Vernon. "I'll make you a guest member."

"Then I'm coming with you," said Vernon. He smiled. "Playing golf is like fishing. It's a waste of time if you don't get to sit around and lie about how good you did."

"I'll just be damned," Lee said softly. He looked Vernon over and grinned. "Let's go tell lies, big brother."

"Show me the way," said Vernon.

Lee kicked open the ragged screen door. "Listen up," he announced. "Me and my brother Vernon here have just shot the damndest nine holes of golf ever played in Finch County. Who's gonna buy the beer to get us to tell you all about it?"

The Liberation of Elsie Watts

Elsie Annette was the oldest of Eva and Mack Ward's fourteen offspring.

At six Elsie was doing the family wash, beating the clothes clean on the rocks of Caney Creek, pressing out the wrinkles with irons heated over the big cookstove. At thirteen she quit school to help at home, cooking and cleaning and caring for the new babies.

Mack Ward held four hundred acres of rugged Eastern Kentucky hillside farm land, and he bred new workers at the rate of one per summer. Eva, willing but weary, was unable to do more than bear the babies, and young Elsie became the surrogate mother. She was the caretaker for the busy household, cook and comforter to the other children, expert at quilting, sewing, soap-making, and canning and cooking.

At thirteen Elsie was prime marriage material, strong and pretty and blossoming, skilled and proven reliable. The first suitors showed up as soon as Mack would permit their visits. They were rawboned young farmers, awkward in starched work clothes, hair slicked with possum fat, rough hands nervously busy rolling Bull Durham. The more wealthy rode up on prancing saddle mares with braided manes and jingling silver bridles, and others hitched their somber mules at the barn and walked the last half mile.

Saturday night meant banjos and fiddles and guitars, and a crowd gathered around Mack's big battery powered Philco radio. There was moonshine and bootleg whiskey, singing and fistfighting, preening for Elsie and serious responsibility to impress Mack.

Elsie was curious, but disinterested, until Harper Watts made his first visit. Harper was twenty, strutting, flashing a wide smile, blessed with curly black hair and dancing eyes. Two days before Elsie's sixteenth birthday they were married, and a week later Elsie was expecting. The first daughter was born, then a son, and Elsie was pregnant again when Pearl Harbor was bombed. Harper enlisted, left for four years in Europe, and Elsie endured.

The second son was born six months after Harper left, and Elsie was expecting again a month after the soldier came home. Harper, after seeing New York and London, was unable to adjust again to Sparks Ridge. He took his growing family west, closer to the edge of the mountains, to a tenant farm near the Kentucky River. Harper farmed, labored on a bridge crew, tinkered with cars and worked as a carpenter, struggled to earn a meager existence for his brood. Elsie bore two more babies, then the twins, and finally the last, a son born just after her thirty-third birthday.

It was Elsie's task to stretch the budget. She worked a two acre garden, tended a flock of leghorn chickens, raised hogs to butcher on Thanksgiving Day, canned beans and blackberries and tomatoes, dressed and cooked the game Harper brought in with his .22 rifle. She sewed the girls' dresses and the boys' shirts, doctored the cuts and bruises and fevers, and sent the little Watts off to school scrubbed and with full bellies.

For four decades Elsie labored, guiding her flock through first loves and graduations and weddings, babies and brawls and heartaches, always available to provide comfort and strength. Harper's hot supper was ready every day at four-thirty, his lunchbox was packed every morning before dawn, and Elsie brought him his pipe and coffee when he stopped to rest.

Harper, as his children left home, was able to finally rest. He cut back to one fulltime job, bought a used color television, and found time again to sip the good Sparks Ridge moonshine. His worn easy chair was his throne, from where Harper presided over the weekend gatherings of his clan. For Harper Watts, the hard part was over.

Elsie was less fortunate.

She served as unpaid babysitter to a dozen grandchildren, chef and dishwasher for the Sunday gatherings, advisor and curtain-maker to nine households, servant to Harper's every whim, and overseer of the small farm. When the youngest, Bub, enlisted and left for the Army, Elsie was also stranded, isolated twenty miles from town and totally dependant upon Harper for any transportation.

Alone at home for the first time in her life, Elsie brooded. Uneducated, unsophisticated, unskilled at any profession, Elsie fretted and simmered. She was over fifty, taken for granted, restless now with her enforced housewifery.

On her 54th birthday Elsie was up at five to bake her own cake, serve dinner to thirty-seven children and grandchildren, and was up to her elbows in soapy dishwater when she made her decision.

Dripping, twisting her apron tails, redfaced and determined, Elsie descended upon the living room assembly.

"Harper Watts!" she screeched. "I've had enough of this!" Elsie wheeled and was gone.

Harper, slackjawed and stunned, stared after Elsie until his cigarette burned down to his fingers. He swore, jerked, and kicked over a table full of ashtrays and coffee cups. Plaintively, he turned to the assembled sons and daughters.

"What do you reckon," Harper asked feebly, "has got into your mommy?"

At first, Harper was quietly proud of Elsie. "For a woman, she's coming right along," he told a neighbor. "Bubby, he's teaching her how to drive, and next week she'll take her test. It ain't like Elsie needs a driving license, you know. I take her anywheres she needs to go, and now we got one of them telephones too."

Bub, home on a thirty day leave, tried to prepare Harper.

"She's looking for a job, Daddy," he warned.

Harper chuckled. "Who'd hire her? Your mommy ain't ever done nothing but cook and clean house and change diapers."

"I'm just telling you," persisted Bub. "Momma is serious about working. She'll find her a job."

Harper grinned. "That'll be the day."

Elsie passed the driving test, so Harper selected and paid for the old Chevy Vega station wagon. "Keeps her happy," he told the children. "You got to humor these mountain women."

Elsie's first solo trip, to Finchburg on Saturday for groceries, went well until she started home. When she reached across the seat to steady a sack of corn meal, Elsie looked back up just as the Vega left the pavement and flew across a deep ditch. The skidding car flattened four fence posts, clipped the legs out from under a water tank, hit a corncrib and rolled, and landed upside down in a muddy pen of squealing piglets. Elsie crawled out the window, slipped and fell in the muck, scrambled to fence to escape the angry sow, and wailed as she watched her little car sink deeper.

After ten minutes Elsie wiped her nose, shooed away the confused sow, salvaged her groceries, and walked stiffly on home.

Harper found the wreckage two hours later. He searched frantically, swore, and drove home in a panic. He found Elsie calmly dishing out supper, expressionless. "You're late," she snapped. "And go wipe the mud off of your feet."

"But you . . . " Harper's temper flared and he sputtered, but he reconsidered after a look at Elsie's face. He washed up for supper. Elsie broke the silence. "I reckon you seen it?"

"Your car?" Harper's lip twitched. "The one up in Jake Howard's hog lot?"

"You and the boys will have to get it out, and fix Jake's fence and water tank." Elsie chewed solemnly.

"I reckon we will," grunted Harper. He finally grinned. "Did you kill any little pigs?"

"No!" snapped Elsie.

After supper they sat beside the fireplace. "Harper," Elsie said after five minutes, "I ain't going to stop driving."

"I don't know about that," scowled Harper. "Appears to me, Elsie, you ought to give it up. Besides, you ain't got nothing to drive now."

"Yes I do," said Elsie. "Roy already found me a Buick."

"You bought a car?"

"Yes."

"But you never asked me."

"No." Elsie smiled. "I never, did I?" She left Harper staring and went off to bed.

The hospital administrator smiled as Elsie left, and called for his assistant. "Do you know that woman who was just here?" he asked.
"No."
"She's 54 years old," said the administrator. "She went to school for less than five years, has never had a job, and I just hired her."
"As a maid?" asked the puzzled assistant.
"Nope." he laughed. "Elsie Watts is the new recreation director for our extended care wing."
"Have you lost your mind?"
"Maybe," grinned the administrator. "But, Maggie, that woman has raised nine children and run a household since she was six. Can you think of any better preparation for taking care of twenty senior citizens?"
"Can Mrs. Watts read and write?" asked the assistant.
"Not like you and me." He chuckled. "But she can sure get a message across."

"You done what?" Harper's fork froze in mid-air.
"Like I told you," said Elsie. "I got a job. At the hospital."
Harper puzzled. "Cooking?"
Elsie glared. "No. I'll be taking care of the older people. Getting them haircuts, and games, and preachers for Sunday, and stuff like that."
Harper grunted. "I'll be danged."
"Is that all you got to say?" asked Elsie.
"I reckon so." Harper finished eating and sat silently.
Elsie spent her first day on the job watching, meeting patients and her co-workers, and didn't get home until after six. Harper met her at the door. "Where the hell is my supper?" he demanded.
"You can set down and wait until I get it cooked," Elsie said calmly. "Or you can fix it yourself, or you can do without." She marched past

him to change clothes, then warmed up Sunday's chicken and dumplings.

"This ain't gonna work," grumbled Harper. "I've damn near starved to death."

Elsie studied hospital manuals until near midnight, then slept in the extra bed.

Elsie's first big challenge came her third week on the job. Sadie Weaver, 86 years old and a terminal cancer patient, disrupted the floor by angrily accusing the head nurse of stealing her baby. Persistent, tearful, heartbroken, the old woman struggled and wailed and was finally sedated. Elsie grieved for her.

"It ain't right," she told the nurse, "to just let Sadie lay there and cry like that."

"What would you do?" snapped the nurse. "Get her a baby?"

"Maybe," said Elsie. "Maybe I would."

The next morning Elsie was early, and she carried a small bundle to Sadie Weaver's room.

"Praise God," cried Sadie. "My prayers is answered, Elsie." Sadie hugged the worn doll close to her breast. "I knowed," she said, "that my baby was here somewheres. That woman stoled it. But you brung it back to me, Elsie."

Elsie blinked back her tears and left quickly.

All day, Sadie proudly showed her baby to everyone in the hospital, and even Eb Weaver gently cuddled the doll when he came to visit. The indignant head nurse went to the administrator. "That woman," she sputtered. "Elsie Watts actually gave Mrs. Weaver a doll. Can you imagine? I've had it. I've never seen anything so outrageous. I insist that you fire Mrs. Watts right now."

The administrator rocked back in his chair and smiled. "How has Sadie been today?"

"She's been too busy holding that doll to cause any trouble," snapped the nurse.

"Sadie didn't cause any trouble at all today?"

"No."

"It seems to me," he said quietly, "that Elsie did us all a big favor."

"Well, in a way," said the redfaced nurse. "Maybe she did. But she violated all hospital routine and procedure."

"Miss Barton," the administrator said gently. "Elsie Watts gave a dying old woman one day of happiness. Isn't that what we're supposed to do here?"

After the angry nurse left, the administrator called down to the personnel office. "Elsie Watts is now a permanent employee," he directed. He smiled. "Today she passed all her tests."

Harper mourned. Elsie's suppers were late, even cold, and she often went back to town for evening programs. Once, for an entire weekend, she went to Louisville for a workshop—her first night away from home since Harper came home from the war, Harper's first night ever alone in the house. Elsie spent her paychecks as she pleased, without consulting Harper, and on Sunday afternoons she drove to visit her family and to attend church services.

"It ain't natural," Harper complained to Priscilla. "Your mommy out running all the time, and spending money like she was rich. She told me she ain't going to cook our Sunday dinners no more, neither." He shook his head sorrowfully. "I don't know what's come over her, Prissy."

"I work," said Priscilla. "Lots of women do now, Daddy. You'll get used to it."

The tension built. Harper compounded the problem by bringing home a dog, a wolfish German Shepherd considered hopeless by its previous owners.

"You'll be sorry," warned Elsie. "That thing'll kill one of the little ones, and then what'll you do?"

Harper ignored her. He kept the dog, and three weeks later Buck did nip a grandchild who ventured too near the food dish. "That thing has got to go," insisted Elsie. "Take him to the woods and shoot him."

"Buck, he's my dog," Harper argued stubbornly. "Besides, he didn't hurt the boy none."

Elsie stormed off to the bedroom.

Even Harper found it difficult to like the clumsy and surly animal, and made only half-hearted attempts to train him. Buck, a drooling dullard, forced the issue. First he killed six of Elsie's hens, then he left a mauled kitten on the front steps. Elsie paled, slipped back into the house, and came out lugging Harper's old double barreled shotgun.

"Come here, Buck," she chirped.

Buck thundered around the corner, skidded and backpedaled, and howled as Elsie's first load of buckshot peppered his flanks. Her second charge spattered around him as he ran, whimpering, for the safety of the barn.

Harper came home, found his subdued and trembling dog, picked out the buckshot, packed his straight razor and shirts, loaded Buck into the pickup, and drove to Priscilla's to stay.

"I left her," he explained angrily. "A man can't live with no woman what'd shoot his dog."

After a week of Harper and Buck, Priscilla convened a gathering of the Watts offspring, and even called Vernon, living in Lexington now after his years in North Carolina. "You all have got to help me," Prissy pleaded. "Daddy is too stubborn to go back, and Mommy's feelings are hurt so bad she won't apologize, and I'm about ready to shoot that damned dog again."

It was Bubby, the youngest, preoccupied as he drove in from Ft. Knox, who unintentionally triggered the solution. Bub lost control of his car on the wet highway, slid into a tree and flipped, rolled out and lay unconscious in the rain.

Elsie took the call from the state police, and arrived at the hospital minutes behind the ambulance, just ahead of Harper and Priscilla.

"They don't know yet," gasped Elsie. "Bub is in there with the doctors." She spoke only to Priscilla. "You tell your daddy."

"I heard her," grunted Harper. "Prissy, ask your mommy did she see Bub when they brung him in?"

Priscilla groaned. "Did you see Bubby, Momma?"

"For a second," sobbed Elsie. "He was all wet, and bloody, and real still." She dissolved into tears and clung to Priscilla. Harper fidgeted, dark and gloomy, and flexed his big hands.

They waited, awkward and anxious, for the half hour before the door opened. "Bub's fine," the doctor said cheerfully. "Cut and bruised some, but more scared than anything. We'll keep him overnight to be sure, but there's nothing to worry about. He's sleeping now, so it'll be a while before he can talk."

"Thank ye, doc," Harper said gravely.

"That's what I'm here for," answered the doctor. "That goes for all of us here at the hospital, including Elsie. I've been meaning to tell you, Harper, what a fine job Elsie does for us. You can be proud of her."

"I am." Harper studied the wall, and Elsie looked out at the steady drizzle.

Priscilla found her coat and umbrella. "I'd better go," she said. "I'll tell everybody Bub's okay. And you can bring Daddy home, Momma."

"Just a minute now," blurted Harper. "I'll ride with you, Prissy."

"You won't either," Elsie ordered firmly. "You'll stay right here. That's your baby laying in that room. You can come back after him, Prissy."

Priscilla surrendered. "Okay," she said wearily. "Call when you're ready, Daddy. I'll send somebody to get you."

Elsie and Harper waited at opposite ends of the room until a nurse finally called them. Bub grinned feebly as they entered. "I guess I'll have to quit making fun of the way you drive now, Momma." Elsie squeezed his hand and stroked his forehead. "How's my car?" asked Bub.

"Don't you worry about no car," said Elsie.

"Was you drinking, boy?" Harper asked sternly.

"Harper Watts!" Elsie spun, spitting mad. "You stop that!"

Bubby groaned. "You stop it, Momma. I'm not going to have any more of the two of you fighting."

"Fighting?" Elsie scowled. "We wasn't fighting, was we?" She looked down at Bub. "I guess we was," she said softly.

Bub chuckled. "You sure were. Like two old setting hens. That's why I was on my way home. We were all going to talk it over and see what we could do."

"We?" asked Harper. "Is that why they was all out to Prissy's?"

"Yeah," said Bub. "She called me, and Vernon, and all the rest."

"Now, dang it all," started Harper, "you all got no business meddling in what me and your mommy does."

"Shut up, Harper," Elsie said gently. "We can talk somewheres else."

They stayed with Bub for another hour, and left him sleeping soundly.

Elsie buttoned her coat and waited at the lobby door. "Harper," she said, "I'm sorry I shot old Buck. Did I hurt him bad?"

Harper shuffled closer. "Naw," he muttered. "To tell you the truth, he's acted lots better since you peppered him." His brown eyes sparkled. "Elsie, I've been missing you."

"Me too." Elsie hesitated. "Harper, are you coming home?"

He took a wary step backwards. "I'm a wanting to," he said. "Are you gonna keep on working?"

"Yes." Her answer was firm and quick. "That's the way it's got to be, Harper."

He grinned and shrugged. "Can't blame a man for trying, can you?" He stepped closer and gently touched Elsie's shoulder. "I'll come home if you'll have me, Elsie."

"I ain't never wanted nobody else," said Elsie. "Not since the first day I laid eyes on you."

Harper coughed. "Let's go home."

"You drive," said Elsie.

"Nope," said Harper. "It's high time I seen for myself how good you can handle a car."

In the parking lot Elsie nervously started the old yellow Buick, edged backwards, shifted gears, gunned the engine and slammed hard into a light pole.

She screamed.

Harper pulled himself up from the floorboard, rubbed his chin, adjusted his cap, and finally grinned.

"Try her again, Elsie," he grunted. "I believe they's a pole over yonder that you missed."

Kentucky Waltz

Bub Watts, otherwise known as WO4 Perry Jonathon Watts, US Army, 101st Airborne, rigged the underside of his Blackhawk helicopter with stereo speakers which blared out Bluegrass music, and there were those who swore he could make the black warplane swing and sway to the rhythm of Bill Monroe's 1946 hit song "Kentucky Waltz."

Bub, the youngest of Elsie and Harper Watts' nine children, grew up on Monroe, Lester Flat and Earl Scruggs, Hank Williams, the Osborne Brothers, Ralph Stanley, and, later, Ricky Skaggs, Tom T. Hall, Keith Whitley, Hank Jr., Johnny Cash, Tammy Wynette, and the many other stars of country, gospel, and bluegrass music—the sounds derived from a heritage of bagpipes, banjos, fiddles, and mandolins—the music of the Kentucky mountains.

Bub Watts had enlisted in the Army at eighteen, already married with a child, and worked his way through the tanks and trainees of Ft. Knox up to a chance to fly the helicopters used for transport, attack, and rescue across the world by the military services. All the while taking classes from Emory-Riddle University in aeronautical engineering, Bub rotated from Oregon back home to Kentucky, to Ft. Campbell, where he also qualified as a test pilot.

His musical whirlwind served Bub well in Granada, Panama, and in the deserts of Iraq, where he would sweep up across the barren dunes with all four speakers roaring, spewing death and destruction to the accompaniment of "Foggy Mountain Breakdown," Bonnie and Clyde in a snarling black machine of mass death, and during that war he stopped reluctantly short of his goal, Saddam Hussein's headquarters, when the president called the battle to a premature end.

Back home, Bub kept up his dual role as test pilot and combat flyer, applied for and was accepted into the "Night Stalkers," the elite 160th Attack and Rescue Team whose "Little Bird" choppers and pilots train relentlessly to live up their "We rule the night" motto.

"By the time you hear about it I've already been there," he told his older brother Vernon. "And we don't know until we're in the air if it's a drill or the real thing."

"Worst thing about secret night attack," he added with a grin, "is that I can't play any music as we go in."

"What a shame," chuckled Vernon. "It'd scare the living hell out of anybody alive if that black chopper popped up out of nowhere with Dr. Ralph wailing out 'O Death' at the top of his lungs."

Four of the Watts brothers were gathered at home in Finch County for the funeral of the fifth, Lee, dead far too young from cancer, most likely a result of exposure to Agent Orange during his Army service in Vietnam, who woke after surgery which removed his stomach and intestines and decided he'd rather not live that way. Lee picked his pallbearers and his burial clothes, turned over and went to sleep forever.

The unexpected reality that they were not, after all, immortal, had stunned the remaining eight offspring of the indomitable Elsie Watts, and hanging even heavier over the gathering was the approaching death of Harper Watts, just seventy-eight, slowing succumbing to congestive heart failure and throat cancer.

Familiar stories about Lee Watts' rambunctious ways temporarily lightened the mood, memories of a brother who lived life his own way, a hard drinker, a hard worker, and hard player. "A few years back," recalled Roy, the oldest, "Lee pulled in out at the Frosty Freeze driving that old red and white Rambler he had. It was pouring rain, and Lee was drunk as a skunk."

"Wanted me to go for a ride with him. I climbed in and he floored it. Never let off. We slid around in the parking lot a time or two before he could get it pointed toward the highway, and then we headed out at about ninety. He missed the road a couple of times and cleaned out some ditches, then over around Tilton he lost it in a curve and we went sliding off the road backwards. Right up into somebody's barnyard, mud and cowshit flying ever which way, us still going backwards with both rear wheels slinging mud."

"Lee held on to the spinner while he finished off a beer, looked over at me and grinned, and said 'Driving this sumbitch, ain't I?'"

Lewis, the twin, laughed. "Puts me in mind of the time Lee and me pulled into the store at Bald Hill about two in the morning and thought we could hear Bub's old van somewhere. Sounded like he was stuck, but he'd wind it out real good and then the motor would die. It was raining cats and dogs, but we kept looking and listening and finally figured out he was somewhere out in the cornpatch."

"We waded out through the mud and cornstalks and finally tracked him down, buried axle deep, with them sunglasses on, stoned to the gills, Lester Flat picking with the sound turned up so loud the windows was rattling. He didn't know he was stuck in the cornfield. He'd put the van in low, floorboard it until he got it spinning good, then shift to second. It'd spit and backfire and die. Then he'd do it all again."

"He finally saw us standing there laughing and said, 'They's something wrong with my van.'"

"We got us a logging chain out of Pierce's shed and pulled him out, about four in the morning. Then we about had to set on him to keep him from driving off."

Bub blushed.

"Hell, Sarge," laughed Vernon. "You don't have to worry. We ain't going to report you to the Army."

"Remember when you wrecked Lee's new car, Bub?" asked Roy. "Only car he ever owned that he didn't tear up hisself."

All three of Lee's former wives, plus the current one, showed up for the funeral service.

One person who did not go was Harper Watts, who sat restlessly in his recliner, smoked, and listened for the military salute to be fired from the nearby hilltop. "I'll be up yonder on that hill with him soon enough," muttered Harper. From the distance came the muted sound of "Taps." "It's done, I reckon," said Harper.

A granddaughter later wrote, of the "Man of the Hour" and the restless time he spent waiting for his son to be buried:

Paintsplashed cap,
Embermarked chair cradles shadowskeleton frame.
He is waiting.
Smokes.

It will be over soon.
He'll see his son soon enough,
No need to go.
He hopes he does not hear the 21 guns.

Nervous.
He is smoking too much too fast
(His dead son's twin sits, too.
And smokes.)

Words hang in the bluehumid haze,
so they stop talking.
Front door creaks;
black suits, black dresses spilling in.
It is done and he did not hear the 21 guns.

The day a round of family:
coming, eating, crying leaving.
He sits, smokes.
Evening.
He has stopped raising the cigarette to his mouth.
It burns down to oakgnarled tissueskin hand
And he lights another one, like incense.
It burns down, too.
And his sons have come to talk squirrel hunting
until the only light
is the streetlamp.

It filters in with the hushed sounds of evening.

He used to be a damned good shot.
He wishes he could have heard the 21 guns.

Quiet.
Cigarette smoke wraps
ghostgray fingers around the night.

As the family scattered, each one knew they would return soon. Harper had, over the previous year, taken each of his offspring aside and given them special gifts, tiny pieces of his life being passed on to the next generation, guns to the sons, other mementos, such as his father's railroad watch, to the daughters.

To Vernon, Harper gave his battered old Mossberg bolt-action .22 rifle, ordered for $9 from a mail order catalog almost sixty years earlier. The rifle had been each son's learning tool, and it was the one Harper had used to strike matches, drive nails, and shatter acorns tossed up into the air.

The worn old weapon now sported a home-made firing pin, fashioned from a finishing nail, and a trigger filed from a piece of flat steel.

"Don't work no more," Harper had said of the rifle. "About like me." He sat down on the old iron bed where six of his children had been born. "But I tell ye, Vernon, that I'm leaving with no regrets. I've done had more, seen more, and done more than any man's got a right to do. I don't owe no man a favor or a cent, and I don't regret a single thing I've ever done in my life."

"I wish I could say the same," Vernon had replied. He was seeing his father's life again, in a different light, remembering the hardships and hard work, the sacrifices and difficulties which had always seemed so terrible.

Harper's father had been killed in a Christmas Eve gunfight when the boy was barely six years old, and he had supported the family by clearing new ground for a quarter a day, by growing a garden he'd cleared and surrounded with a split rail fence to keep out the deer, by killing squirrels for the cooking pot with a crude slingshot.

An ill-tempered stepfather, a few years later, went into the woods with Harper's three year old brother, Dean, and did not return. Searchers found the little boy playing in a neighbor's yard and asked about his father. "The old bastard is over'n the creek dead," Dean had replied.

The old bastard was.

Harper managed to finish eight grades then helped his brothers and half-brother go to school. Paul went on through high school and became a US Navy pilot. Dean joined the Army on his seventeenth birthday and was soon captured during the Battle of the Bulge. Harper left shortly after Vernon's birth for service during the invasion of Europe, where he made an abortive effort to rescue Dean but was stopped by MPs who wondered why such a heavily armed soldier was traveling alone on foot.

All three survived the war, though Dean spent eighteen months as a German POW, then Paul was lost when his bomber was lost near Korea in 1947.

Harper moved his family to Finch County after WW II and sent all nine through high school, worked without vacations as a carpenter and raised tobacco on the halves, and finally had retired and bought the house in town.

Harper had been married for over fifty years to Elsie, and he now proudly watched over a large flock of grandchildren and great-grandchildren.

Vernon caressed the old rifle. "My son will get this," he said. "Then his sons. And their sons."

"I know," said Harper, grinning. "That's why I give it to you."

Vernon went back to his job at the university, and Bub drove homeward wondering just how the youngest child, the baby of nine, could pay a tribute to his father that would do justice to the man and the moment.

Two months later Bub had his answer.

It was a routine flight for the Blackhawk, from Ft. Campbell to the Bluegrass Army Depot near Richmond for minor updates to the electrical systems, but when Bub had the chopper back up in the air he turned east instead of west. He turned to the two technicians flying with him.

"You are hereby ordered to forget everything that happens for the next hour," said Bub, as he switched off the radios. He swung the helicopter toward the Kentucky River. "Close your eyes if you don't want to see what happens."

"Where are we going?" asked one of the soldiers.

"If I told you that," said Bub, grinning, "then I'd have to have you court martialed." He looked down at familiar countryside. "Where we're going," he finally said, "is to salute an old soldier."

Over Finch County Bub slowed the Blackhawk and swung out in a lazy arc to stare down at the small town spread below them, crisp and clear under October sunshine. He switched on the cassette tape player.

"What in the hell?" asked the soldiers.

From under the Blackhawk the music that blared forth was not Bluegrass, but it was the ancestor of the music of the hills. The drone of a bagpipe, then the shrill notes of "Amazing Grace" filled the October air as the Pipes & Drums of the 48th Highlanders of Canada gave full voice to the most beloved song of rural America.

Bub swung the warship around and down, came in over the county courthouse and dropped lower, found what he was looking for and eased down, hovering, lower and lower until the Blackhawk was blasting the treetops with propwash and the thunder of engines was rattling windows.

Harper Watts roused himself when he heard the shrill pipes, coming from above, and for a minute he wondered if he were alive or dead, then began his slow struggle to pull himself up from the hospital bed. Harper had rigged one of his leather belts to make a pull strap, and now he groaned with the effort as he worked his frail body upwards.

Elsie came running from the kitchen, apron twisted, face flushed, grabbed Harper's shoulders and helped him rise up. "What is it?" she asked, listening as the roar and the whine came closer and closer.

Harper struggled over to the window sill. "By hell," he muttered. "It's Bubby."

The huge black shape of the Blackhawk dropped down into view, and from the pilot's seat WO4 Perry Jonathon Watts snapped a crisp salute to his father and held it as he hovered.

Sheets flew off Elsie's clotheslines and shrubs flattened as Bub held his position, and with a broad grin Harper Watts drew himself shakily erect and returned the salute with a trembling arm and toothless smile.

Bub, tears streaming, held the position for a few more seconds then hit the throttles, scattering debris and leaves as he climbed and turned.

The bagpipes stopped and Earl Scruggs' banjo notes filled the air as the Blackhawk circled for a final pass over the house and headed west at treetop level.

Cows, horses, dogs, and chickens scattered as Bub climbed up to a cruising altitude.

"You can turn the radio back on in twenty minutes," Bub told the two soldiers riding with him. "Tell 'em whatever you've got to."

"About what?" said the technician, grinning through tears. "Did you see anything, Jess?"

"Me?' The other soldier wiped his eyes. "Not a damn thing, sir."

Bub's tape switched over to "Kentucky Waltz" as they crossed over the Kentucky River at Boonesborough, and anyone watching from the ground would have wondered at the lilting, graceful movements of the fearsome attack helicopter that danced across the sky, waltzing its way back to Western Kentucky.

Harper sat down slowly, stunned.

"If I'd a knowed he was coming," he finally said weakly, "I'd a put in my teeth."

Finchburg's two police cruisers screamed madly through the streets, going no place in particular but going there at full throttle, responding to frantic calls swearing that the Russians had attacked the town. Troops were on the ground near the stockyards, said one report, and bombs from an attack chopper had destroyed the Chevrolet dealership.

Tanks were reported rumbling past the sewer plant, insisted a frantic caller, and paratroopers were floating down onto the golf course.

The VFW post had alerted all its members and the veterans were assembling, some armed with Enfield rifles and some with pump shotguns, but when somebody opened the bar the volunteer force quickly lost its foot soldiers.

The Finchburg Volunteer Fire Department rolled its pumper and tankers, but could not locate even any smoke in need of immediate attention.

Four Kentucky Sate Police troopers were sipping stale coffee at the Stockyards Restaurant, blissfully unaware that the county was at war. The publisher of the weekly paper was out and about, busily snapping news pictures, but as usual he had forgotten to load film into the camera.

The county's judge-executive was in a Frankfort motel room, comforting an over-made lobbyist who did not look nearly so good in harsh daylight as she had the night before in the dimly lit bar at the Holiday Inn. The mayor of Finchburg was huddled in his office with the lights off and the phone off the hook, hoping he would not be discovered until the current crisis had ended.

That left the chief of police in charge, on the front lines, and the chief finally figured out that whatever had happened was over and called in the cruisers and firetrucks.

A grizzled farmer called in to report, fairly accurately, that "some damn fool in black helicopter scattered my cows from here to kingdom come," and that his mules had dragged the sled through a bob-wire fence and into the farm pond by the crib.

Vernon Watts was on the phone, laughing until he cried, listening to Elsie's accounting of the afternoon attack on Finchburg. "Tell Bubby I won't write a word," he promised, "until he says it's okay."

Late in the evening Bub called home to get Elsie's reaction and her pledge of silence, especially if anybody came around from the US Army asking questions. "I won't," she promised. "Do you want me to wake up your daddy so you can talk to him?"

Bub hesitated. "Not tonight," he finally said. "I've already told him goodbye."

There was a final goodbye two months later, as four sons and three grandsons, four in uniform, carried the heavy, flag-covered coffin to the hilltop for burial beside the still-raw grave of the son. From the car Elsie watched as her sons and grandsons did their duty, and could not help telling those in the car with her, proudly, that "I sure did raise me some good looking boys."

The graveside words were brief. The seven rifles, manned by American Legion and VFW members, crashed three times, almost in unison. Those in uniform came to full attention to salute the flag and to salute Harper Watts as "Taps" echoed softly from the hilltop.

Lewis and Bubby Watts precisely folded the flag and Bub, as the senior officer present, made the formal presentation to his mother.

The hilltop slowly emptied.

The immediate family lingered, then slowly scattered, but returned four days later to honor Harper's wish that the family spend Christmas day together as was the longstanding tradition.

On a sunny Sunday afternoon the following spring, Vernon Watts drove alone to the cemetery, to the hilltop gravesites now lush and green with an American flag whipping above the headstones.

There were fresh flowers on both graves, a cement bench, and curios on the graves that served as ample evidence that this was a site often visited.

Vernon sat with his father and brother for over an hour, and was standing up to leave when he thought he heard the whump-whump-whump of a helicopter and what sounded like Bluegrass music wafting down from above.

The black chopper came in from the west, dropped to circle the hilltop, the strains of the fiddle and mandolin ringing out below the roar of jet engines, Bill Monroe and the Bluegrass Boys celebrating the springtime sun and the flowering meadows.

The chopper swung in low, hovered, and Vernon could see the pilot behind dark sunglasses, grinning as he brought the Blackhawk closer.

Vernon twisted his head to listen, trying to identify the music, then broke out into a wide smile when he recognized the high lonesome sound of the father of bluegrass music playing for the father of the Watts family.

Vernon took a few hesitant steps, then swung his imaginary partner into a waltz, lilting steps and swoops across the green green grass of home.

Bub grinned, let the music play for half a minute more, then shoved the throttles and swung the Blackhawk about, climbing steeply, quickly, then turning to make another pass over the gravesite.

And, as only he could do, Bub Watts used his fierce black warplane to dance across the ridgetop to the haunting strains of "Kentucky Waltz."

Final Liberation

For six long and lonely years after her son, Lewis, and her husband of 55 years, Harper, died within months of each other, Elsie Watts quietly worked and mourned, drove her little gray Chevette five days a week to work in the county library, lived alone in what now seemed to be a large empty house, worked her flowerbeds and suffered the companionship of her grouchy cat "Hidy."

Not "Heidi," as most people assumed, but a shortened version of Elsie's morning greetings to what was once a tiny kitten.

"Hidy, little cat," she'd say, and the name stuck despite the Siamese cat's unfriendly advances toward visitors and her frequent wailing demands for more food.

Elsie bristled at any suggestion that someone should live with her, and snapped at her daughters for calling far too often to see if she was okay. Despite diabetes and arthritis, high blood pressure and a mild stroke fifteen years ago, Elsie kept to her schedule, working twenty hours a week, hosting the family gatherings, shopping for her meager supply of groceries, sewing fancy braids and lace onto her clothes.

Mostly, though, Elsie Watts was lonesome, grieving for Harper, and nobody could fill the void in her life. Other men simply were not a consideration. "When you've had the best," said Elsie, "you don't ever want nothing else."

As the years slowly passed Elsie gradually became more forgetful, and more than once the children found food in the oven that had been there for weeks. Elsie ate less and less, lost weight, began to repeat herself and to forget who had come to visit.

Peyton, Elsie's granddaughter, had lived with Elsie and Harper during her college years, after her mother died, and one room of the house in Finchburg was still know as "Peyton's room." Elsie had fretted when Peyton married and chose to have a career before having babies, so when the children finally came after 10 years Elsie was delighted and full of advice on the care and raising of twins.

She was also pleased when Vernon, the third child and second son, moved back home after forty years and then moved into the farm house in the county where Elsie and Harper had lived for a dozen years.

The family celebrated Elsie's 80th birthday at the farm, a yard filled with family and friends, all of Elsie's sisters, and the long-time neighbors from the closely knitted farm community. Elsie's eight living children, most of the grandchildren, and a half-dozen great-grandchildren were there, plus a sprinkling of current and former in-laws who filled the tables with gifts and food. Elsie arrived for the surprise party in a long white limousine, which did not impress her at all, but the crowd waiting there for her did make Elsie happy.

Just six months later, Elsie suffered a major heart attack, was rushed to the local hospital and then to a medical center in Lexington. She survived, but kidney failure, persistent infection, and her rundown condition prolonged her stay to two months. Elsie came home facing dialysis three times a week plus the reality that she could no longer work or even take care of herself. She could not or would not eat, and in her frustration and depression would lash out angrily at whoever was handy.

Her memory of events sixty or seventy years past actually improved, and her stories of growing up in the mountains had new detail. Born in a log cabin, oldest of fourteen children and her father's favorite, Elsie Ward had lived a life that most observers would consider impossibly difficult, washing clothes in the creek, riding a horse to school, cooking for the family and caring for all the brothers and sisters, but her father had found ways to brighten Elsie's life.

Mack Ward covertly brought home lipstick and makeup to young Elsie, and when his World War I bonus came he sat down with the wishbook and let Elsie select any dress she wanted.

Elsie chose a beaded model, which when worn made a clucking noise that led her brothers to label it "the turkey gobbler dress," which brought out the "half-bear" in Elsie, sending the brothers retreating to the safety of the woods.

Elsie shipped the dress back for something less flashy, and was wearing the new dress the night young Harper Watts first saw her walk out the door of the church at Stark. "That's the girl," he told his best friend Manuel, "that I'm going to marry."

He finally did, after Elsie engineered most of the courting. One rainy Saturday she worked all day cleaning up the "courting room" of the new dogtrot cabin only to find two of Mack's prize foxhounds wallowing on the lace bedspread.

A furious, sobbing, screeching mountain girl chased out the hounds and went looking for Mack. "What do you want me to do?" he asked plaintively. "Kill them?"

"Yes," wailed Elsie.

He did.

In maybe the most powerful expression ever of his love for his feisty oldest daughter, Mack led his two hounds up on the mountain and shot them.

Later that spring Harper was late for a Saturday night date, but at dusk Elsie's mother peered down the wagon road and burst out laughing. Dressed in a white shirt visible from across the hillside, Harper Watts was wobbling from one fence post to the other.

"Drunk as a skunk," reported Evie.

Which was a condition both women easily recognized, having waited up many nights to make sure Mack made it home, a task made possible by the old white mare that knew the route and took care that she didn't dislodge her well-lubricated, full-voiced passenger.

Mack's graveled voice echoed off the cliffs and mountainsides, Old Regular hymns made somehow more satisfying by large doses of potent moonshine.

Mack's still on Caney Creek was off-limits to females, but Elsie and her cousin Madge often slipped though the underbrush to watch the men at work.

Over sixty-five years later, in his mother's kitchen, Vernon Watts jokingly said he'd love to have a good stiff drink then nearly fell out of his chair when Elsie reached into her potato bin and produced a fifth of Kentucky bourbon.

"For making candy," she explained.

Vernon had his drink, then put the bottle back.

In contrast to her vivid memory of the past, Elsie's perception of current events suffered and she seldom could remember what had happened on any given day. She did not lose her sense of humor, though, or her ability to laugh at herself. An old friend, well aware of the many Watts children's divorces, remarked wickedly that "I reckon your youngens is all growed up and married now, ain't they?"

Elsie hesitated, then answered, "Sometimes they are."

When Elsie would be brought to the farmhouse on Sunday afternoons, Vernon's two female Huskies, Molly and Dolly, would abandon their normally aloof and wolfish ways to lick both Elsie's hands as they gently escorted her from car to front door.

She called Vernon to ask about Harper's old rifle, the one he'd ordered from the Montgomery Ward catalog for nine dollars when he was a teenager. A woman living alone, opined Elsie, had need for a weapon, and the old Mossberg .22 was the only gun she knew how to shoot.

Then she told the story again, of the Sunday morning gunfight in their front yard while Harper was in the war, when three young men died, when Elsie nailed her windows shut, loaded the old .22, and sat awake for three days to protect her babies.

Elsie had used her sheets to cover up the bodies, and Mack Ward was part of the posse that finally shot the last of the killers out of an oak tree.

"Daddy gave me the rifle," said Vernon, "but it won't shoot."

"Shoot?" asked Elsie. "Shoot what? Do you remember the time your daddy went off on Friday night to get you some canned milk and didn't come home 'til Monday?"

Vernon grinned, glad the rifle was forgotten. "I was two months old."

"He got over in a barn somewheres, drinking and playing poker. When he come home I told him if he ever took another drink me and you babies was leaving."

Harper had believed her, and backslid only late in life when his sons served as his bootleggers.

As more months passed, Elsie took on a look that seemed, to Vernon, that of a caged animal, a once-free spirit doomed to a life of confinement and medical treatments that finally included antidepressants. "Keeping old people alive past their time ain't all it's cracked up to be," she told Vernon on one of the rare occasions when they were alone.

"I can't shoot you," replied Vernon, trying to joke. "They'd send me to prison."

Several years earlier Vernon had called Elsie to say that he had bad news, that he was getting a divorce, and Elsie had sniffed and said, "Is that all? If you ever get married again, marry you a woman who can cook beans."

Barbara Ann, the blue-eyed coal miner's daughter from deep in the Kentucky hills, was that woman. Elsie loved her immediately, and spent many hours talking with her new daughter-in-law about the loneliness of life without Harper. When Barbara Ann's oldest son was killed in a wreck, the two women shared the grief that only a mother can know, and Elsie repeated what she had earlier told Vernon. "No mother should live long enough to bury a child. You know I loved Vernon's daddy better than anything in the world, but it was easier to see him go than it was to lose Lewis."

Elsie then told Barbara Ann that shortly after Vernon was born his father, Harper, left to fight in World War II and didn't come home for almost two years. "Vernon is the only one of them that I raised by myself," she said. "That's why he was always my baby."

Then, with a smile, she added, "He still is."

For Christmas Day Elsie dressed up. "In real clothes," she said, her brightest seasonal outfit, to host the gathering of family and friends. The twins came, crawling and climbing, and Elsie's gift to each of her children was new color portrait.

Two days later Vernon took a phone call, climbed into his truck and rushed to Lexington. Elsie had not, he found, had the reported heart attack, and seemed to be in great spirits and in control of her thinking. She asked for and received the forms to sign forgoing any life support.

"Except the water," she added. "I sure do like my water."

In the hospital room Elsie asked Vernon about his shoulder surgery scheduled for the next week. "I'll have to learn to drive with one hand," he grinned.

"You learnt that back in high school," laughed Elsie. "With that Sarah Collier girl."

Vernon smiled. "You won't believe it, but I heard from her not too long ago. She said she wishes she'd caught up with me between wives."

Elsie's grin was almost evil. "Tell her," she said, "to not give up just yet."

Elsie's spirits remained high for the rest of the day. Vernon went on home, called his daughter to update her, and Peyton suddenly decided she'd drive to Lexington Sunday morning. "I'll call you," she said.

She did. The call was not what Vernon expected.

"She just died," sobbed Peyton. "She was smiling, and talking to Harper and Lewis and to her father, and then she was gone."

"She's where she wants to be," Vernon finally said softly.

Monday morning the surviving Watts offspring were not where they wanted to be.

Gathered at the funeral home in Finchburg, seven of the eight brothers and sisters agreed that the funeral would be on Wednesday, that the sons and grandsons would be the pallbearers, and that the one night of visitation would be on Tuesday.

Vernon, with his shoulder surgery scheduled for Friday morning, worked on Tuesday to get caught up before being gone for two months, and did not go near Elsie's house. He did not talk to any family members until the evening of the visitation, when he and Barbara Ann showed up early for the family viewing.

Even in death, in her pink coffin, Elsie Watts was petite and feminine, and her face no longer showed the pain and frustration. As family and friends gathered, Vernon reached to hug a high school classmate and was suddenly bent double with pain, the left shoulder dislocated, grimacing and pale as he struggled. The shoulder quickly snapped back into place, and Vernon breathed again.

He suddenly was aware of the shocked onlookers, most looking as though they'd just witnessed a heart attack, and grinned feebly. "Didn't want Mommy to get all the attention," he said hoarsely. "I'm okay."

Somebody brought water and pain pills, and Vernon slumped to a chair.

On the day of the funeral, Vernon protected the sore shoulder as best he could, not an easy task during such an emotional time. He had plenty of help, people who would pull him back if he forgot and started to reach out. He flatly refused to excuse himself as a pallbearer. "I've got another arm," he grumbled.

A minister who could not pronounce Elsie's name preached a short service. A fifty-year friend and neighbor eulogized Elsie, smiling as she described how one of her sons insisted that "Miz Watts" was the prettiest woman he'd ever seen. A son-in-law sang "Amazing Grace."

As the brothers and two grandsons prepared to move the closed coffin, Vernon took up a spot on the left side so he could use his good right arm. There was snow on the ground, and slick dress shoes could not get a grip. Stubbornly determined, aware of watching eyes, Vernon stayed on his feet and carried his share.

On the way to the cemetery, Barbara Ann said, quietly, "You don't have to do that again. Don't hurt yourself."

"Can't hurt no worse," Vernon said doggedly. "I'll do my part."

He did, switching sides, treading carefully, eyes down.

The brief ceremony ended, and there was food and family back at the church.

Already, Vernon was aware that an era had ended. There was no Watts family home any more. There was just a house, and now it was lifeless.

When the meager estate was settled, Vernon wound up with an aunt's painting of the old Ward homeplace, his grandmother's old cedar chest, the bottle of Maker's Mark from the potato bin and other stuff, but mostly he valued the photographs that surfaced. His favorite, still framed and on display in Vernon's living room, was of a young Elsie Watts holding up her youngest-at-the-time, Vernon, smiling proudly and showing him off to the world.

Six months after Elsie's funeral, Barbara Ann took three of Vernon's grandchildren to visit what they termed "the Mamaw's" gravesite, and young Gene, born two years after Harper Watts' death, could not understand the other occupant. "Who is this Harper?" he asked, "and why is he here next to Mamaw?"

Barbara Ann explained, as best she could, then drove home and watched as Gene marched straight to where Vernon sat. "You've got no parents," he sternly informed Vernon, "and you're missing a brother."

Vernon quietly agreed.

"How many are you?" asked Gene.

"How many what?"

"How many years?" Gene said.

"Sixty," replied Vernon.

"How many was the Mamaw?"

"She was 82," said Vernon.

"Then you don't have much longer to live," Gene yelled back as he ran outside to play.

"Probably not," whispered Vernon as he watched the white-haired boy trot happily out into the early spring sun. "As if I needed reminding."

Hellcat

When the REA snaked its lines up Sinking Creek in 1947, Verl Rose stole enough electrical cable and hardware to string power to his new four-seat outhouse.

Even before he added the yellowed light bulb and scratchy Philco radio, Verl's privy was by far the most elegant in all of Caster County. The solid foundation was of creosoted railroad ties, the exterior walls were red brick tarpaper, and the roof was sparkling galvanized tin. Inside, Verl pasted up rosebud wallpaper, laid a blue linoleum floor, and installed four hinged pink toilet seats he ordered from the Sears & Roebuck wishbook.

Verl was working on a heater, too. Already he had rigged a rotating fan, with a switch which worked off the door to turn it on as you entered and off as you left.

Sometimes, Verl would sit on one of his thrones and study the wishbooks, but most of the time he just sat and stared at the big color poster Paul Skaggs had brought him in 1943. The poster was of a snarling F6F Hellcat, the US Navy's superb little fighter plane, the blunt-nosed hotrod which flew off carrier decks to shoot down over 5,000 Japanese Zeroes in three years of action.

Paul, Orb Skaggs' boy from up on Mauk Ridge, shot down fourteen of the those 5,000 Japanese fighters before one of them got lucky and got him. Paul's Hellcat blew up before he could bail out. Paul's body was recovered and shipped home to Kentucky. Orb got Paul's medals, after the war, and a letter which told all about how good Paul had been. Paul Skaggs was Verl's hero.

Verl had tried hard to join up, in '42, but the Army refused his application for the Air Corps. "Read, hell," Verl had snorted. "What's reading and writing got to do with flying a airplane?" Not even as a mechanic would the Army take Verl. He had walked the six miles home from Olive Hill angry and ashamed, and two weeks later asked Buck Cox, over at the Mauk Ridge Store, just what the hell was "mentally deficient" anyhow?

Buck took a chew, spat, and finally allowed as how it must have something to do with the way a feller's hammer hangs, and gave Verl the wheels off an old girl's bicycle which had broken in two in the middle.

To a remote mountain county short on young men, spare parts, and cash, Verl Rose's tinkering was crucial to keeping the old Fords, sawmill engines, radios, and coal trucks going while the war was being fought. In bits and pieces, in payment for his work, Verl had acquired a flat-head V-8 Ford engine and transmission, a leather aviator's cap and goggles, a pair of WW I cavalryman's boots, a pair of balsawood oars, six old shotguns, a pile of scrap metal, and a truckload of planed white oak lumber.

Verl used some of the supplies to build his elegant outhouse, and kept the rest neatly stacked and stored in the barn behind the homeplace. Verl's mother, Lily, staunchly defended Verl from gossipy neighbors who wondered just how a man who never even went to war could have got shellshocked. Lily also encouraged Verl's friendship with ten year old Benny Lee Skaggs, Paul's youngest brother, grateful that her eccentric son could relate to at least one fairly normal person.

Benny would listen for hours to Verl's worshipful stories about Paul Skaggs, and it was Benny who collected every available scrap of printed information about the Hellcat warplane. "They was over 12,000 built," Benny said with authority. "The Hellcat, it'd outrun, outclimb, and outshoot any other old airplane they ever was. Why, one pilot, it says, he shot down fifteen Japs in one fight. All by hisself."

"Paul, he could have done that too," insisted Verl. "Paul was the best pilot what ever lived."

"Yeah," agreed Benny. "I reckon he was, at that." He sat, pondering. "I wish they was somewhere we go to see us a Hellcat. I'd give a bunch to look at a real one."

Verl searched quietly, but couldn't locate a live Hellcat. "They couldn't even land one in these parts if we was to get one," he grumbled. For two more weeks Verl studied it over, then made his announcement. "Benny, I aim to build us one."

"Build us one what?" asked Benny.

"A airplane," said Verl. "A Hellcat. Just like the one Paul flew."

Benny stared suspiciously at his friend. "You don't know how to build no airplane, Verl," Benny finally said. He waited. "Do you?"

Verl beamed. "I got parts, ain't I? I got a picture to go by, don't I? Are you gonna help or ain't you?"

"I ain't so sure," said Benny. "Where you going to put it?"

Verl grandly pointed. "Right yonder," he said. "Right up in the top of that big old oak tree."

Two days later Caster County deputy sheriff Will Davis eased his dusty Ford coupe off to the side of Sinking Creek Road and crawled out laughing. "What are you up to this time, Verl?" he yelled.

Verl, from thirty feet up into the roadside oak, yelled back. "It ain't none of your business, Will. But, if it was, I'd tell you I was up in here building me a airplane."

Will peered up at the treetop, being rapidly leveled out by Verl's busy saw, and at the homemade ladder nailed to the tree trunk. "Lord have mercy," sighed Will. "This time I reckon Verl has gone plumb crazy." Will climbed up cautiously, and was surprised to look up and see Benny Skaggs grinning down at him. "Not you too, Benny," groaned Will. "Look here, Verl Rose. It's one damned thing if you want to fall out of this tree and break your own fool neck, but you ain't got no business dragging a boy up here."

"Verl never drug me nowheres," protested Benny. "I'm helping. And when we get it ready to go I'll be the co-pilot."

Will sighed, shook his head, climbed down and drove back to the courthouse. His laughing report sent scores of vehicles up Sinking Creek during the next two weeks, and there were daily courthouse-steps summaries of Verl's progress.

The Hellcat was taking shape.

Verl carefully built the frame from steamed and bent hickory, braced by sturdy white oak, and even the distinctive folding wings were made functional by two pairs of iron barn door hinges on each side. But, before he added the final outer cover, Verl rigged a block and tackle.

"What now?" wondered Will Davis.

Verl and Benny sweated and struggled, loaded the Ford V-8 motor and transmission onto a low sled and borrowed Lester Whitt's mule team to drag the load into place just under the oak tree.

"Surely," pleaded Will, "you ain't going to try that."

Verl nodded stubbornly.

Will swore, shrugged, spat on his hands and threw his two hundred pounds into helping pull the chain. The engine inched slowly upward. "You're crazy as hell, Verl," Will gasped. "This whole contraption is going to fall right on top of us."

"No it ain't," said Verl. "You gonna talk, or work?"

To Will's relief, the platform held the engine and transmission without a quiver. "Solid as a rock," beamed Verl. He toyed with the long gearshift lever which stuck up from the transmission case. "When we get done," Verl said proudly, "this here airplane is going to look exactly like the one Paul flew in the war."

Next Verl rigged a short driveshaft and a hand-operated clutch, brought up a gas can and an old battery, and started up the coughing old engine. "We need us a muffler," Verl yelled into Benny's ear.

"That ain't the half of what we need," Benny yelled back. "Where's the propeller?"

Verl shut down the rasping engine. "First things first," he announced. Ten feet of wellpipe and the muffler from a wrecked Reo truck quietened the motor. "Now," said Verl, "we'll get us that propeller." He retrieved a pair of doublebladed oars from the barn loft, and grinned at Benny. "With a little fixing, these here will do just fine."

Before dark, Verl had finished mounting his new four-bladed propeller. He connected the driveshaft. "Will that really work?" asked Benny.

"Stand back," ordered Verl proudly, "and I'll show you." He started the motor, engaged the clutch and shifted to bulldog low, and gently opened the throttle as he released the clutch. The propeller shuddered and started to turn. Will opened up the throttle.

"It works!" Benny yelled happily. "It's going, Verl."

Verl wiped his hands and grinned. "Told you it would," he said modestly.

As they washed up in the rain barrel, Verl explained the workings of gears and driveshafts. "We can run her in low gear and the propeller, it'll go slow. We shift her up, she'll go faster." Verl winked. "If we ever hit high gear, Benny, that thing'll take off and fly right across the ridge yonder."

"Yeah," whispered Benny. "We can fly our Hellcat to Ashland and back."

The next day Verl and Benny nailed on the thin outer boards and mounted the old bicycle wheels. The Hellcat looked even more real than they had dared dream. "Durn," Benny said admiringly. "It looks like it's really flying, Verl."

"Swooping right down at the road," cackled Verl, "diving down to shoot up anything what comes up this here hill." He smiled vaguely. "One thing we ain't put in yet, Benny, is the guns."

"That's 'cause we ain't got any guns," Benny said absently, staring up at the Hellcat. "God, Verl, she sure is pretty."

"We got guns," Verl muttered to himself.

When Benny arrived the next morning, Verl was already up in the Hellcat working. "Looky here," he said proudly. Benny stared. Six rusted .12 gauge shotguns, two of them double-barreled, were mounted—three to each side of the cockpit—linked together on a swivel mount.

Verl giggled as he demonstrated. "Swing 'em up, swing 'em down, go to either side, just like this. And this rod here, it's hooked to ever one of the triggers. You can shoot 'em one at a time or all of 'em at onct." He beamed. "Ain't that something, Benny?"

"Are they real guns?" Benny nervously fingered the control rods. "Will they shoot, Verl?"

"Hellfire yes they'll shoot!" laughed Verl. "Want me to show you? I brung shells."

"Naw," Benny said quickly. "Let's finish the painting."

They painted the Hellcat bright US Navy blue, and copied insignia from Paul's old poster. "One more thing," Verl said shyly. "Paul's airplane. Didn't he name it 'Bad Bessie'?"

"Yeah," said Benny. "How'd you know that?"

"Me and Paul, we was buddies," beamed Verl. "Paul, he told me about everthing."

They lettered the name across both sides of the Hellcat's nose, then added fourteen red dots. "For fourteen Zeroes," explained Benny. "Paul shot down fourteen of 'em."

Will Davis came that afternoon to admire "Bad Bessie," but his smile faded when he came to the six shotguns. "Them don't work, do they?" Will asked sharply.

Verl cut off Benny. "Heck no they don't work, Will. Them's old ones I had down on the barn."

"That's okay, then, I guess," said Will. He smiled again. "Just don't you boys get no ideas about hanging a bomb onto this thing." The deputy left chuckling, looking back, shaking his head.

"Why'd you lie to Will about the guns?" Benny demanded as soon as the deputy was out of hearing range.

"Wonder what we could make us a bomb out of?" Verl answered thoughtfully. He grinned at Benny. "It wouldn't be real."

"It'd better not be," said Benny. "Why'd you lie, Verl? About the guns?"

"Aw, old Will would have made us take 'em off if he knowed they'd work," protested Verl. "It wasn't no real lie, Benny. It don't matter."

"Maybe not," Benny said skeptically. "But you better not ever start shooting."

Verl worked most of the night, by lamplight, building his torpedo shaped bomb. Two sticks of ten-year-old dynamite went into the center. "What Benny don't know won't hurt him none," Verl whispered. He finished mounting the bomb on the plane's belly as the first car of the morning came bouncing up Sinking Creek Road. It was Buck Cox, grinning ear-to-ear. "By damn, Verl," Buck finally announced, "you've done it. Coming up the hill yonder, that things looks just like a real fighter plane swooping down at you." He chuckled. "And, a body'd think that bomb on the bottom was the real thing, too."

Traffic picked up. For a week, a string of dusty Fords and Chevies paraded up the hill. Verl's Hellcat drew visitors from as far away as Morehead, and one young newspaper reporter talked Verl into posing in front of the plane wearing his aviator's cap. Benny Skaggs wore Paul's old flight jacket and goggles proudly, and gave detailed technical explanations to anyone who would listen.

The newspaper story drew even larger crowds, and Verl began to fidget. "Sometimes," he said to Benny, "I get the idea that them people is making fun of us."

"Me too," complained Benny. "I wish they'd just all go away."

Verl's patience wore thinner. Benny stopped coming by altogether, and the steady flow of chuckling gawkers drove Verl to paint signs warning people off. No one paid the least bit of attention.

On the third Sunday, Verl took more direct action. He scrambled angrily up the ladder with a box of No. 6 birdshot, loaded all eight barrels, and snarled as another convoy of cars came laboring up the hill.

First Verl fired just one gun.

Buckshot spattered off windshields and fenders, and the lead car slid to a stop.

"Git, goddamn you!" squalled Verl. This time he pulled two triggers, and laughed as he reloaded. Cars were trying to back up and turn around; horns were blaring; people were cursing hysterically. "Take this, you sonsabitches!" screamed Verl. All eight barrels thundered at once, shaking the Hellcat and sending the last of the crowd running frantically downhill.

Verl reloaded, but kept a wary eye on the highway. When the coast was clear he scrambled down and ran to the barn. Verl came back wearing his high-topped cavalry boots, aviator's cap and goggles, and an old .32 revolver strapped to his waist.

From Verl's neck streamed a long red silk scarf.

He climbed the ladder with a bubbling, stuttering Rebel yell. The old engine clattered to life, the propeller began to turn, and Verl's shotguns swiveled to cover the battlefront.

Will Davis slammed his brakes when Verl's first round of gunfire shattered his windshield. Will shoved open the door and dived headfirst into the deep ditch. He crawled out covered with sticky mud. "Verl, damn you!" Will bellowed. "Come down out of there!"

Verl swung his guns around to bear on the angry and wet deputy, but held up as Benny Skaggs ran into the field of fire.

"Get down, you little fool!" yelled Will. Benny dived into the ditch.

"Don't you shoot Verl!" Benny shrieked.

"Shoot him?" growled Will. "Hell, son, it's Verl that's trying to do the killing." Will peered up over the edge of the ditch. "What's he doing now?"

The roar of the Hellcat engine was louder, and the propeller was spinning fast.

Benny peeped out. "He's going to fly away," whispered Benny. "Verl's really going to fly."

Will sighed. "You're as crazy as Verl, boy." But he stared at the blur of the Hellcat's propeller. "That thing won't really fly. It won't, will it? Benny?"

"Naw," Benny said nervously. But he watched closer now. "At least I don't think it will."

Verl shoved the clutch and shifted to second gear. The plane shuddered as the propeller picked up speed. Verl shoved the throttle wide open, and the Hellcat struggled against its moorings.

"My God," whispered Will Davis.

The old V-8 was screaming. Verl's scarf, whipped by the propeller wash, flew back from his clenched teeth and tearstreaked face.

Then Verl smiled and shifted to high gear.

The propeller shrieked.

Then there was a sudden, sharp crackle as Verl's blue Hellcat broke free from the oak tree's limbs. The stubby fighter plane leapt out into space, rattled and bellowed, dipped hard to the left and nose-dived, pieces of hickory and oak streaming behind.

"Bad Bessie" slammed nosefirst into Caster County's most elegant outhouse.

Two ancient sticks of dynamite exploded. There was a blinding flash, a muffled roar, and a shower of hot splinters and metal shards.

Will Davis crawled weakly up out of the ditch and stared. "What happened?" he whispered. "What in the name of God just happened?"

"It flew!" Benny scrambled up trembling. "The Hellcat flew," he repeated disbelievingly. "Verl's airplane really did fly."

Fire crackled through dried oak and hickory timbers.

"The poor soul," whispered Will. "Poor old Verl."

"No." Benny tugged at Will's sleeve. "Don't you say that."

"What?" Will put a strong arm around Benny's frail shoulders. "Easy, son. They ain't a thing we can do for Verl now."

"We don't have to do nothing for him." Benny was smiling, beaming through a stream of tears. "Verl done it already. Don't you see? Verl finally got to fly a Hellcat."

Benny was almost strutting now, his chest thrust out proudly.

Will shook his head.

Smoke curled up from the wreckage, and drifted slowly down toward Sinking Creek. Benny Skaggs suddenly stopped, snapped to attention, and threw a crisp, military salute to mad Verl and Bad Bessie.

Hellcat II: The Burying

What was left of Verl Rose was buried in a flag draped pine box with near military honors. Buck Cox provided the faded American flag, salvaged from a Decoration Day parade in Ashland; Will Davis rounded up five more veterans who could still squeeze into dress uniforms; and Benny Skaggs wore Paul's flight jacket as he led the procession.

Right behind Benny came Lester Whitt's dress mule team, matched young sorrels with polished harness, pulling Orb Skaggs' new lightweight yellow and green Studebaker wagon with the coffin roped securely to the bed for the steep climb up Rose Gap to the graveyard.

Lily Rose led the long procession which straggled along behind the wagon and the honor guard. Neighbors, relatives, the morbidly curious, and a handful of newspaper reporters swelled the ranks of the mourners who struggled up the narrow twisting trail.

Lester led his stiff-legged young mules up the final steep rutted cut, then solemnly followed Benny across the flat to the rounded grassy knoll and the Rose family's graveyard. The honor guard assembled rigidly in sweat-soaked wool uniforms, and rested at ease leaning on Winchester carbines. The pallbearers, Orb Skaggs, Lester Whitt, Mark Cox, Sam Leedy, Jim Barker, and Tom Rose, easily lifted the coffin off the wagon and onto the sawhorses. Mourners assembled near the open grave. Brother Nicodemus Harmon wiped sweat, shuffled forward, took out his worn Bible, coughed importantly and read, without looking, the familiar words:

The Lord is my shepherd, I shall not want; he makes me lie down in green pastures. He leads me beside still waters; he restores my soul.

The stooped old preacher paused, eyed the strangers in the flock, coughed again, and finally spoke in quavering tones. "Brother Verl Rose didn't fear no evil on this earth, and he ain't a fearing none now. Verl, he's off up yonder a flying right now, got wings of pure gold, a swooping down across them heavenly hollers and hillsides, batting them big old wings and a soaring up past the clouds, just a sailing along right now, grinning ear to ear, wondering why we're standing down here on this old hilltop crying over him."

Benny, surprised by the turn of the sermon, now listened wide-eyed.

"Verl, he's free now," continued Brother Harmon. "Free as a bird, free to fly right up to wherever he's a wanting to go, singing the songs of angels. More than likely Verl's done oiled the hinges on the Pearly Gates, and rigged up a way for St. Peter to get 'em open and shut with a motor of some kind, and probably Verl's done got some kind of machine built so's God can shell his corn without getting calluses." Brother Harmon smiled at Benny. "Hit's the pure truth, brothers and sisters. Verl Rose has done flew home, done gone to where he can rest free from the wagging tongues and the judgment of men on earth, free from the torment and the laughing we set upon him." The old minister swayed and spoke louder, more firmly. "Verl Rose, he was borned a child of God, and he stayed one for all of his natural life. Verl's gone home now, gone to home in a blaze of glory the likes of which we ain't never seen afore in all of Caster County."

The weary old man slumped. "God rest his soul." He looked up, then lowered his eyes. "Amen."

Will Davis, Purple Heart and Silver Star proud on his chest, barked orders. The veterans sort of swung into attention. "Fire!" yelled Will. Three times the Winchesters cracked and echoed. Will and Jessie Binion folded the tattered flag and handed it to Benny Skaggs. Benny stumbled twice on the way, but made it to Lily Rose and made the presentation. He backed away and saluted as Gillus Macfarland slowly plucked out "Taps" on his five string banjo.

Then it was over. Verl's box was lowered into the grave, and clay thudded down.

Benny was the last to leave Verl's mountaintop grave. He trudged slowly down the trail, to the foot of the gap where his mother and father were waiting with Lily Rose. Orb's '41 Oldsmobile was parked near Verl's oak tree where a dozen or more people still lingered, whispering and chuckling, wondering aloud how a boy and a halfwit could have built a flying machine from scrap metal and dressed oak timber.

Benny bristled. "Leave 'em be, boy," Orb ordered quietly. "It's all over."

Lily Rose handed Benny a thick scrapbook. "Verl, he'd want you to have this," she said. It was Verl's collected newspaper clippings about Paul Skaggs, from high school basketball hero to Navy ace. Benny nodded through tears and mumbled his thanks.

"Let's go home," Lorena Skaggs said gently.

Benny slid numbly into the back seat of the black Olds. No one spoke as they crunched through the thick new gravel of Sinking Creek Road, the car laboring uphill in second gear then low as Orb slowed and downshifted for the hairpin turns cut into the cliff face. Finally, after a last hard pull, they topped the gap and rolled easily down the winding ridgetop. After two miles Orb swerved left onto the narrow wagon path worn deep by years of use, threaded the car across another spiny ridge, then drove slowly downhill to the sprawling Skaggs homeplace. He parked near the woodshed.

Benny sat in the car for a half hour more, alone. He clutched the ragged scrapbook close, stared off over the mountaintops toward Verl's remote graveyard, and for the first time gave in to the tears.

Orb and Lorena stood on the stilted porch, twenty yards away, to watch. "He's just a baby," Lorena whispered defensively. "Our baby."

"And Verl Rose wasn't nothing but a boy in a growed man's body," said Orb. "I don't aim to raise up another one just like him."

"You're not," said Lorena. She watched Benny climb stiffly out of the car. "Benny, he's more like Paul than anything. Don't you see how much they're the same? When Paul was Benny's age he just wanted to read and learn about stuff, and he followed Buck Cox around for months asking about the war in Germany."

"And you see what it got him," snarled Orb. "Burnt to death five thousand miles from home." He snorted. "Burned alive, just like Verl Rose."

"It wasn't the same," Lorena whispered.

"No, not to you and me it wasn't," Orb said gently. "But I ain't sure Benny knows the damned difference between a hero and a halfwit."

"He knows," Lorena said.

"I hope to hell so," snorted Orb.

Benny walked stiffly inside, climbed the steep steps to the sleeping loft, and hid the scrapbook in Paul's old sea chest. He hung the flight jacket on its peg of honor and slipped downstairs and out the kitchen door. Benny went looking for his grandfather, Lorena's father, Sam Wheeler. Sam's farm lay to the east, the other side of Mauk Ridge, five miles by the twisting roadway but just thirty minutes by foot on the path which crossed straight up and over. Benny found Sam, a slouching large man in bibbed overalls and sweat-stained straw hat, in the barn feeding Bess, the weathered old mule. Benny slipped close to peer through the slats of the stall, careful to keep his fingers clear of long yellow teeth, and watched the wary, solemn mule crunch methodically at a nubbin of corn. "Did that old mule really kill a man once?" he asked. Sam Wheeler took his time cutting a chew from the block of tobacco he always carried in his overalls pocket. "I've had Bess twenty year now," said Sam. "Now, I ain't saying she's a pet, but that mule won't ever hurt nobody."

"But did she?" insisted Benny. "Grandma, she said so. So did Uncle Billy." Benny waited. "Did Bess really stomp a man to death?"

Sam leaned against a barn beam and stared at his bony, scarred old mule. "Bess, she ain't a killer," he finally said quietly. "But, yeah, when she was about three year old, Bess kicked a man in the head and killed him."

Benny's eyes widened and he backed away from the stall.

Sam went on. "Feller over at Stark, name of George Lewis, he owned Bess back then. That would have been, let's see, about 1930." Sam spat and continued. "Lewis was a drinking man. One that got whiskied up and mean. He whipped that mule just like he beat his woman and his youngens. One Saturday he'd been over to Soldier, come home drunk, and was trying to unsaddle the mule when he got tangled up and fell. Lewis went to yelling and cussing, then he picked up a board and whacked Bess across the head."

Benny leaned closer. "Bess was scared, just trying to get away from George Lewis and his club, is the way George's boy told it. Lewis fell down and Bess kicked him right behind the ear. Bess was shod. Most riding mules was, back then." Sam's gentle face hardened as he remembered. "Them fools were fixing to shoot Bess. Thought they'd have to, to get Lewis's body out of the stall."

Sam turned to stare off at the hillside. "One of the Lewis girls come and got me. I was at the church house. I run over and settled Bess down, and led her outside so they could get to George. Then I had to stop 'em from shooting the mule, right there in the barnyard." Sam shook his head. "Just young and scared, was all she was."

"Then what happened?" asked Benny.

"They was the god-awfulest uproar," said Sam. "People come from all over to look at the killer mule. That's what they called her. Poor old thing got poked at and yelled at so much she turned ill tempered, and that just made 'em worse about tormenting her. I offered Sarah Lewis fifty dollars for the mule, ever penny I had, and I brung Bess home. Folks showed up on and off for three or four years, looking for the killer mule, and I reckon that's how come Bess still don't take to strangers getting close to her."

Benny peered in at long ears and teeth, skinny legs, and a harness-worn back. "She still looks mean to me," he whispered.

"I've worked Bess for twenty year," said Sam, "and I ain't been bit or kicked yet. Bess has worked hard. She's wore out three younger mules."

"Is that how come you got the horse?" asked Benny. "I never saw anybody else work a horse and a mule in the same team."

Sam chuckled. "I got the horse sort of the way I got Bess. He was too wild, they all said, to ever be broke to work. I just hitched him up beside of old Bess and she broke him for me."

"It looks funny," said Benny, "to see that old mule and that young horse hitched to the sled."

"It works out good," said Sam. "The old mule don't get around so good, and the young horse ain't got good sense yet. Last summer, when I was mowing that hillside over by the creek, where it's so steep I have to put a board across the mower and set on the high end to hold the mower down, we mowed into a hornets' nest. They swarmed all over, and that horse, he went crazy. He tried to run off, and would have took us right over the cliff, straight down a hundred feet, except for old Bess. She just dug in and stood there, held that horse back, and kept us all from getting killed." Sam chuckled. "Bess don't run, ever. Not even to get away from a mad hornet." He grinned. "That team of mine, they're a lot like you and me when we work on the crosscut saw. You're young and full of vinegar, and me half crippled, but between us we can cut up them logs pretty good, can't we?

Benny thought it over then grinned, and followed Sam out into the bright sunlight. Across the hollow the horse looked up from his grazing, nickered, and came trotting sideways to the barn. "He's pretty," said Benny. "He looks just like Roy Rogers' horse Trigger."

"I reckon he does, if you say so," chuckled Sam. He reached into a pocket for an apple, cut it in two and gave half to the horse. "He'd make a good saddle horse, too, if they was ever anybody wanted to ride him."

"I don't ride so good," Benny said.

"You'll learn," said Sam. "It's in your blood. Your brother Paul, when he was young, he rode like a wild Indian."

"I kind of remember," said Benny. He turned to inspect Sam's grizzled, craggy face. "Were you in a war?" he asked.

Sam sighed. "No. I never had to go. When the first war started I was already too old for the draft."

"Don't you wish you could have gone?" asked Benny. "Didn't you want to fight?"

"No," Sam said softly. "I never was much of one for fighting."

Benny squirmed. "Are you afraid?" he asked anxiously.

Sam smiled. "No, boy, I ain't any more afraid than the next man. If it's got to be done, I'll do it. But most men don't go out looking for a fight neither. They just get pushed into it, or they see a good reason for going to war. They're all scared, but they go anyhow."

"Paul wasn't scared," protested Benny.

Sam smiled. "You got a lot to learn, Benny. They ain't a man alive who don't get scared. A brave man, like your big brother, he's the one that'll go ahead and do it anyhow, even when he's scared." He took out his knife, found a thick hickory splinter, and started peeling off thin shavings. "All of your uncles, and your brother, they're brave men. They had to be, to do what they done." He stared off at the hillside. "Most of what gets called brave," continued Sam, "ain't nothing but scared. Man gets scared enough, he'll do just about anything. He don't care no more what happens to him. He don't care, or don't even know. Just wants to get it over with." Sam smiled. "You'll be more of a man, Benny, the day you learn that you don't go looking for a fight. Try everthing else first."

"That's being a sissy," said Benny.

"No," Sam said tightly. "That's being a man. Don't fight until you have to." His gentle face hardened. "Then, when you do have to fight, you got to win. They ain't no such thing as a fair fight. Do whatever you got to do to win."

"You mean fight dirty?" asked Benny.

"Ain't no such thing," said Sam. "Fighting is fighting."

They walked on together and sat down in hickory chairs on the trellised porch. "You buried Verl today, didn't you?" Sam asked gently.

Benny nodded.

"Verl Rose was your friend," said Sam, "and don't you ever go feeling like they was anything wrong with that."

"They all say Verl was a halfwit," mumbled Benny. "That he was shellshocked without ever being in a war."

Sam sighed. "Verl, he done things a little different. Seen things his own way. But he was a good person, Benny. Good to Lily, and to you. And I reckon Verl figured Paul hung the moon."

"Did Paul really tell Verl all that stuff?" asked Benny. "And give Verl things? Was they really friends, like Verl always said?"

"Does it matter?" Sam asked softly. "Verl worshipped your brother. Paul, he was good to Verl, the way you were."

Benny studied. "The way Verl died, was it like when Paul got killed? I mean, they laughed at me when I said Verl finally flew the Hellcat, that that'd make him happy, that they ain't no need to feel sorry for him."

"Your brother and Verl both died doing what they loved to do," Sam finally said. "Flying." He cut a fresh chew. "It was different but some the same. Paul, he was a real pilot, a hero, and Verl was just doing the best he could. But in some ways, Benny, what Verl done took as much brains and as much nerve as what Paul did. Don't let people tell you that being

Verl's friend was wrong, Benny, or that flying that contraption out a tree didn't take some sense. Verl, he was different, but he wasn't bad."

Benny grinned slyly. "Verl did make that old thing fly," he said proudly. "Nobody else could have."

Sam chuckled. "That's the God's truth. 'Course, nobody else would have tried it, neither."

Benny studied Sam, almost asleep now in the old hickory bark-bottomed rocker. "How come you know so much?" he finally asked.

Sam stopped the rocker. "I don't," he said with a grin. "I've just been around for a long, long, time."

Fire On The Mountain

He caressed the fiddle, turning it gently in his calloused hands to inspect every detail. The back and sides were birdseye maple, painstakingly formed and sanded to glossy smoothness, and the top, with its ornate sound holes, was spruce, geometrically striped, carefully cut and fitted. The slim neck was sturdy maple, gracefully tapered, and the tuning pegs were black walnut.

"It play good?" he asked.

"Try it," grinned Willie. "Here's you a bow."

"Druther use my own, if you don't mind." Asa Horner, six foot eight and deceptively graceful, cradled the new fiddle under his chin and touched his bow to the strings.

The sound was sweet and sharp, full throated, and the cabin rang with joyous sounds. He played snatches of "Sourwood Mountain" and "Cotton Eyed Joe," swung into "Red Wing," switched to "Shove That Pig's Foot a Little Closer to the Fire," and slowed to finish with "Amazing Grace."

"Kin ye do 'Little Log Cabin in the Lane'?" begged Willie. "Hit's my favorite of all."

Asa played the request, threw in "Cluck Old Hen," and broke into two minutes of "The Devil Went Down to Georgia."

"Mighty fine, Asy," said Willie. "You shore do play good."

"Damn good fiddle," grunted Asa. "How much?"

"Bein hit's you, Asy, I reckon three hundred'd do it."

Willie watched closely for Asa's reaction. "Worth twict that, ye know."

"I know," grinned Asa, his yellow buck teeth protruding. "Next summer, when the tourists get here, it'll bring you five hundred."

Willie frowned and shifted the blanks he was shaping for the next fiddle. "Two hundred seventy five?"

"Two fifty," said Asa. "Cash money."

"You're a robbin me, Asy," moaned Willie.

"You could keep it," said Asa. "Next summer, you could . . . "

"Take it, damnit," sighed Willie. "Two fifty and a quart of that shine you get."

"Sold," said Asa. "I'll be back after supper."

"You'll be bringin the shine?"

"One quart, one hundred eighty proof, clear as spring water."

"Where do you git that stuff, Asy?"

"I ain't tellin.", said Asa. "Feller could get hisself shot, tellin where his moonshine come from."

"Ain't it the truth." Willie bit off a fresh chew. "I mind the time me and Ezry went over to . . . "

"I gotta go, Willie," interrupted Asa. "Tonight we'll talk." He smiled. "And I'll play some more, if you can spare me a toddy to get me going."

He left quickly, and drove off humming the tune to "Fire on the Mountain." Slouched in the narrow bucket seat of the blue Jeep he resembled a graying bullfrog, heavy jowels drooping, belly squeezed in under the steering wheel, stringy gray hair hanging below the corduroy hunting cap.

Asa carried three hundred pounds on his elongated frame, and his clothes had stretched to bag loosely. The red jacket, with cartridge loops and game pockets, was soiled and wrinkled. The shapeless trousers had once been green, and were worn shiny at the knees and seat. Heavy boots with thick yellow sponge soles were laced to midcalf, and he carried a Buck knife on his belt.

The Jeep was muddy and dented, showing hard use and minimal care. The back, with the jump seats folded away, was cluttered with an assortment of wrenches, pipe, rain gear, blocks of wood, a rusty skillet, an axe, and a tangle of rope. A battered case cushioned the old fiddle, and a .30-.30 Winchester carbine rode standing between the seats.

The engine growled as he downshifted to cross the creek, knobbed tires slinging mud and water as he exited, gunned up the steep cut, and dropped down the road to the gravel roadway.

The narrow lane followed the crest of Hogback Mountain for five miles, then dropped and curled its way down five thousand feet to connect with the paved highway beside the railroad track. Asa was home in thirty minutes, none to soon to suit the waiting young delivery man.

Asa helped the laconic youth unload and store the shipment, paid him, and stood waiting as he methodically counted. "That's got it," he said, tucking the cash inside his thick wallet. "We got us a problem, though, Mr. Horner."

"What's wrong?" asked Asa.

"Pap don't want me to deliver no more," he said. "Too risky, crossin the state line all the time. We're gonna just sell to them what comes and gets it."

"I don't reckon I got any choice, then," said Asa. "Tell your pap I'll be down in two weeks for my load." He watched the old Chrysler rumble away and cursed his bad luck. That evening he asked Willie how a man went about hauling moonshine.

"Where from?" asked Willie.

"South Carolina."

Willie chuckled. "How much at a time?"

"Fifty, eighty gallons. More when I can get it."

"Git ye a big old car," advised Willie. "A Mercury or Buick or Chrysler, and git one of them Asheville mechanics to fix you up with a motor and springs and brakes. Then you bring it up here and I'll finish 'er up fer ye. You want to haul bottles or in tanks?"

"Which is better?" asked Asa.

"Tanks is easier to hide. Ye kin stick 'em into the floor and sich." Willie spat into the fireplace. "Bottles, they git broke too damn easy."

On his way home Asa pondered the possibility of going back to his old job, leaving the moonshine market to younger and braver men.

For twenty years Asa Horner had taught mathematics at North Carolina State University in Raleigh, pursuing his love for folklore and fiddling on the weekends and during the summers. The little house on the mountain over Asheville had been a friend's summer cottage, borrowed often by Asa, purchased three years ago when the friend took a job on the west coast. After two years of driving back and forth and winterizing the house Asa resigned, packed his few belongings, and moved.

His savings evaporated, and in six months Asa was almost broke. The fiddle earned him only ribbons, and Asa was ill qualified to handle most available real jobs.

His supplier, a lanky farmer from Old Fort, sat Asa up as a moonshine distributor, arranging the reliable South Carolina source and referring Asheville area customers to the cottage on the mountain. The profits were sizable and tax free. Asa paid forty dollars per gallon, delivered in bulk, and re-sold the shine at upwards of forty dollars a quart. He bought the new Jeep, ran water to the cottage, and now had over ten thousand dollars inside the lard can under the floor.

He could not quit now.

The Cadillac was baby blue with a white roof, a 1972 Coupe DeVille with a solid body and blown engine. Asa paid two hundred, plus a thirty dollar tow bill to move the car to Banjo's in West Asheville.

The estimate was seven thousand dollars.

"What do I get for that?" gulped Asa.

The grizzled banjo ticked off the changes. A new five hundred horsepower engine; heavy duty radiator, brakes, and transmission; a tuned racing suspension, with air shocks to level heavy loads; belted steel tires and a "thirty-thirty" warranty.

"Thirty feet er thirty seconds," grinned Banjo.

"What about a paint job?" asked Asa.

"Best to leave it be," advised Banjo, "specially if ye ain't wantin nobody to notice ye."

Asa blushed. "Reckon you're right."

It took three weeks. Asa gambled, and drove the Jeep across the line to pick up his scheduled shipment. He sweated and his stomach churned until he was safely home and unloaded.

"It's not worth it, Asa," insisted Penelope Nye, his semi-steady lover. "Why do you put yourself through such things?"

"Money," said Asa. "To buy me free time to fiddle and lay around in bed with you."

"Pull out," she begged.

"Can't," he said. "Paid Banjo four thousand dollars already."

Penelope drove Asa to pick up the Cadillac and followed him up the mountain to Willie's.

"Down by the river," Willie told Asa, "we kin get tanks and hoses and stuff. You better bring about five hunnert cash." They came back with the Jeep stacked full, and Willie's work took four days.

He showed it proudly. "Four twenty-five gallon tanks, all hid in the body. Ye fill 'em up over here, inside the panel. Drain plug's under the frame there. She's all set, Asy. When's yer first run?"

"Tomorrow," choked Asa.

That night Asa's fiddle was mournful, and not even Penelope's wet kisses could dispel his fears.

Asa was up at dawn, checking and rechecking the Cadillac, topping off the gas tank, gauging the tires, cleaning the windshield. At noon he could wait no longer. He strapped his leather pouch—with four thousand dollars inside—to his left leg, and drove south.

The car was responsive and agile, flatly slipping around the tight curves, accelerating with a rush, stopping with the touch of the brake. He suddenly realized he was speeding, slowed to the limit, and drove through Greenville at one.

Loaded up and on the road toward home by three, Asa stopped to pump up the air shocks and eliminate the sag. Even with its hundred gallons aboard the car was easy to drive, and Asa hummed fiddle tunes as he climbed up the mountain toward Flat Rock. The roadblock was a total surprise; he braked, swallowed, and tried to stay cool.

The trio of gray uniformed troopers looked larger than life, standing casually by the roadside, checking each vehicle closely. Asa had his license ready.

"You the fiddle player?"

Asa glanced up on surprise.

"I saw you last summer at the folk festival," said the trooper, "and I liked the stuff you played."

"Why, thank you," said Asa. "Come by sometime and I'll show you my collection of old tunes."

"I'll do that, Mr. Horner." He waved Asa through. "Have a good trip."

Asa's underwear was soaked through, stuck to his bottom and dampening his pants. He drove cautiously, and was home in less than an hour. At Willie's, he drained the shine into the new storage tank buried behind the cabin.

They sipped a sample. "Damn," said Willie. "This is better'n what you been gittin."

For two months, until spring began to break, the new deal worked perfectly, with Willie taking ten percent for his work. "Shore pays better'n fiddle makin," he observed. "Asy, we could handle twict as much, now that we got the car fixed and the tank in place."

"Forget it," Asa said firmly. "We can't risk any more, Willie."

"Hell, I kin drive," Willie muttered to himself as Asa left. "Ain't no sense in me a doin without when they's easy cash to be had."

He scratched his chin thoughtfully, and the next day drove his old Chevy to the store to use the phone and arrange a pickup. "It'll be atter dark," he told them, "and I'll be drivin."

Asa and Penelope left for Asheville to hear a new young fiddler play, and the cottage was dark when Willie arrived. He took four thousand dollars from the lard can, leaving an IOU, and found the keys to the Cadillac. Twenty miles down the road he stopped and leaned on the horn ring. "Hurry it up, Bessie," he howled. "You and me's got a date." He waved a half empty bottle. "Brung along some antifreeze." He drank again as she ran to the car.

Bessie Cole had serviced Willie's needs for twenty-five years, and she loved nothing better than a night ride and some sipping whiskey. Willie provided both. The bottle was empty before Flat Rock, and another from under the floor mat kept them happy. Willie drove with grand, sweeping movements, tires screaming. Bessie snuggled close.

After the tanks were filled Willie felt even better. The Cadillac was humming, Bessie was warm and willing, and April freshness blew in through the open windows.

At the base of the state line mountain Willie saw the flashing blue lights behind him.

"Hang on, Bessie!" he yelled. "Revenooers." The engine roared as he punched the accelerator, and the Cadillac surged away from the surprised South Carolina highway patrolman. He grinned and accelerated, figuring to quickly overtake the old car and make the arrest. As his speedometer passed 115 he peered after the vanishing taillights. "Damn," he muttered. "That thing must be doing 130 or more." He radioed the North Carolina patrol. "White on blue Cadillac, North Carolina tags, headed your way at about 140. No known warrants. I just wanted to tell him his brake light was out, and he took off like a bat out of hell. He's all yours, fellers." He turned at the state line and drove back south, smiling.

Willie slid up the ramp to I-26 with his foot on the floor, almost rear-ending the waiting cruiser before he swung to the left and passed. Willie drove with one hand, stroking Bessie with the other, singing at the tops of his lungs. He left the interstate at the Asheville airport exit, took US-25 to the Blue Ridge Parkway, where a pair of Park Rangers joined the chase. Radios crackled as the frustrated law officers tried to coordinate their pursuit.

Willie lost a headlight when he broke the roadblock at US-70, shunting a cruiser off into the woods and sending two troopers diving for cover, and ripped off a muffler as he bounced and skidded across the cement barriers. After three miles he braked hard, swerved right, and followed the narrow road beside the railroad tracks. He switched off the headlights.

"Lord!" screamed Bessie. "You're gonna kill us both!"

Two tons of metal soared up into the air as they topped a sudden rise. "Damn," grunted Willie. "Forgot all about that hill."

The front tires hit hard, flattened, and exploded. The Cadillac skewed sideways, hubcaps flying, clipped a row of bushes from the muddy bank and finally stopped, rear wheels dangling over the edge of a steep bluff.

Willie grabbed Bessie in a fierce hug.

"What the hell are you a doin?" she screeched.

"Tell them cops," said Willie, "that we's jist out here a parkin."

A patrol car followed Asa up his drive. "Mr. Asa Horner?"

"Yes. What's wrong?"

"Do you own a 1972 Cadillac, white on blue?"

"It's mine," said Asa. "What's happened?"

The trooper relaxed into a slow grin. "Some drunk old coot used your car to outrun every policeman from the South Carolina border to Swannanoa."

Asa blanched. "Willie Sims?"

"That's him. Don't know as we'd ever have caught him if he hadn't had a blowout."

"Is he hurt?" Asa asked weakly.

"Not to speak of. Just a bump behind his ear. We had to subdue him. He's over at the jail, asking for you."

"The car?"

"Being towed. You can claim it in the morning at the highway patrol garage."

"Was Willie—why were you chasing him?"

"Started out with a busted tail light." The trooper laughed. "Now, they got a list of charges ranging from drunken driving to resisting arrest to damaging public property."

"What damage?"

"He killed a cruiser. Took that old Caddy and knocked it clean off the highway and into a ditch."

Asa groaned. He saved the crucial question for Willie, still groggy as they sat in the visitors cubicle at the county jail. "Did you have a shipment?"

"Hunnert gallon," hissed Willie. "So far they ain't noticed it."

Asa was trembling. "You mean they've got a hundred gallons of moonshine sitting out there at the station?"

Willie grinned. "They ain't a goin to know it lessen you tell 'em. These young fellers, they ain't got good noses."

Asa bailed Willie out, and early the next morning they were at the patrol garage to claim the Cadillac. Sagging to the front, it sat alone in the gravel lot behind the garage. The headlight dangled, and broken limbs clung to the rear bumper. A spreading puddle was beneath.

"My God," groaned Asa. He crawled under to check the leak. "Valve's busted," he muttered. "It's steady comin out."

"Mornin, fellers." Asa slammed his head into the frame as he scrambled out. A man in oily coveralls stood grinning. "Ya'll come to git the old Caddy?"

"Yes," said Asa. "I paid the tow and storage."

"Better git to a shop," said the garage foreman. Git that hole in the transmission plugged up."

"I will," said Asa, taking the man by the arm and leading him away. "Say, can I use your telephone to call a wrecker?"

The Cadillac had been gone for thirty minutes when one of the mechanics stopped to light a cigar and tossed his burning match into the gravel.

Flames leapt, blue and flickering, spreading with a sudden "swoosh" and blast of air. "Yeeoow!" screamed the mechanic. "What in the hell is this?"

He danced clear of the flames, slapping at his smoking pants legs. "What damn kind of transmission fluid does that son of a bitch use?"

The fire slowly died down and left a circle of scorched rock.

The Cadillac rested on concrete blocks.

Willie rigged a hose and opened the valve, drained the clear liquid into milk cans, and loaded them onto Asa's Jeep for the trip to Hogback Mountain.

Willie tabulated gloomily. "Four cans is eighty gallon, and half another'n makes ninety. Spilt ten gallon, more or less, Asy."

"That's four hundred dollars, Willie. Plus two tires is $250, and $175 for the muffler and pipe makes $425, and fixing the fender will run $175 or so. You owe me $675 for the car." Asa grinned. "Ninety gallons will bring about $11,000, and your cut is $1,100. Pay for the car and that leaves, oh, $525. Your fine will be maybe $1,000, so you're out about $500 for the night. Was it worth it?"

"Damn near," swore Willie. "Lets get this stuff up to the tank." He drove the Jeep carefully, protecting the valuable cargo.

F our men in a dusty Bronco followed the Jeep.
"They're gonna take us right to it, George," said the driver.

Two federal agents and two sheriffs deputies huddled to peer out the window.

"That old fool thinks we didn't notice," chuckled George, the senior deputy. "Hell, everybody in two mile knowed what he was haulin. That old Cadillac musta had fifty gallons hid in it somewheres."

Agent Earl Smith, at the wheel, grunted. "Shoulda arrested him while we had 'im with the stuff." He downshifted for the steep climb.

"Naw," said George. "Willie's gonna show us where the rest of it is now. We'll git maybe a hundred gallon, and put old Willie away fer five years."

"What about that other Feller?"

"Horner? Hell, he wouldn't know shine if he was settin in a tubfull. He's one of them rich fellers that come up here to live the simple life."

"You sure he ain't the man in charge?"

"Hell, he don't need the money," said George. "All he wants to do is play the fiddle. Willie's our man."

A sa backed the Jeep close to the rhododendron thicket, and together he and Willie emptied the cans down into the concealed inlet.

Willie cackled. "Ain't nobody'd believe we got a 500 gallon tank down under there." He closed the spout and pulled the limbs back to cover it. "Yessir, Asy, me and you, we done it right. Got it on tap, right under their damned noses, and can't none of 'em see a thing."

Asa pulled the Jeep down to the cabin. "I could use a drink," he said.

Willie rinsed out two peanut butter jars, and opened the door under the kitchen sink. He stooped, twisted the faucet concealed under a towel, filled both glasses, and lifted one up the light to inspect it.

"Clear as water," he said. "Asy, this was some fine idea, runnin a line into the kitchen here. Hell, nobody'd ever believe it."

They drank, gulping the raw whiskey.

"Bring out a fiddle," said Asa. "and we'll damn well celebrate."

Asa refilled both glasses and shut the door.

The three mudspattered men crawled back into the Bronco.

"Goddamnit, Smitty, next time I'm doin the drivin," growled George.

"How am I supposed to know," protested Smith, "that they ain't but one place to cross? That creek don't *look* deep."

"Shut up and drive," grunted George. "We've done give 'em time to hide the stuff.'"

Willie raised his hand, shushing Asa.

"Somebody comin," he said. He quickly rinsed the glasses and stepped out to the porch to watch the muddy Bronco park beside the Jeep. "It's the law," he whispered. "Keep a fiddlin, Asy."

"Mornin, fellers," sang out Willie. "What brings youens up to Hogback?"

Asa scraped busily, playing "Fire on the Mountain" extra fast.

"You know why we're here, Willie," said George. "Save us all a lot of trouble iffen ye'd jist show us where ye keep the shine."

"Shine?" Willie shook his head sadly. "Law, George, I ain't had no good sippin whiskey in fifteen year."

Asa played "What a friend we have in Jesus," dragging the bow mournfully across the strings.

"Willie, we know ye was haulin last night. What's in them milk cans up yonder?"

"Nothin," grinned Willie. "That's some old cans Asy got fer me. I paint 'em up and sell 'em to the tourists. Good money. Why, I recall that onct . . ."

"Shut up, Willie," grunted George. "And tell that fool to stop playin the fiddle."

"Fool? George, that yonder's Asy Horner, what teached at the university fer twenty year. He's a wondrous smart man."

Asa put down the fiddle and walked outside. "Howdy men. Something I can do for you?"

"You the one that owns the Cadillac?" asked George.

"It's mine."

"You're under arrest."

"What for?" asked Asa.

"Runnin moonshine," snapped George.

Asa chuckled. "That old Caddy is down at the house up on blocks. And, gentlemen, you won't find any moonshine anywhere in it."

"That's the damn truth," muttered George. "We watched 'em empty it all out."

"Search this area," ordered Smith. "The stuff has to be here."

"Hep yeself," grunted Willie. "But ye ain't gonna find nothin."

The search lasted two hours, and was fruitless.

"Tol ye," grinned Willie. "You fellers want some coffee?"

Penelope and Bessie came for the celebration, and the liquor flowed free and quick. Willie built up a fire to ward off the night chill, and Asa played with a new intensity.

He used up his repertoire by midnight, and started over.

Asa fiddled fast, slow, soft, loud, sad, and happy. Greased by liberal doses of 180 proof, his hands fairly flew, and the sweetest of sounds flowed out across the mountain. He played "Old Dan Tucker," "Sally Ann," "Fox on the Run," and a wailing assortment of Bob Wills tunes, sweating profusely and tapping until his toes ached. He fiddled "White Lightnin," "Sugar in the Gourd," "Sallie Goodin," "Turkey in the Straw," and "Bucking Mule."

Willie danced, pranced, kicked and wheeled around cabin, swinging Bessie and yelling encouragement.

"Listen at 'em," said George. "Them in there all warm and raisin hell, and us layin out here freezin."

"Don't go blamin me," grunted Smith. "I wanted to get 'em while they was loadin up. *You* the one wanted to foller 'em up here. Lead us right to it, you said."

"Damnit, iffen you could drive, and hadn't got stuck, I'd a caught 'em red handed."

"Hell," scoffed Smith. "What's that tune, George?"

"Red Wing," said George. "He sure does play that thing good."

"At least we're gettin us a free concert," said Smith. "We ain't gonna git nothin else."

By three Asa was slowed, dragging the bow softly, blinking by the firelight, barely able to lift his head.

"Do 'Little Log Cabin'," said Willie.

"Bring me another drink first," said Asa. "I'm powerful thirsty."

Willie stumbled to the kitchen.

"Look at that, would you?" Smith whistled. "A damn faucet, right in the house. No wonder we never found it. They got a straight line to wherever it's hid."

Willie filled Asa's glass, but did not get the faucet closed. The moonshine continued to run slowly, spilling out across the floor, trickling through the doors and spreading.

Smith shoved open the cabin door, his .38 in his hand. "You're all under arrest!" he yelled.

"Son of a bitch," groaned Willie. "Hits that revenooer again."

"We got you this time, Willie," smiled George. "We seen ye drawin shine out of that tap in the kitchen."

Asa fumbled for a match to light a cigarette.

"Here," grinned George. He flipped a box of wooden matches to Asa. "You might as well smoke afore we take you in."

Asa sucked the cigarette to life, then wearily tossed the match to the floor.

The fire exploded.

The moonshine had run through the kitchen into the living room, a quarter inch deep in the floor, and now the flames leapt to the ceiling.

"Run!" screamed Penelope.

Asa looked to Willie. "The tank!"

They jumped to the door, followed closely by George and Smitty, and dived for the bushes, dragging the women.

Asa clutched the fiddle as he rolled.

The five hundred gallon tank, three fourths full, lifted a half acre of mountain as it ignited.

George stared, his mouth open.

As far away as Asheville and Old Fort, there were reports.

"Ball o' fire," said one caller to the highway patrol. "Hit lit up near alla Hogback, I swear."

A Delta captain called the Asheville airport to ask about the orange glow, swinging his 727 south to miss the turbulence.

From Montreat, Blue Ridge, and even Lake Junaluska, frightened callers warned of the end of the world.

Billy Graham, thankfully, was not at home.

The fiddle sang sadly, piercing the night with its wail, drawing out the deepest emotions from the five listeners. The ashes of Willie's cabin glowed, snapping on occasion, letting the fire die gradually.

George and Smitty lay on the charred slope, grateful to be alive, wondering if they'd have to pay for the smoking Bronco.

Bessie was curled in Willie's arms, still sobbing, and Penelope sat close to Asa, ducking the bow as he fiddled.

The moon was full, and across the ridges of the Smokies dogs howled in sympathy.

Asa stopped abruptly.

"Why ain't you fellers gone?" he asked of Smitty. "We'd druther be alone, if you don't mind."

They left quietly, walking toward lower ground.

Willie groaned through the darkness.

"Hit's all gone, Asy. My house, my car, everthing."

"We still got the Cadillac, partner," said Asa. "We can start over."

"Somehow that don't hep a whole lot right now," said Willie. "You still got the fiddle?"

"Right here," said Asa.

"Would ye play 'Amazin Grace' fer me?"

The fiddle recalled the bagpipes of the highland settlers, and Willie wept softly.

Then they sat in total silence.

It was midsummer, the peak of the tourist season, and Willie stood kneedeep in sawdust, humming as he shaped the pattern for another fiddle. Asa's back porch was a good workshop, close enough to the city for the tourists to visit, and sales were booming.

The Cadillac, still up on blocks, was weed-choked and rusty, a picturesque prop to entertain the buyers.

Asa budged the wheelbarrow closer, shoveled it full of sawdust, rolled it to the bin near the cellar door, and dumped. He returned, stood on the porch, and wiped sweat from his brow with a sopping handkerchief. "Seen 'em today, Willie?"

"Two. Up on the hill yonder, same place as always."

"They ain't givin up, are they?" said Asa.

Willie chuckled. "Makes it all a little more fun, workin right under their noses like this."

"Sawdust burner works mighty fine," said Asa.

"Yep," said Willie. "Hits a fine way to keep the place clean."

Asa took another load to the bin, then slipped inside the cellar.

The sawdust fired burner, built with the expert assistance of technicians from North Carolina State University, would also be the furnace, come winter. A series of traps and afterburners eliminated all smoke; a fan sucked away any odors and vented them into the sewer line. The coil was disguised as water lines; the new still was totally modern and ecologically sound, a tribute to contemporary technology and Willie's master knowledge of distilling.

On a shelf sat small rows of boxes. "Blue Diamond Fiddle Strings." Each box contained a full set of strings, as promised, plus a tin pint container labeled "Fiddle Wax." Most of the "wax" was 180 proof.

Asa tasted the clear drops collecting in the vat, and rejoined Willie. "Good run," he grunted.

A dusty car rolled up the drive, and two middle aged farmers climbed out, one carrying a battered fiddle case.

"Howdy, Jacob," said Willie. "Good to see ye again, Enos."

"Howdy do," said Jacob. "I'm a needin strangs fer this here fiddle, Willie. And some more wax."

"How many sets you be needin, Jacob?"

"Bout four, I spect."

Willie bagged the four cartons in a sack printed "Sims & Horner Music Supplies" and sat it on the railing. "That'll be fifty dollar, Jacob," he said. "Strangs, they went up some."

"Hits worth it, to git the gooduns," grinned Jacob. He counted five wrinkled tens from a leather pouch. "You tune this here fiddle fer me, Asy?"

"Sure thing, Jacob," agreed Asa.

He held the worn instrument gently, plucking and adjusting, then reached for the bow.

The younger agent groaned. "Is that the only song he knows?"

His partner grinned. "Hell, at least we get free entertainment while we're settin up here."

"We gonna stop that car?"

"What for? Hell, it'll just be more fiddle strings. I'm gettin tired of all these musicians cussin me out. Willie ain't sellin no shine down there noway. Only reason we're up here is Smitty still ain't got over that night up on Hogback."

Asa's foot was tapping and the bow danced across the strings. Willie grinned his approval, and Jacob and Enos nodded in rhythm.

In squeaky, leaping cadence, the music sang out across the trees.

"What the hell is the name of that tune?" grumbled the younger agent.

George chuckled. "That'un? It's called 'Fire On The Mountain.'"

Big Game

Eb Willard thumbed red Remington shotgun shells into the cartridge loops of his faded hunting jacket, bent to re-tie his boots, slurped the last drops of coffee from the cracked saucer, and walked restlessly to the foot of the stairwell.

"Jasper," he yelled. "Ain't you and Teddy ready to go yet?" Eb waited, then yelled again. "Git on down here! We're late already."

Eb tugged his cap down, collected his new shotgun, turned again to the stairs, and scowled as his two sons came tumbling down. "Got everthing?" he asked gruffly. "Got your gloves, Jasper?"

"I got 'em, Daddy," replied Jasper. He carried Eb's old 12 gauge double-barrel. "What's Teddy gonna use? My old rifle?'

Eb grinned as his younger son struggled awkwardly into the Jasper's old Mackinaw coat. "Teddy, he don't need no gun. He'll just trip and fall on them rabbits."

"Don't want to go nohow," mumbled Teddy. "Do I have to." He rubbed his puffy eyes and watched Eb. "I'd druther stay at home."

"You got to come, Teddy," laughed Eb. "They ain't nobody else scrawny enough to crawl under the brush and spook out the rabbits."

Jasper handed Teddy a small .22 rifle. "Here," he said. "Try to not shoot off your own foot."

"I shoot as good as you do," argued Teddy. "Better'n you did when you was twelve."

"Shut up and let's git," ordered Eb. "It's daylight already and Bud's waiting for us."

Eb scraped ice off the windshield and waited as Teddy dawdled. "Hurry up!" he snapped. "Put that rifle in the back seat and help me push."

Jasper slid importantly under the steering wheel, pulled out the choke button, and shifted to low gear. "Ready," he announced. "Get to pushing, Teddy."

"You ain't the boss of me," grunted Teddy.

"Hush it up and push," ordered Eb.

The cigar shaped old Buick broke away from the frozen mud in a crackling, slow motion crawl. "Faster!" yelped Jasper. Teddy slipped and fell face-first on the icy mud. The Buick picked up speed and lumbered heavily down the rutted roadway.

"Let out the clutch," yelled Eb.

The car lurched, backfired, and started. Jasper jabbed the brake and the Buick skidded, stopped, idled too fast and belched out a cloud of steam. "Push in the choke," yelled Eb. "You're about to blow it up." Huffing, he caught up and reached for the frosted door handle. "Scoot over, Jasper."

"Let me drive," the boy begged. "I can do it."

"You can play hell, too," replied Eb. He feathered the choke and tapped the throttle. "Where'd Teddy git to?"

Teddy, stumbling, wiping his nose, crawled silently into the back seat. Eb gunned the reluctant engine and sent the Buick bouncing down the frozen farm road.

Bud Willard was waiting by the mailbox, in front of his trailer, stomping to stay warm. He tumbled heavily into the back seat. "Colder'n a witche's tit," he laughed. "Where you boys been all damn day?"

"Like to never got these two runts up out of bed," said Eb.

"I was ready," said Jasper. "But Teddy still ain't awake."

"Am too," grumbled Teddy.

"Why hell yes this youngen is awake," chuckled Bud. He tapped Teddy's shoulder. "Pay no mind to Jasper, Teddy. Big brothers is like that. When me and your daddy was boys, I used to have to whup his butt about onct a week."

"He tried it about once a week," said Eb. "As I recollect, though, it was always me that done the whupping."

Eb parked at the foot of Cole Mountain. Zack and Willie, and Willie's two boys, were already there. The hunt began under a bright winter sunshine, a stiff-legged march across the frozen stubble of last summer's hayfield. Eb walked closer to Bud.

"You watch that Jasper today," Eb said softly. "That boy has turned hisself into a good shot." He watched Jasper, matching them stride for stride, and grinned. Then Eb remembered, searched for Teddy, and found him struggling, dragging the unloaded rifle. "Damnit, boy," hissed Eb. "Git on up here." He checked the rifle, snorted, and fitted a cartridge into the worn chamber. Eb slapped quickly, and Teddy's ear burned bright red. "You come on now," warned Eb. "The least you can do is act like you want to be here."

"But I don't," protested Teddy. "I want to go home."

"Wipe your nose," said Eb. "And git up here where I can keep a eye on you."

The morning's first rabbit broke from cover and four shotguns barked. "Lord have mercy," laughed Eb. "That'n will weigh ten pound, you all have filled him so full of lead."

The hunters spread in a ragged arc, and took a dozen rabbits in an hour. Jasper downed two, firing smoothly and confidently. Teddy hung back, sullen and distracted, rushing to catch up only when he caught Eb's angry glare.

Bud chuckled. "Teddy, he ain't no hunter, Eb. That boy don't like this one bit, does he?"

"He's just sleepy, is all," growled Eb. "I like to never got him up out of bed."

"If you say so." Bud uncapped his flask, drank, and offered the pint to Eb. "Hell, big brother," he said softly. "It's okay if the boy don't want to hunt. Maybe Mabel can learn him to wash clothes and keep house."

"Shut it up, Bud," snapped Eb. "Just shut your mouth."

Bud grinned and walked jauntily away.

"Teddy!" yelled Eb. "Get your skinny butt over here and shake down this brushpile."

Teddy clutched his rifle with numb fingers and kicked at the tangle of underbrush. A rabbit sprang from under his feet and Teddy jumped aside, startled. Jasper fired. Lead shot stung and splattered, and the rabbit crumpled.

"You like to have shot me!" squalled Teddy. "You watch out, Jasper."

"Don't worry," said Jasper. "I'll kill them mean old rabbits afore they can hurt you."

Teddy glared. "Don't you shooot so close to me no more."

Eb, ten yards away, started to speak by didn't.

Teddy moved on, stepping carefully, ears burning, and almost didn't hear Bud. "One right in front of you," whispered Bud. "Drop him."

A fat buck rabbit stopped fifteen feet away.

"Hurry," said Bud.

Teddy swung up the rifle, fumbled for the trigger, and fired. The rabbit's ears twitched, and he took a tentative hop. "Be damned," snorted Bud. "You missed him."

Teddy was working, clumsy and cold-fingered, to reload. He dropped the cartridge and bent to search in the tangled grass.

"Good Lord," snorted Bud. He brushed past Teddy and fired, dropped the rabbit, and turned. "Sorry," he said lamely. "I was afraid he'd get away."

Eb glared and chewed his lower lip.

By midmorning, every hunter but Teddy had bagged at least two rabbits. They stopped, on a sunny knoll, to rest and compare counts. The men passed bottles and bragged, laughed over missed shots, cleaned and reloaded shotguns. Teddy, frozen and miserable, hoped they'd decide to call off the hunt and go play poker in the stripping room.

Bud grinned and passed his pint to Jasper, who eyed Eb for approval and got it, and took a long pull. Bud howled as Jasper coughed, turned red, and gagged, but kept the whiskey down. Jasper swallowed again, grimly, and blinked back tears. "Not too bad," he gasped. "A little weak, is all."

"That boy, he's a chip off the old block," Bud said admiringly. "Jasper can shoot and drink damn near as good as his daddy."

"He's growing up," Eb agreed proudly.

"Hey, Teddy," called Bud. "If you're so danged cold, come over here and take a swaller of this stuff."

Teddy studied his toes. "Don't want none," he mumbled.

Bud chuckled and took a sip. "You don't know what you're a missing. This here stuff'll make a man out of you."

"I said I don't want none," replied Teddy.

"Leave the boy be," ordered Eb. "Did you all come out here to hunt or to talk?"

They hunted methodically, through scattered underbrush, worked slowly up the mountainside, and took fewer rabbits as the growth thickened. Teddy, warming now, kicked idly through the thickets and rattled the brushpiles, lost in his own thoughts as he wandered through the middle of the firing line.

He kicked out a rabbit which ran, stopped, and scooted sideways. Teddy raised his rifle, saw Jasper across from him, and held his fire. Jasper didn't. Hot pellets clipped the dry weeds and stung at Teddy's calves. He screamed, grabbed his legs, looked and realized that there was no blood, and came up crying and cursing. Teddy charged past Jasper's flailing arms and drove the bigger boy backwards. They tumbled over a log and fell, screeching and clawing, into a briarpatch.

Eb arrived first, snatched Teddy by the collar and tossed him, squirming and screaming, back across the log. Bud grabbed Teddy and pinned him to the ground, laughed as the boy cried and clawed, then swore as the boy spit in his face. Bud's big hand smacked and stung. Teddy blinked, glared, but finally relaxed and lay flat.

"Are ye done?" gasped Bud. "You through fighting, boy?"

Slowly, Bud released Teddy and backed away to wipe his face. "Damnation," Bud said, half admiringly. "Teddy's wilder than a old wet she-wildcat."

Teddy lay flat, whimpering.

"What happened?" somebody finally asked.

Bud rolled up Teddy's pants leg, stared at red welts and looked up at Jasper. "Well," he said softly. "You sure as hell shot him, Jasper."

"He ain't hurt bad," Eb said gruffly. "Hush the squalling, Teddy, and git up from there."

Teddy climbed slowly to his feet and glared at Jasper. "He tried to kill me," said Teddy. "Jasper shot me."

"It was a accident," Eb said stiffly. "Jasper never meant to hurt you."

Jasper's face was red. He retrieved his own gun, found the old .22 and took it to Teddy. "I didn't see you, Teddy, " he whispered hoarsely. "I swear I never."

"I seen you," sputtered Teddy. "What if I shot you in the legs?"

Eb put a pint bottle into Teddy's hands. "Drink," he ordered. "This'll settle your nerves." Eb turned to Jasper. "Let this be a lesson to you," he said. "A gun ain't a toy. Knowing how to shoot don't mean a damn thing is you ain't man enough to handle a gun. And, by God, you ain't so big but what I can't still turn you over my knee."

Teddy, watching, sipped from the bottle. He gagged, then blinked at the sudden warmth which trickled down through his body. He drank again, grinned, and slipped the bottle into his coat pocket while all eyes were on Eb and Jasper.

"Can you do better now?" Eb demanded of Jasper. "Or do you want to go to the house?"

"I want to stay," Jasper said quietly.

"All right, then." Eb shouldered his shotgun. "What the hell is everbody looking at? Let's hunt some rabbits."

Eb waited until the others moved on, then stopped to check on Teddy. "You okay?" he asked.

Teddy nodded.

"Then let's move," said Eb. "And this time try to not get in nobody's way."

"I never did," argued Teddy. "That was Jasper's fault."

"He never meant you no harm," Eb said firmly. "And don't you say so much as one word about all this to your mommy." He walked briskly away. Teddy stared dully after Eb, then turned and found Jasper waiting.

"I'll get you," warned Jasper. "When we get home I'm going to beat the hell out of you." Jasper wheeled and stalked off to rejoin the hunt.

Teddy wiped his nose on a ragged sleeve, remembered Eb's pint bottle, took it out and greedily sucked down the remaining two inches of bourbon whiskey. He shuddered, grinned, tossed the empty into a thicket and trailed slowly off after the hunters.

Teddy giggled, stumbled, caught himself and plunged through thick brush. He was plenty warm now, sweating, and the cheerful tingle washed away the sting of Jasper's buckshot. He tripped over a dead log and sprawled. Teddy wallowed in dry leaves, staggered back to his feet, and bent to pick up the old .22 rifle.

"Never hurt it one bit," he mumbled. Teddy's tongue was big and numb. "Didn't hurt Jasper's dumb old gun at all."

Carefully he picked his way through a grove of locusts, grinning and giggling, his head spinning. He found a stump at the crest of a ridge and sat down heavily to watch the hunters fanned out below him. "Look like a bunch of pissants," he giggled. "Crazy old pissants."

He saw Jasper, tall and arrogant and important, and twisted his lips. "He's going to whup me," groaned Teddy. "Sure as hell, Jasper is going to thrash my butt."

Teddy lifted the rifle, aimed carefully, and giggled.

"Could have shot Jasper," he mumbled. "Right in the leg, the way he done me."

The idea delighted Teddy, and he leaned on the old .22 to laugh. He peered down again at the circle of hunters. "I could shoot all of them from up here," he said. Teddy giggled and hiccupped. "Shoot ever one of them durned old pissants."

He dropped down off the stump, lay flat on his belly, and aimed. "Pow!" Teddy laughed. "Got Bud, that time, right through the head."

He swung the barrel around and centered the sights on Jasper.

Teddy was suddenly weary. His eyes were bleared. The ground tried to roll slowly out from under him. Teddy groaned and hugged the cold earth. "It's all your fault, Jasper," he whispered. "All your fault."

Teddy focused his eyes with an effort, blinked, and located Jasper's back. He lined up the gun sight, and steadied the battered stock. He squinted. Then, very gently, as he'd been taught, Teddy squeezed the trigger.

New York, New York

Joggers, winos, weirdos, and other big city creatures came crawling out from under the shrubbery of Central Park at daybreak. Angular Josh Whitt squatted under an oak tree, much the way he'd hunker down back home in Kentucky to hunt squirrels on a Sunday morning, to watch. Two people, and Josh couldn't tell what sex they were, were bathing. Nude. One red-eyed derelict was shuffling from trash can to trash can, sucking at emptied beer cans and wine bottles, muttering angrily to himself.

Across the street, past the Mayflower Hotel, paraded a busy stream of young corporate females, dressed-for-success but wearing somehow sensuous sweatsocks and sneakers, marching in healthy, swinging strides which Josh decided must have been the parade step of General Sherman's Civil War soldiers. Pinstriped executives, gawking tourists, stumbling street people, policemen, buses, taxis, delivery trucks, whooping emergency vehicles, garbage trucks, and assorted oddballs were busy above ground and under, where a constant rumbling marked the passages of the subway trains.

A braless jogger pounded past, sweat-soaked, grimly determined. Josh chuckled, and decided that the brawny young woman could either outrun or outfight the Park's sleazy inhabitants. The dogwalkers filtered over from nearby apartments with happy little house dogs on dainty leashes, and Josh wondered what they'd think about his two big rowdy hounds, and what Buck and Lockjaw would do if he turned them loose in Central Park. Probably, Josh decided, the two fierce coon hounds would cower under the brush and watch.

"Just like me," chuckled Josh. One of the newly awake occupants of a nearby bench stared and grinned. "Hey," shrugged Josh. "A man's got to talk to somebody that understands him. Right?"

The toothless little black man scooted closer and Josh stiffened, but the man suddenly stood and walked to the trash bin, searched, and brought out two wine bottles. He sucked greedily, found a beer can and drained it of whatever was left, smiled brightly at Josh and went woozily on his way. Two uniformed officers in a four wheel drive vehicle bypassed the staggering wino but stopped to glare suspiciously at Josh. Josh glared back. The patrol truck lurched away.

"They think I'm strange," growled Josh. He quickly checked to see if anybody had noticed him talking to himself again, then lit a cigarette and walked back toward the hotel. Josh Whitt was tall, with powerful sloped shoulders and big, muscled forearms, and he walked with the lazy, surefooted woodsman's gait. He wore faded jeans, soft boots, and a longsleeved white dress shirt with the sleeves rolled up to his elbows. Josh's leathery tan, sunbleached hair, high forehead, and dark, solemn eyes added to the perception that here went a cowboy, lumberjack, Indian, or cross-country trucker, someone whose existence depended largely on brawn, cunning, sweat, and some sort of rowdy pioneer resourcefulness. In reality, Joshua Eli Whitt was the sales manager for a small Kentucky manufacturer of wooden desk accessories, in New York for the Gift Show, and a sometimes writer of very regional fiction who wasn't sure anymore whether he maintained the casual, rugged image more for effect or for comfort.

Josh grinned as two of the street citizens eyed him then decided to make plenty of room on the sidewalk. Josh squared his shoulders and tried to look even more like a cowboy movie gunslinger. Slow and dangerous. New York's street hustlers weren't sure what to make of a rawboned, slow moving rustic, so they gave Josh lots of elbow room.

The day before, Josh had flown into LaGuardia and inspected New York City's filth and traffic during the taxi ride to Manhattan. After a quick shower Josh had walked up Broadway to Times Square, through break dancers and hookers, watch peddlers and tourists, cops and busy hustlers. He'd paid $20 for a beer and a hamburger, picked up a fake

Rolex for $30, declined an invitation to join a gay threesome for an evening at the theater, and tried not to look at the hooker who screamed obscenities at his back for half a block. Josh rested at Columbus Circle, then walked to Lincoln Center. There, he saw what he would always remember as the perfect image of the contradictory New York City lifestyle. A beautiful young blonde in a white gown rode up on a rusty bicycle, parked and locked the bike, took slinky heels from her backpack and sat down to change, stuck the sneakers into the pack and marched elegantly in to be seated for the opera. Wearing the backpack.

This morning Josh had been up at five, had found coffee at John's near Lincoln Center, then drifted back to the Park to watch the animals. The human ones. Now, from his window seat in the Mayflower coffee shop, Josh watched the hustling doorman flag cabs and direct traffic. The waitress was young, with a dramatic face, and she'd made Josh repeat his order three times. Finally she'd smiled at her difficulty with the Kentucky drawl and brought strong bitter coffee.

Josh finished off breakfast, went back to the room for his battered briefcase full of tools, tape, and price lists, and rode the hotel limo to the Javits Center. The big plywood crate was waiting in the booth. An hour later, Josh was distracted from his work by a soft, huskey, female voice. A definitely Southern, throaty, familiarly accented voice. He looked for the owner. Across the aisle two young women were setting up a sales display, and Josh listened, until one of the girls caught him staring. Both she and Josh blushed. He went quickly back to work, and finally finished setting up his display late in the evening. Outside the Center it was dark; there were no shuttles still running, no cabs, and no one to ask for directions. But there were three equally anxious women also looking for transportation.

Josh approached them hesitantly, then realized that two of them were the women from across the aisle. He blushed again. "Excuse me," Josh finally said. "Would you all have any idea where a body'd have to go to catch up with a taxi cab?" He moved closer. "I'm Joshua Whitt, from Kentucky. The reason I was staring at you today is that you're the first people I've heard since I got here that don't talk funny." He waited. "I don't mean to be forward, but I don't have any idea how to get away from this place."

The oldest of the three smiled warily. "Maybe if you walked eight or ten blocks that way," she said, "you could find a taxi." Josh twisted to stare at the bleak, shabby, empty row of streets. "That is," the woman added, "if you it make through there alive." She relaxed. "I'm Jessica Greene, and these are my daughters Beth Anne and Lucy Marie. If you do decide to walk through there, could we go with you?"

"Sure," grinned Josh. He eyed the deserted streets. "I think I'd feel better with some company."

As they walked, Josh learned that the mother and daughters were from Georgia, that their family marketing firm had grown to the point of being able to support the New York marketplace, and that this was also their first time in New York. "And our cab driver this morning," said Beth Anne, "got started ranting and raving about the prostitutes and AIDS and bums and winos and just about everything else, and got himself so worked up he bumped right into another cab. Then there was a traffic jam and there was a fire truck behind us blowing its horn so our driver got out and screamed at the fireman so the fireman got out and hit the cab driver and then fifty people just started fighting right there in the street."

"When we finally got out and across the street," added Lucy Marie, "we were waiting for a light to change and some man grabbed me by the behind so I squalled and stepped right out in front of a police car."

They were all talking too much, too fast, to cover their apprehension about the dimly lit streets. They were walking fast, trying not to look too closely at their surroundings. "I wonder what all is down under us," shuddered Beth Anne.

As if a switch had been flipped, Beth Anne got her answer. Suddenly, savagely, the rats were everywhere, a horde of leaping, snapping, shrieking, oversized sewer rats who scampered frantically across the grillwork beneath them, hundreds of redeyed squeaking and leaping little monsters who stormed past and were gone as suddenly as they had come.

"My God," Josh finally whispered. "Those things are bigger'n possums."

"Shut up and walk faster," growled Beth Anne. She hesitated. "On the other side of the street."

Five blocks later there was finally a taxi. At the hotel near Times Square Jessica Greene invited Josh to join them for a drink and a snack. "I need a drink," Josh said gratefully. "And then I'm going to go somewhere and buy me a pistol and a Bowie knife." He gulped down bourbon and sent for more. "I wonder," Josh finally said, "just what else is running around down under there?"

"Whatever there is," Lucy Marie said firmly, "I don't intend to find out. I'll never set foot on the street again except to walk out to the bus in the morning."

When Josh left an hour later he started walking, looked around, and decided to flag a cab. He slept fitfully, dreamed of little red eyes and thousands of little sharp bloody teeth, and woke up worn out an hour before dawn.

Josh killed time, had coffee, and caught the first shuttle to the Center. Halfway there he saw what he first thought were majorettes, dressed in short, tight, sequined outfits, and wondered why a parade would start at eight o'clock Sunday morning, then got closer and realized that two, then four, hookers were working the intersection, banging on car windows and screaming at the men who passed them by. Josh's jaw dropped, and the woman seated across from him giggled. Josh stared back out the side window. He didn't look at the woman as he hurried off the bus.

Josh spent a half hour haggling with union electricians and finally paid $93 to have his booth electricity plugged in. Grumbling, wondering why he'd ever agreed to come to New York, he busied himself with final display arrangements.

The Georgians arrived laughing. "On the way here," explained Lucy Marie, "some bum asked Beth Anne for a dollar. She wouldn't give it to him. So he spent the next five minutes telling her, as loud as he could scream, that she was the ugliest, stingiest, meanest woman he'd ever seen."

"Then, " added Beth Anne, "there was this woman on the bus who didn't have anything on under her jacket." She blushed. "She was painted. From the waist up. That's all."

"Painted?" Josh grinned. "What color?"

"Blue," said Beth Anne. "Navy blue with white trim."

"Just what part," Josh asked, "was trimmed?"

Beth Anne blushed furiously. "Her neck," she blurted, "and I'm not saying what else."

At ten the crowds came, flocking buyers from all over, and for six hours Josh was on his feet talking, writing orders, forcing a smile and ignoring the ruder visitors. When, after four, he was finally free and dropped to his chair, Lucy Marie came over. "Don't you need a break?" she asked. "I'll watch your booth."

"Thanks," Josh said gratefully. After the bathroom he looked at long food lines and decided to do without until closing. The final half hour was calm, then there was a stampede to the shuttle buses. Ninety minutes later Josh staggered into the hotel and went straight to the bar. Three beers later he looked up. "Rough day?" grinned the bartender.

"You wouldn't believe it," grunted Josh. He ordered a hamburger, ate, had a half dozen more beers and went off to bed. The next morning Josh stubbed his cigarette as the bell rang and the elevator arrived. He stepped quickly to the open door then stopped, halfway in, frozen. In the elevator a young woman was bent over, dress hiked up over her shoulders, hands reached back to adjust pantyhose or waistbands or something. She didn't let Josh stop her. She looked up at him and smiled. "Good morning," she said brightly.

Josh stumbled on into the elevator and tried unsuccessfully to not watch as the girl tugged and squirmed. At the lobby level she stood up, wiggled her dress down just as the door opened, smiled at Josh and said "Have a nice day."

He stepped out numbly, stood and watched as the girl walked briskly away, finally grinned, shrugged, and allowed as how there were some things about New York which were a joy to behold. The second day of the Gift Show was slower, with time to meet more nearby exhibitors and share more funny stories with the Georgians, and by closing time Josh felt that he was an old hand at the trade show business. The group of Kentucky craftspeople in the next row invited him to join them for dinner.

"Where?" asked Josh, mentally calculating his dwindling cash reserves. Two hours later, happily drunk on cheap beer in the Beefsteak Charlie's at Times Square, Josh was telling rowdy stories about rats, hookers, and beautiful girls on elevators. The next day Josh woke up reluctantly, painfully, and made it to the booth just at opening time.

"Oh, my God," drawled Beth Anne. "What happened to you?"

"Beefsteak Charlie's. Sardi's. Someplace called Jim Bob's or Billy Jack's or something like that, and I don't exactly remember what all else." Josh groaned. "Kentucky did downtown. Back home they'd have put us in jail early and I wouldn't be feeling so bad."

Lucy Marie joined the teasing. "You look like," she told Josh, "that you finally met the woman with the painted top. Did you have blue paint on you when you woke up this morning?"

"He looks more like he ran into some of the majorettes," Beth Anne said thoughtfully, "except that he still had money left for coffee."

"Go away," moaned Josh.

"Are you going to write a story about New York when you get home?" asked Beth Anne. "Or do you think you'll remember anything?"

"I'll remember a few things," grinned Josh, "and a few people."

"Will I be in your story?" asked Beth Anne.

"Sure," said Josh. "You'll be the painted lady." She blushed. "And you," Josh said to Lucy Marie, "I'll describe as a majorette with the back quarter of your head shaved."

"You wouldn't," laughed Beth Anne. She reconsidered. "Would you?"

Josh grinned. "I would."

On the last day the Show ended at noon. In thirty minutes Josh had his booth disassembled and was ready to pack up and leave, but his crate wasn't there. "How do you get your packing boxes?" he asked the Georgians.

"You wait," Beth Anne said grimly, "until some union worker feels like dragging them out here to you."

For another hour Josh drank beer, wandered around watching and helping, then sat glumly in his booth for another thirty minutes. The crate still didn't come. At four, a little drunk and thoroughly disgruntled, Josh went looking for his crate. He found it, in the rear of the building at the loading docks, sitting with other packing cartons stacked on top. Josh decided to push the load out by himself. A brawny red-faced man came running.

"You can't do that," bellowed the dock hand.

"Why not?" asked Josh. "It's mine. And I've been waiting four hours to pack up."

"If you move your own crate," said the dock man, "what'll all these guys do? We got to make a living too, you know."

"Hell," growled Josh. "I'll pay you to not work. That's what I had to do with the electricians. I just want my crate." He moved into position to shove the load out onto the floor. The dock hand sent for a foreman.

"You can't do that," warned the crew boss.

Josh looked up and grinned angrily. "Just watch me," he snarled. The foreman stepped closer but stopped, reconsidering when he saw Josh's cold smile, then shrugged. "What the hell?" said the foreman. "Take it on, cowboy."

"Thanks," Josh said dryly. "You've been a big help."

Josh went down the aisle distributing cartons and finally uncovered his own heavy crate. Before he was finished packing the Georgians came to say goodbye. "We'll see you next time," said Beth Anne, "and if you get to Atlanta give us a call."

Josh wiped sweat. "Do you have big rats down there too?" he asked.

"No," smiled Lucy Marie. "Just real possums."

"If you're not busy tonight," said Josh, "maybe we could have dinner."

"We've got a 9 o'clock flight," said Beth Anne, "and I can't wait to get home. Are you staying over?"

"Have to," said Josh. "Obviously, planes don't go into Kentucky after suppertime."

"Well, be careful tonight," giggled Beth Anne. "Don't get any more blue paint on yourself."

It took Josh another hour to finish packing and to arrange for shipping, and by the time he went outside it was dark and the shuttle buses had stopped running. The street was deserted. "Not again," groaned Josh. After forty minutes a cab finally came, and Josh made it back to the hotel. He showered, went down to the bar for a drink, then went looking for food. Finally Josh settled for ribs in a crowded restaurant off Columbus Avenue where the waiter rushed him through the meal to make room for larger seatings. The walk back to the hotel seemed to take forever, and the street bustle had lost its charm. Josh packed, drank the last of the beer from the noisy little room refrigerator, and slept restlessly.

The 5:30 cab sped to the airport, and after a stopover in Pittsburgh the jet streaked toward Kentucky. During the approach to Lexington Josh watched gratefully as open green fields, trees and fences, and patches of timberland came into view.

The man beside Josh chuckled. "I know it's pretty down there," he said, "but you look like you've just seen heaven."

"Close to it," grinned Josh. "Home."

"Been to New York?"

"For a week," sighed Josh. "Longest week of my life."

The pilot lowered the flaps and landing gear, lumbered into Bluegrass Airport, bumped down and reversed the engines, finally slowed and turned and rolled awkwardly to the terminal. Josh collected his luggage, stopped just outside the door to take a deep breath, then walked happily to the long term parking lot. The muddy high wheeled Chevy Blazer finally started, coughed and clattered, blew a cloud of smoke and settled into a rumbling fast idle. Josh eased out into the traffic, caught New Circle Road around Lexington to I-75, and headed south across Clay's Ferry Bridge and past White Hall. Just outside Berea, Josh caught his first glimpse of mountains. "Lord," he grunted. "Them old hillsides ain't never looked so good to me." An hour later Josh left the main highway and rolled to a stop in a graveled parking lot.

The truck stop waitresses met Josh at the door, clamoring for information about what it was like up in New York City. "Feed me first," laughed Josh. "Country ham, gravy, biscuits, fried potatoes, and fried apples. Near as I can tell, they ain't a hog or a skillet in all of the state of New York, and I haven't had any food you could taste since I left home." He sat at the counter. "And you don't know how good it feels to hear people talk that don't sound funny."

As he ate, Josh told about big rats, Central Park, Sardi's, tall buildings, painted women, and union electricians. "Cost me $93 to get an extension cord plugged in," groaned Josh, "and a hot dog was six dollars. You got to keep a pocketful of money, 'cause everbody you see has got his hand out."

"Did you see the Statue of Liberty?" asked Millie.

"Nope," said Josh. "Except from about 2,000 feet up. Come to think of it, I didn't see much of anything except the insides of that big old building."

"Would you ever go back?" asked Millie.

"Sure," said Josh. "But not until I've eat my fill of fried meat, let my nerves settle down some, and dried out from all the drinking."

"I swear," sighed Millie, smiling. "I just can't imagine it. Josh Whitt up in New York City, riding subways and going to Times Square." She frowned. "You didn't go up there and wear them old blue jeans all the time, did you?"

Josh shrugged. "They don't care what you wear, what you look like, or what you do, long as you keep forking over cash money." Josh wiped his plate clean with a biscuit and lit a cigarette. "New York," he said contentedly, "is one hell of a town." Josh smiled. "But I'll tell you what. I wouldn't swap an acre of Kentucky for the whole durned island of Manhattan."

"We're glad you come home," said Millie.

"Not half as glad as me," said Josh. He stood and stretched. "Now. I got to go feed two hungry old hound dogs and sleep for about two days." He went out the door whistling. At the door to the Blazer he stopped and chuckled when he realized what the tune was, then swung in and drove away still happily whistling "New York, New York."

The Bitter Creek Appalachian Symposium

Buddy and The Bootleg Bandits reverently played that old Appalachian folksong, "Get Martha White self rising flour, the real all purpose flour," and the music flowed happily. Clarence Whittimore led the way on his steel guitar, and Alfred Cox followed on creaky fiddle. Buddy tugged down the brim of his black ten-gallon hat, glared out from behind wraparound sunglasses, and sang in a nasal monotone.

Most of the crowd was already noisily drunk. Buddy grinned wolfishly and dragged the tune out two more minutes. He finished with a flourish. "Thankee, thankee," Buddy growled into the microphone. "Ya'll a nice crowd. Real nice. We appreciate it."

The Third Annual Bitter Creek Humor & Folklore Society's Appalachian Symposium was in full swing. Buddy and the Bandits had already played "All My Rowdy Friends," "I Like Beer," and "Don't Let Your Babies Grow Up To Be Cowboys," and now they were ready to do some authentic mountain music.

"We're gonna do a little thing for you now that my granddaddy learned me," announced Buddy. "Grandpa, he never did see the words wrote down. He just learned her by listening." Buddy grinned. "Now, what Granddaddy was listening to, it was a stereo cassette tape. Grandma's new microwave oven has got a digital alarm clock, a dual tape deck, and chimes that play 'My Old Kentucky Home.' Anyhow, this is a old mountain song my grandpa picked up while he was out in the kitchen heating up a pizza. Ready, boys?"

"The Devil Went Down To Georgia" featured Alfred's frantic fiddle-work and Buddy's busy vocals plus tight harmony on the "Fire On The Mountain" segment.

As the tune ended, to rowdy applause, George Peters was trying to locate a parking place outside The Maverick Club. George finally edged the silver Volvo into a slot between a jacked-up four-wheel-drive pickup truck and a sleek yellow '57 Chevy Bel Aire. "Here we are," George announced grandly. "The elegant Maverick Club, on the weedy outskirts of suburban Pikeville, Kentucky."

The tall woman sniffed suspiciously.

That's Bud Wilson's fish fry," chuckled George. "Deep fried catfish and hushpuppies with French fries. You won't see a whole lot of yogurt and alfalfa sprouts at the Bitter Creek Symposium." Dr. Amanda Coldiron, PhD in Rural Sociology and visiting professor in the University of Kentucky's Appalachian Center, uncoiled gingerly from the big Volvo seat. "What have you done to me, George?" she asked with a half-smile. She cocked an ear to listen. "Are they handling snakes in there?"

George grinned. "Not yet."

Amanda shuddered. "Are you sure this is safe?"

"Just don't get near Lem Stephenson," cautioned George. "Lem thinks all outside women are like some of the girls who came here in the sixties with VISTA. Lem laid stoned, in bed for three years, and he still gets a glazed look about him when he hears a city accent."

"Very funny," said Amanda. She hesitated. "Which one is Lem?"

"He looks like Little Abner," grinned George, "and talks out of the corner of his mouth. Like Elvis."

"You're kidding." Amanda laughed nervously.

"Am I?" George grinned. "There's just one way to find out. Ready?"

As they walked closer to The Maverick Club the noises were even louder. Somebody was vomiting between two trucks, and giggles and groans came from inside a red and black Monte Carlo. "Don't look now," advised George, "but it sounds like Lem has met another anti-poverty worker." He led Amanda to the front door. "After you," George said gallantly, "and welcome to the Bitter Creek Appalachian Symposium."

Amanda stopped halfway inside. "My God," she whispered. George shoved her on in, and followed. Buddy looked up, stopped the music, and pointed. "Here he is, folks," bellowed Buddy. "The poet laureate of the Bitter Creek Humor & Folklore Society — George Peters."

George waved to Buddy and somebody stuck a bottle of beer in his hand. "We'll hear more from George later," promised Buddy. "He said he'd read us a poem. Bitter Creek Breakdown." There were groans and boos. "But first," continued Buddy, "let's turn Clarence loose on the steel guitar."

Buddy left the band onstage, shucked his guitar, and worked through the maze of cords and connectors to greet George and Amanda at their table. "Dr. Amanda Coldiron," announced George, "meet Dr. Edward Chase."

"Dr. Edward L. Chase?" asked Amanda, staring blankly.

"Buddy to my friends," he laughed. "How's the beer?" Buddy poured from a plastic pitcher. "The Maverick is fresh out of white wine."

Amanda sipped, still awed by Buddy's presence. "Dr. Chase," she finally said, "I've read all your books."

"The name's Buddy," said Buddy, "and I've read all of yours too, but that doesn't mean we can't be friends." Buddy drained his mug and beamed. "So, Dr. Amanda Coldiron, what brings you to Pikeville tonight?"

"I thought George was serious," Amanda said weakly, "when he told me about the Bitter Creek Symposium. He said to come here if I wanted to meet some real Appalachians." Amanda stiffened. "I didn't know I was coming to an orgy. What is this place?"

"A genuine redneck honkytonk," grinned Buddy. "One that nobody has put in a book yet, so a body can still come here and have some fun."

"But," stammered Amanda, "what kind of symposium is this?"

"According to Dr, Chase," explained George, "a symposium, in the original sense of the word, was a time when a lot of people got together and did a lot of hard drinking."

Amanda glared. "So it's all just one big, not very funny joke. The symposium, the Bitter Creek Humor & Folklore Society, and your presence here."

"Not exactly," laughed Buddy. "It's sort of a conditioned reaction. The Appalachian Studies Conference, the New River Symposium, the Appalachian Humor Festival, and Saturday night in Eastern Kentucky all rolled into one. With lots of beer, music, dancing, and laughing right out loud."

"I should have expected something like this from George," sniffed Amanda. "But not from you. Dr. Chase, you're a very respected scholar and professor."

"That's the cross I must bear," groaned Buddy. "Don't hold it against me. Want some more beer?" Buddy called for another pitcher, refilled the mugs, and leaned close to Amanda. "Dr. Coldiron, every person in this room is a native Appalachian. People from families who've lived here eight, maybe ten generations, people who've never read your books, or my books, who wouldn't know Harry Caudill if he fell through the door screaming. But they'd buy Harry a beer." Buddy smiled. "There's not one dulcimer player, Danish folk dancer, academic storyteller, or ballad singer in the building. Just truckers, clerks, waitresses, bankers, coal miners, farmers, schoolteachers, a few bootleggers, and not more than a dozen used car salesmen. Take a good look, Dr. Coldiron. Like it or not, these are the people you study and write about."

Amanda looked around the room and sniffed distastefully. "Does anybody ever get killed during your symposium?"

"Not so far," said Buddy. "We've had some broken jaws, bloody noses, some food poisoning, and a few pregnancies."

"I understand now," said Amanda. "This is all research for you. You're going to put it all in a new book."

"No way," scowled Buddy. "That wouldn't be right. I leave that kind of writing to George, only he calls it fiction and the editors give him hell for not writing about believable characters. George's weirdest stuff is just the pure truth with the names changed."

"The Maverick Club is a beer joint," George said quietly. "That's all. It's like the ones I grew up in, a few counties over. Call it a settlement school for rednecks." He chuckled. "When I went off to college, I had to hunt all over for a place where I felt at home. I found the old White Horse Tavern over in Richmond, but then had to quit going there when the bartender shot a customer. After that they checked IDs, and a seventeen year old couldn't get in."

"Does everybody in Eastern Kentucky spend their time in places like these?" Amanda asked weakly.

"Lord no," George said quickly. "My mother would burn this place down. But, I'd say attendance here comes in a close second to church services." He shrugged and grinned. "Lots of the same people at both places, too." George smiled. "Here, they let Buddy bring his band and have some fun. Sometimes a student or two will wander in, but the Maverick is too rough for kids used to rock bars, so it's pretty much just the natives who come back."

"So why did you drag me up here?" asked Amanda.

"To round out your education," grinned George. "The hillbilly bars in Lexington that you go to are patterned after places like this, but you needed to see the real thing. In person. This is pure, scholarly research."

"I'd better get back to the band," said Buddy. "They're slowing down." Back onstage Buddy brought Alfred and a wolfish young mandolin player up closer to the microphone. "We're going to do a number now for Dr. Amanda Coldiron," grinned Buddy. "This one's for you, doc. Ready, boys?"

The band leapt into a wailing, hard-driving bluegrass version of "Long, Lanky Woman".

George howled, and Amanda bristled. "I've certainly learned the truth about Dr. Edward Chase," she snapped. "Monday morning his books come off the reading lists for my classes."

"Settle down and have a beer," suggested George.

Amanda sipped numbly and stared out across the dimly lit cement block dance hall.

George chuckled. "You'll see more Kentucky Cluster diamond rings, polyester, pancake makeup, sideburns, and gold chains in here tonight than you could find back in New Jersey in a month of Sundays. And, any one of those big trucks out in the parking lot costs more than you paid for that Saab."

Amanda studied George, slumped happily back in his chair, and smiled. "You don't belong here," Amanda said triumphantly. "Your blow-dried hair and plain glasses are a dead giveaway. Not to mention that fifty dollar sweatshirt and the scuffed up sneakers." She smiled, a little drunk and evil. "You, George Peters, are a fake. You're no more Appalachian than I am."

George shrugged. "Once I open my mouth all is forgiven. Once a hillbilly, always a hillbilly. No matter what you look like."

"Don't you find the term 'hillbilly' degrading?" asked Amanda.

"From you I would," said George, "or from anybody else who meant it as a slur. But I was a hillbilly, and damned proud to be one, a long time before some scholars and bureaucrats decided I was an Appalachian."

"Then why don't you live here?" Amanda asked. "And why don't you have sideburns down to your neck?"

"Couldn't make a living here," grunted George.

"You could work in the mines," persisted Amanda. "Sell mobile homes. Teach English."

George grinned. "But then I'd never get to meet people like you. Besides, I like my running water and central air."

"They've got that here now," argued Amanda. "Plus satellite television, VCRs, fast food, cocaine, and venereal diseases."

"True," grinned George. He drank again, and sighed. "We've been given that kind of progress in Eastern Kentucky. I grew up on a hillside farm with nine brothers and sisters, an outhouse, and a big old heatstove. The happiest day of my young life was when they ran electricity and my parents brought home a used cookstove. That meant I didn't have to split kindling and carry coal all summer. Now, the kids eat pizza and walk around with earplug radios, drive Camaros, and work at Druthers. Half of them can't read or write above a third grade level, but they're overweight, healthy as horses, and sexually active from the time they're twelve."

"Weren't you?" smirked Amanda.

"I sure did want to be," George said mournfully. "I just couldn't get anybody to cooperate."

"Why did you leave?" asked Amanda. "Seriously, George, why didn't you just stay at home?"

"College, I guess." George swirled his beer and pondered. "I wanted to go to school some more. I figured there had to be more to life than driving a truck or growing a crop, and it seemed to me that the only way out was college. I had good grades and test scores, and scholarship offers, but I still couldn't afford school in Lexington so I went to Berea."

"The school for Appalachians," smiled Amanda.

George grunted. "When I was there, most of the faculty tried to make me over into a mid-western missionary. They didn't like anything about the way I talked, acted, or thought." He poured more beer. "But there were some professors who liked me the way I was. One even let me write about Eastern Kentucky while everybody else was imitating J.D. Salinger."

"I've tried to read your fiction," said Amanda. "You use too much dialect, too many stereotypes, and far too much crude humor."

"Thank you," said George. He signaled for more beer. "Drink up, Dr. Coldiron. You get graded on class participation."

"You're already drunk," said Amanda. "How are we going to get back to Lexington?"

"On the great Bert T. Combs Mountain Parkway," George said grandly. "We'll crash the Winchester Wall at about ninety then cruise right on up I-64 to the beautiful city built by the people who moved away from Hazard."

"What's the Winchester Wall?" Amanda asked anxiously.

"The Winchester Wall," George said solemnly, "is the great invisible barrier which keeps Eastern Kentucky from polluting the sacred bluegrass. They don't dare bring the Japanese carmakers past the Wall. If they did, we might shoot them. Some of us haven't forgotten Pearl Harbor." George leaned closer. "The Winchester Wall, Dr. Coldiron, is the line the Kentucky politicians drew when it came time to divide up the power and money. Eastern Kentucky gets the shaft. Always has, always will. We're outnumbered, outvoted, and outspent. New industry goes to the golden triangle, Lexington and Louisville and Cincinnati, and our coal severance taxes help pay for getting them there."

"That's sort of a one sided evaluation," smiled Amanda.

"I can be one sided if I want to," mumbled George. "I'm a deprived minority."

Buddy and The Bootleg Bandits played "Blue Moon Of Kentucky" and George sang along.

"You're very drunk," observed Amanda.

"Part of my heritage," grinned George. "I come from a long line of men who got very drunk now and then."

"Since you're so wound up," smiled Amanda, "what warped view of the future do you have? What comes next for Eastern Kentucky?"

"In a hundred years," George announced profoundly, "this place where we're sitting will be in the middle of a desert. Or a garbage dump. When the coal is all gone, we may become the refuse depositary for all of the eastern United States."

"My God," laughed Amanda. "Now you've turned morbid."

"A genetic defect," said George. "I'm descended from the scum of London, you know."

"Such a pessimist," said Amanda, smiling gently. "Don't you see any hope? Any changes that could make things different?"

George shrugged. "Schools. But that won't happen until parents and taxpayers decide to value education enough to foot the bills, and that's not likely until there are jobs here for the ones who do get educated. But we can't get the industry until we improve the schools, so it's sort of a hopeless, vicious circle." He sighed. "In my home county, unemployment runs about twenty-five percent. Half of the ones who do work commute. A hundred to two hundred miles a day, for low-end jobs. The counties themselves are a big part of the problem. Too many, too small and poor to support good schools and services, too crooked to change."

Amanda grinned. "What about the welfare system? I assume you hate it too?"

"No," said George, "I don't. At least now nobody starves to death, or freezes, and thirty years ago that happened. I don't like the way the system penalizes the ones who want to work, but anything is better than the misery some people used to endure."

George rocked his chair back and continued. "I'll tell what kills me. It's the hopelessness. You see so many people who've given up. They won't try any more. They've been whipped, then whipped again, and now they've quit. It all changed so fast, after World War II, that some families never did adjust. Up 'til then you could live pretty good without cash money. With enough kids to do the work you could scratch a living out of a hillside farm. Grow or shoot your own food, order whatever else you had to have from the Sears & Roebuck catalog, and survive if you'd work hard enough. That ain't so any more. You can work your butt off and still have to have help."

George drank more beer and stared morosely at his hands. "I'm one hell of a scholar. I preach doom, practice raising cain. I love Eastern

Kentucky but won't live here. I want it to change but I want it to stay the same. I'm full of questions, but I don't have one single damned answer." George smiled wearily. "Welcome to the Bitter Creek Appalachian Symposium, Dr. Coldiron."

Amanda watched George , emptied the beer pitcher and signaled for one more. Buddy came back to the table. "Have you two solved all the ills of Appalachia, or have you said the hell with it and got crocked?"

Amanda had kicked off her sensible shoes, crossed long legs, and had opened the top buttons of her silk blouse. Buddy grinned. "Enjoying yourself, Dr. Coldiron?"

Amanda nodded and smiled sadly.

"I can tell. Old lonesome George has been on the stump." Buddy chuckled. "Fill George full of beer and he'll preach until somebody stuffs a towel in his mouth. The drunker George gets, the more sense he makes. Or is it the drunker I get the more sense George makes?" Buddy laughed. "Whatever. I guess George told you about the vast wasteland?"

"In detail," Amanda said thickly.

"George Peters is a walking contradiction," said Buddy. "He was too old to be a good hippie, and he's too young to be a proper mountaineer. George is smack-dab in-between. About one more pitcher and he'll want to sing with the band. Did you ever hear a slobbery drunk try to sing 'Amazing Grace'?"

Amanda giggled. "Maybe we'll do a duet."

"A new George and Tammy," grinned Buddy.

"Who's that?" asked Amanda.

"You poor thing," grinned Buddy. "You just ain't been educated."

"Dr. Coldiron has led a very sheltered life," George said. "Until tonight she didn't even know about hillbillies."

"And she's learning from you?" Buddy snorted. "This man here," he told Amanda, "drinks beer for breakfast. He can shoot like Daniel Boone but ain't killed a squirrel or rabbit in thirty years. He's got a '59 Ford pickup and a new Volvo. He keeps a pack of red tick hounds out back of a house that came right out of *Architectural Digest*. George would die without air conditioning. He writes fiction. How could you believe a word George Peters says? He's about as much of a hillbilly as I am a cowboy, except I come closer because I at least got boots and a hat."

"I got a cap," protested George.

"And it says 'Eat More Possum' right across the front." Buddy grinned, and leaned close to speak softly to Amanda. "I've heard rumors that George Peters listens to classical music and goes to aerobics classes. I know for a fact that he drinks Perrier water and orders boots from LL Bean."

Amanda giggled.

George scowled.

"Have you seen George's bumper sticker?" Buddy asked. "The one that says 'Minor Regional Writer'?"

Amanda nodded.

"In George's case," said Buddy, "that sticker is the honest to God truth."

George nodded his agreement. "But it ain't my fault," he added, "that I write about such a minor region."

"My God," said Amanda. "I've stumbled onto the set of 'Hee Haw.' Where are the dancing pigs?" She stopped George. "Please don't answer that question." Amanda shook her head and sipped at the beer. "How," she asked, "are we ever going to get back to Lexington? George can't possibly drive, and I'm a little too drunk to try it."

"Just get a little drunker," grinned Buddy, "and drive like the natives do. Stop and shoot up a few road signs. Pull off in the ditch to puke and sleep it off. If the sheriff gets you, all you have to do is spend the night in the Pikeville jail."

Amanda grimaced.

"It ain't all that bad," shrugged George. "You get pork and beans twice a day and a shower once a week."

"How would you know?" asked Amanda.

"Research," grinned George. "Pure scholarly research. Working on a paper. 'Famous Kentucky Jailhouses I Have Known.' We'll get Appalshop to make the movie, with Ned Beatty." He yelled for more beer and studied Amanda. "Well, Dr. Coldiron, how do you like the real Appalachia? Will this change the way you teach?"

Amanda peered over her glasses at the two men who sat smiling at her. "Not really," she finally said. "But I might bring my class to your next Symposium."

"You do that," Buddy said wearily. "Bring the youngens to see the hillbillies up close. Have them write essays about how the mountaineers drink away their frustrations." Buddy drained his mug. "Ready, George?"

"Ready for what?" mumbled George.

"Your poetry reading," beamed Buddy. He shoved back his chair. "This here's the serious part, Dr. Coldiron. Literature. Classy stuff." Buddy wobbled to the stage, stopped the band, and bent to the microphone. "Here's what you've all been waiting for, folks," he said dryly. "It's time for George." Buddy waved away the groans. "Here he is."

George shuffled up to the mike, pulled a tattered paper out of his hip pocket, coughed, and blushed. "I'll make it fast," he mumbled. "This is 'Bitter Creek Breakdown.'" George bent over close to the mike and read:

Up here on Bitter Creek
The water runs green and acid yellow
Clogged by Pampers and Clorox jugs
Refrigerators and shells of old Chevrolets.

The government run us a water line
In 1968, so we got a mobile home,
And Uncle John's Black Lung check
Pays the bills
Ever since we voted wet
And a body can't make a living no more
Bootlegging.

Cousin Jeff grows marijuana
Over on Poosey Mountain
But he says it's hard to make any cash money.
Last year some old boys from Hazard stole half his crop

And this year the cows got in
And et it.

They give mighty good milk for a while,

*Jeff said,
But then they got all sniffly and redeyed
Went to wearing red bandannas
And writing poetry.*

*Brother Ben went to Vietnam
And come home a hippie.
Beard, hair
Old Army field jackets
And a strange look in his eyes.*

*But now they made him a memorial
Over in Frankfort
And the lottery, it's going to get Ben a hundred dollar bonus
So I guess it's okay
That he still don't sleep at night
Can't hear out of one ear
Or hold down a job.*

*There's work up around Lexington, they say
If a body'll drive two hours each way
Build Japanese cars
Or sweep up floors for one of the coal companies
That owns most of this county.*

*No work here, though.
Mines are about shut down,
Timber's all cut,
And the government's idea of how to get us all back to work
Is to have us make quilts, whittle, spin and weave,
And peddle our stuff to the tourists.
Ain't no tourists here, though.*

*And factories, they say,
Won't come to the mountains.
Bad roads, bad water, bad schools,
And we're all too damned ornery to work*

When it's squirrel season.

So here on Bitter Creek
We got to go it on our own
Scrouge out a living somehow
Hang onto this hillside
And 80 acres of scrub timber.

You ask me why?
Why, this here land's been ours for 200 years.
Up in that graveyard they's markers
Ten generations that lived here
And died poor.

So I got to stay.
Got to keep the strip miners out
Of Grandpap's graveyard
Scratch out enough cash money
To send the youngens to school
And get 'em a little Christmas.

But don't you worry none.
When it's all over,
When the coal's give out,
The creeks is dry,
And the do gooders have done
Give up and gone

We'll still be right here.

George folded up his paper, stepped back, nodded to the audience, and waited, uneasy in the sudden silence.

"Goddamn," Buddy finally growled. "You'd take the fun out of a funeral, George. Why'd you have to go and read that?" Buddy waved to the band. "Play," he ordered. "Give us a little bit of 'Foggy Mountain Breakdown.' George, get your skinny butt down off of that stage."

As the band leapt into the driving music George walked slowly back to the table and sat down heavily. "Beer," he said. Dr. Amanda Coldiron poured.

"I think you need this," she said. "For what it's worth, George, I liked your poem."

"Me too," grinned Buddy, "but I couldn't let everbody stand around all embarrassed, and this bunch ain't much to show it when they get serious."

George shrugged. "Hey, it's a symposium, right?"

"Right," laughed Buddy. "We all came here to learn, didn't we?" He leaned closer to Amanda. "And what I want you to learn next is the words to a song. I want you to do a number with us."

"Me?" Amanda stared.

But, thirty minutes later, with George Peters swaying beside her singing harmony, Dr. Amanda Coldiron belted out a gutsy rendition of "It Wasn't God Who Made Honky Tonk Angels," and the Bitter Creek Appalachian Symposium was back in session.